SISTER
FRIENDS
FOREVER

SISTER FRIENDS FOREVER

a novel

KIMBERLA LAWSON ROBY

GRAND CENTRAL
PUBLISHING

NEW YORK   BOSTON

Copyright © 2022 by Kimberla Lawson Roby

Cover design by Elizabeth Yaffe. Cover copyright © 2022 by Hachette Book Group, Inc.

Grand Central Publishing
Hachette Book Group
1290 Avenue of the Americas, New York, NY 10104
grandcentralpublishing.com
twitter.com/grandcentralpub

First Edition: August 2022

Grand Central Publishing is a division of Hachette Book Group, Inc. The Grand Central Publishing name and logo is a trademark of Hachette Book Group, Inc.

The publisher is not responsible for websites (or their content) that are not owned by the publisher.

The Hachette Speakers Bureau provides a wide range of authors for speaking events. To find out more, go to www.hachettespeakersbureau.com or call (866) 376-6591.

Scripture quotations taken from the (NASB®) New American Standard Bible®. Copyright © 1960, 1971, 1977, 1995 by The Lockman Foundation. Used by permission. All rights reserved. www.lockman.org. Scripture quotations also taken from King James Version.

Library of Congress Cataloging-in-Publication Data
Names: Roby, Kimberla Lawson, author.
Title: Sister friends forever / Kimberla Lawson Roby.
Description: First edition. | New York : Grand Central Publishing, 2022. |
Identifiers: LCCN 2022004310 | ISBN 9781538708958 (hardcover) | ISBN
    9781538708972 (ebook)
Subjects: LCGFT: Novels.
Classification: LCC PS3568.O3189 S59 2022 | DDC 813/.54—dc23/eng/20220204
LC record available at https://lccn.loc.gov/2022004310

ISBNs: 9781538708958 (hardcover), 9781538708972 (ebook)

Printed in the United States of America

LSC-C

Printing 1, 2022

In Loving Memory of

My dear aunt
Mary Beasley,
for all your unwavering love
and support and for always being
there for me my entire life. I will
miss you always, and I love
you with all my heart.
July 3, 1939 – August 15, 2019

My dear aunt
Shirley Jean Gary,
for loving me as your
biological niece…from the moment
I married your nephew, Will. You will
forever be missed, and I love you
with all my heart.
May 15, 1940 – May 10, 2020

My dear aunt,
Marie Tennin,
for all your love and all the
happy times I spent at your home
as a child, during our annual summer
vacation trips. You will forever be
missed, and I love you with all my heart.
January 13, 1932 – February 7, 2022

SISTER
FRIENDS
FOREVER

CHAPTER 1

Serena

S erena was forty, had never been married, and was lonelier than she'd ever been in her life.

And she knew why.

It was because she still hadn't found her soul mate—if there was such a thing—and the fact that she had just learned three days ago that her so-called significant other, Tim, was sleeping with another woman. Which might not have been so surprising had Tim not been claiming for months—nearly a year, to be exact—that he loved her and that she was everything any man could want in a woman. Although now, as Serena thought back on their overall re-lationship, she couldn't deny how obsessive and protective he had been when it came to his smartphone. He'd almost always kept it on silent, claiming that he didn't want a single thing to interrupt the quality time they spent to-gether, and he also rarely checked his phone in front of her for missed calls or text messages. Worse, there had been a few times when Serena had traveled to out-of-town speaking engagements, and she hadn't been able to get in touch with him at all. But then, like clockwork, he would finally call her back the next morning, waking her up and apologizing for dropping off to sleep a lot earlier than *usual* or for not seeing that she had called him until that very moment.

Serena had, of course, been suspicious, the same as she had been of every man she'd dated, but this time around, she had tried to be more trusting. She'd told herself that being paranoid, skeptical, and insecure wasn't good, and that maybe Tim really did love her as much as he said he did. She had also decided that he didn't seem like the kind of man who would be unfaithful, not with his regularly talking about his belief in God and the fact that he seemed to have a huge amount of respect for her and her decision to remain celibate.

Of course, this hadn't always been Serena's normal way of thinking, but then a couple of years ago, she had begun making her relationship with God a much bigger priority in her life. Then, after she and one of her best friends, Michelle, had attended this amazing Christian women's conference, they'd both decided they would no longer have sex outside of marriage. They'd talked about it for two days, both by phone and in person, and what had truly sealed the deal for them was when the keynote speaker had said, "When you have sex with someone, you willingly give them a part of your soul that you can never get back. So why not wait for the one man who genuinely loves you and who wants to spend the rest of his life with you?"

But again, Serena had thought Tim was fine with her celibacy decision and that they were good. That is, until his *other* woman had obviously found out about Serena and had decided to record the audio of Tim and her having sex, and then had sent the file to Serena's website email address. At first, Serena had wondered how the woman had even known who she was. But it wasn't as though Mitchell, Illinois, was some huge metropolitan city, and for all Serena knew, this other woman could have seen her and Tim out on one of their many dates. It also wasn't as though most people in the city didn't know who Serena was, what with her having a popular lifestyle blog and being a nationally known speaker.

Serena dropped down onto her navy blue leather sofa, leaned back into the corner of it, pulled her knees up close to her body, and rested her elbows against the tops of her thighs. She pulled her ponytail around and onto her left shoulder, and without warning, tears flowed down her high cheekbones. She was so unhappy, and the more she mentally replayed that raunchy, X-rated audio recording and tossed one awful thought through her mind after another, she wondered what was wrong with her and why after all these years of dating—one man after another—she hadn't so much as been engaged before. In fact, no one had ever even asked for her hand in marriage—that is, unless you counted that time when one of her former high school classmates had seen her dining at a restaurant...and out of nowhere...declared how much he had secretly always loved her, how he had never *stopped* loving her, and that if she would have him, he would marry her anytime she wanted. Serena had been stunned, to say the least, and while she hadn't wanted to hurt his feelings, all she'd been able to think about was how not only did she barely remember him, he also wasn't her type. Not even close.

And the even bigger truth? She could tell he didn't earn at least a six-figure salary.

But there was something else that had bothered her, too: the grayish-blue short-sleeved maintenance shirt he'd worn. Not to mention the fact that the name of the plumbing, heating, and air-conditioning company he worked for had been stitched on the upper left-hand side of it. His working attire had told Serena everything she'd needed to know, and since she had hired that very company in the past for some of her own heating issues, she'd known her former classmate wasn't the owner of it.

And yes, she also knew that success and wealth didn't mean everything, but she had decided a long time ago, back when she'd been a small girl, that once she became an adult, she would live a completely different kind of life in comparison to the horrible one she'd been forced to endure while growing up. If she could help it, she would totally forget about her penniless, project-housing upbringing. She would forget about the fact that she and her younger sister, Diane, had sometimes gone to bed starving... as well as about being forced to wear secondhand clothing, all of which the other children at school had ridiculed Serena about daily. Of course, this latter part hadn't been something Diane could relate to because unlike Serena's deadbeat father, whom Serena still had never met, Diane's father had taken her school shopping at the start of every school year. He'd gifted her with some of the best clothing money could buy, and then he would give Diane even more clothing at Christmastime. And if that hadn't already been enough, he also made sure to buy Diane a whole new summer wardrobe at the end of every school year.

But as much as Serena had tried with all her might, for years, to forget about her unfortunate and unfair childhood, she hadn't. And as much as she hated to admit it, deep down, she still resented her sister for having a much better father than she'd had—a father who had loved and adored her, spent time with her one to two weekends every month, and who had willingly made his child support payments on time, without fail. Serena knew that her mother's choice to date and sleep with Diane's father—a much more responsible man than Serena's father—wasn't her sister's fault, but what Serena hadn't been able to deal with was the pathetic way Diane had always bragged about *everything*. From having the better father to receiving all the beautiful clothing to all the summer vacations her father took her on annually, Diane had bragged, bragged, and bragged some more, and Serena had never truly gotten over it or forgiven her sister.

So no, Serena couldn't and wouldn't settle for just any man, and if she could help it, she would, with no exceptions, marry the man of her dreams. A man who was well-educated and one who could financially bring to the table as much as she did. In particular, a man like Tim, who was chief financial officer for a large insurance company. And if God answered all Serena's prayers, her future husband would ultimately be able to provide her with a whole lot more than that, and the beautiful son or daughter they would have would experience a much better childhood than she had—a son or daughter Serena would need to have very soon, because her biological clock was now ticking pretty loudly.

More than anything, though, Serena wanted to live the absolute best life she could, and she wanted to begin doing so, much sooner rather than later. Although, she couldn't deny that whenever one of her three best friends, Michelle, Kenya, or Lynette, brought up the subject of marriage, she pretended that marriage couldn't have been further from her mind. Why? Because she didn't want any of them to know just how unhappy she was being single. Especially since Serena knew a good number of women who preferred being single and that many of them were happily living their lives to the fullest.

And there was another reason, too, why Serena didn't let on to her friends about how much she wanted to be married: all three of them thought her standards were set way too high and that, on far too many occasions, she had overlooked some of the kindest, caring, and most respectable men around. Men who had been very interested in Serena, yet Serena had still either turned them down the very moment they asked her out on a date. Or if she did agree to date them, she would do so only one or two times and then basically—according to her friends—dump them as quickly as possible.

But the thing was, it was all because Serena knew what she wanted, and this was also the reason that she was willing to wait for as long as she had to—even if it meant spending another holiday all alone and in tears, the way she was doing now on Memorial Day. Her sister had invited her over to celebrate at her house, but to be honest, Serena didn't feel like being around Diane and her boyfriend—two lovebirds who acted as though they were young teenagers who had just fallen in love for the very first time. Actually, Serena didn't care to be around her sister on *any* day, let alone a holiday, but still, today it was mostly because of the whole lovebirds thing. Serena had also declined cookout invitations from Michelle, who was happily engaged, and Kenya, who was happily married. And the only reason she wasn't getting together with Lynette, who was happily divorced, was because Lynette and her two teenage girls were away visiting Lynette's parents in Mississippi.

The more she thought about it, though, it was so amazing how Serena, Lynette, Kenya, and Michelle had met at church when they were small children, became best friends, and remained best friends for more than three decades, yet they still led very different lives. But in many ways, they were also very much alike. For example, they had all turned forty this year—Serena and Michelle in January and Kenya and Lynette earlier this month; they all shared very similar Christian, family, and moral values; and with the exception of Lynette, who was a stay-at-home mom, they all had great careers or owned their own businesses. But again, when it came to their relationship statuses, they couldn't have been more different. Serena was single, Michelle was engaged, Kenya was married, and Lynette was divorced. Which just went to show that every human being had a very specific and preordained destiny. Still, being single at the age of forty was not the destiny Serena had been expecting or hoping for, and she prayed with everything in her that God had something much better planned for her future. Yes, He had blessed her with a wonderful college education and two degrees from Yale, as well as a wonderful purpose of writing and speaking, and she was grateful to Him for everything. But what she was also beginning to realize more and more was that success didn't mean much of anything—that is, if you didn't have someone to share it with.

Someone you loved.

Someone who loved you back.

Someone to take vows with.

Of course, it was true that Serena didn't want just any man, but she also didn't want to continue being alone. What she wanted was to be married. And while she knew there was no such thing as having a perfect marriage or a perfect relationship of any kind, she wanted to find the man who was perfect for *her*.

What she wanted was to get married and live as close to happily ever after as she could.

CHAPTER 2

Michelle

This was by far one of the best Memorial Days ever. The reason? Michelle was finally engaged, and in just over three short months, she and Dr. Christopher Blake III would become husband and wife. They would soon be joined by five hundred of their family members and friends, and they would be well on their way to creating a lifetime of wonderful memories. Needless to say, Michelle couldn't be happier. Especially since God had blessed her with the opportunity to meet one of the best men she had ever known in her life. Yes, it didn't hurt that he was one of the most knowledgeable cardiothoracic surgeons in the country, but more important, he was kind, loving, and compassionate, and he genuinely loved God. He also loved *her*, and he showed her just how much on a consistent basis. From flowers to chocolate-covered fruit to jewelry, he regularly showered her with gifts for no reason other than to let her know how special she was to him.

So yes, God had truly blessed her in more ways than she had even prayed for, and she was grateful. And while she, too, worked in the medical field in her dream job as a geriatric nurse practitioner, that wasn't how she and Chris had met. It had been her father, Larry, who had introduced them instead. Of course, in all honesty, Michelle shouldn't have been surprised, what with her father's and mother's adamance toward Michelle meeting and marrying a man who came from a prominent family. So when Chris had hired on Michelle's father to handle the entire negotiation process for the partnership offer he had received from his employer, Larry Jackson hadn't hesitated mentioning his daughter to his new client. Then, as it had turned out, the more Larry had gotten to know Dr. Christopher Blake III, the more he had liked him and discovered that Christopher III was *perfect* for his only child. Lucinda, Michelle's mom, who, like her husband, was a top attorney, had felt the same way, and the next thing Michelle had known, her parents had invited Chris over to their home for dinner. They'd also basically *told* Michelle what time she should be there, too.

This hadn't been a surprise, though, because for years, Michelle's parents had regularly tried playing matchmaker when it came to her love life, except none of the other men they'd set her up with in the past had been her type. They hadn't as much as come close to choosing the right person for her, but she did have to admit that with Chris, they'd done exceptionally well, and she was grateful to them.

Michelle glanced over at her father, who was turning meat on the grill and laughing and talking with Chris and his dad, Christopher II. Then she walked closer to the patio table where her mom, Michelle's future mother-in-law, Audrey—who had already become her mother-in-love—and Michelle's Aunt Jill were sitting.

Michelle placed her hand at the top of her forehead, blocking out the bright, hot sunshine, and she was glad she'd gotten her hair cut in a super short but elegant hairstyle.

"Once Daddy finishes the last of the grilling, we should be good to go."

"Well, I'm definitely ready," Audrey said.

"I'm ready, too," Aunt Jill agreed. "Usually when I cook a lot of food, I'm not hungry at all. You know, because of all the tasting that goes on. But I'm hungry today."

All of the women laughed, and then Lucinda said, "I really appreciate all the work you put in for us, sis, because you know I'm certainly not the cook in our family."

Aunt Jill chuckled again. "No, you're definitely not, and you know I was glad to do it."

Michelle smiled because for the first thirty years of her life, even though her parents had lived very well and resided in what most people would consider to be a mini-mansion, the three of them had celebrated nearly every single holiday at her Aunt Jill's. Michelle had always been thrilled about it, though, because for one, Aunt Jill could cook absolutely anything, and two, while her house wasn't all that spacious, she had a very special way of making everyone feel right at home. She was simply an amazing woman, and that was the reason that some of Michelle's fondest memories included all the times they'd spent at her aunt's home.

Now, though—at least for the past ten years, anyway, once Michelle's parents had built and moved into their current home—Aunt Jill had begun spending the night with her sister and brother-in-law on the evening before any big holiday. That way, she could cook huge meals in their picturesque, custom-style gourmet kitchen. Aunt Jill loved everything about it, and she always seemed so happy when she was there in her element, doing her favorite thing, which was cooking for the family she loved. Especially since she didn't have a husband or any children. Although, it wasn't as if Michelle was complaining, because this was part of the reason that Michelle and her aunt were so close, and the reason Aunt Jill was more like a mother to her than an aunt.

Michelle saw her father removing more meat from the grill and placing it in a large tinfoil cooking pan. Then, Chris picked it up and headed across the multicolored rock-textured patio toward the house, and Michelle followed behind him so she could place the meat in the oven until the rest of it was done. But as soon as they walked inside and Michelle slid the patio door closed behind her, Chris set the pan of meat onto the granite-topped island and pulled her into his arms. "Have I told you how much I love you?"

Michelle crossed her arms behind his neck, smiling and admiring how handsome he was. "Not in the last few hours."

"Well, I do. Baby, you're my world, and I love you with all my heart. And I always will."

"I love you, too, baby, and I thank God for you."

"And I can't wait to marry you. I can't wait for you to become Mrs. Christopher Blake the Third."

"Neither can I, and thankfully, we only have a little while to go."

Chris grinned at her.

"What?"

"It's actually twelve weeks, five days, and a few hours from now."

"Wow, talk about detailed."

"Well, when you've waited for as long as I have, you can't help but count down to the big day. I mean, don't get me wrong. I am totally on board with you wanting to honor God. But I'm still human and I still want...more than anything...to make love to you."

"I want the same thing, sweetheart," she admitted. "Believe me, I do."

"And I'll tell you something else. It hasn't been easy. Not with me loving you as much as I do. I love you more than I ever thought I could love anyone, Michelle, and you mean everything to me."

Tears filled Michelle's eyes, and Chris kissed her with what seemed like more passion than he ever had, and she kissed him back with the same intensity. But when their kissing stirred up the kind of fiery feelings that made them both want to do so much more, Michelle pulled away.

And Chris sighed with frustration. "Like I said, this isn't easy."

"I know. But it's like we just talked about, it won't be long."

Chris shook his head and sighed all over again. "Well, right now, it feels like it's going to be forever."

For the next few minutes, Michelle and Chris laughed and chatted about the "wait," the wedding, and their honeymoon in Jamaica. But soon after, Chris grabbed a bottle of water from the refrigerator and went back outside to see if Michelle's father had finished grilling. Michelle stayed behind, double-checking to make sure she had pulled out enough dipping spoons from one of the utensil drawers for the side dishes, but it wasn't long before she thought about something she'd tried her best to not think about ever again: the chance meeting she'd had just a few days ago with her first love, Steven Price.

She had run into him at a grocery store, and while it had been years since the two of them had seen each other, their meeting had felt as though they'd never spent much time apart at all. They had seemingly picked up where they'd left off, and then once they had said their goodbyes and headed down the paper products aisle in separate directions, Michelle had glanced at her watch and seen that more than thirty minutes had passed by without her realizing it. She and Steven had chatted for much longer than they should have, and while Michelle couldn't help feeling guilty about it, she had told herself that there was nothing wrong with catching up with an old friend. That there was nothing inappropriate about conversing with someone she had simply run into by coincidence—even if it was the former love of her life.

She had also told herself, for what seemed like a thousand times...that there was nothing left between her and Steven. Nothing at all. But no matter how hard she tried believing her own conviction, there was something else she just couldn't get over.

And it worried her.

In truth, it terrified her because there was no denying it. She and Steven still had noticeable chemistry between them. And not just a little bit of chemistry, either. No, the chemistry *they* shared was strong, comfortable, and familiar, and although Michelle had tried her best to push everything about Steven completely out of her mind, she found herself thinking about him multiple times every single day. And checking his Facebook profile and postings...every single day. She even thought about what could have been had her parents not interfered in her and Steven's relationship. Had they not believed Steven's high school education and fast-food management position weren't good enough for their only daughter. Had they not threatened to disown her...if she married the man she loved with her entire being.

Sadly, Michelle thought about a lot of other things, too, but more than anything else, she thought about the loving, compassionate, caring man who had just hugged and kissed her and confessed his undying love for her. She thought about the love she had for him, too, and how blessed she was to be marrying him. Which was the reason that from this moment on, she would focus on Chris and the incredible life they were going to have together instead of focusing on some previous relationship that had ended years ago.

She would become the best wife she could be to Chris, and she would forget about the fact that Steven and *his* wife were now divorced. She would also ignore something else that she had thought about every single day since running into Steven, which had everything to do with her feelings for Chris. Because while she certainly did love Chris, God forgive her, she wasn't so sure she was *in* love with him. She even worried that maybe she never had been, and until now, she also hadn't thought too much about the fact that there was a very big difference between loving someone and being *in* love with them. There was a huge difference indeed, and it was that part, in and of itself, that frightened Michelle the most.

CHAPTER 3

Kenya

It was bright and early on Tuesday morning, and the Griffin household was still and quiet. Kenya had gotten up about an hour ago, washed her face, pulled her long, thick, wavy hair into a bushy ponytail at the top of her head, thrown on her workout clothing. Then, she'd made some coffee. Of course, her initial plan had been to sit outside on the stairs of their wooden deck to enjoy it and then head back inside to get in her workout on the treadmill, but here it was more than thirty minutes later and she was still sitting there basking in the warm sun, which had now completely risen. This actually was her morning ritual, all spring and summer unless it rained, and the only reason she had skipped sitting outside early yesterday morning was because she and her husband, Robert, had spent time preparing for their holiday guests. And, oh, what a wonderful holiday celebration it had been. Especially for their two children, Elijah and Alivia—whom everyone referred to as Eli and Livvie—as they loved nothing more than having over a few of their cousins for a pool party. They'd had an amazing time, and the adults had equally enjoyed themselves as well, relaxing around the in-ground pool and watching the children both swim and play all sorts of water-related games. Kenya and Robert hadn't invited a huge number of people, but just having over Kenya's dear, sweet parents-in-law, a couple of Robert's first cousins, their spouses and children, and Kenya and Robert's next-door neighbors had been more than enough guests to have a great time. The food had been delicious, too, which was another reason Kenya knew she couldn't skip her workout regimen today, no matter how tempted she was to do so.

But as she continued basking in the sun with her eyes closed, one thought led to another, and before long, she couldn't help thinking about her mom and dad, who had both passed away when she was just in her thirties. They'd died two years apart and well before either of their sixtieth birthdays, and sadly, they'd both been diagnosed with cancer. Uterine for her mom, and colon for her dad. Still, no matter how much time had passed, Kenya couldn't believe they were gone, and she missed them every day of her life. Worse, Kenya had been an only child, so while she loved her husband and children with all her heart, there were still times when she wished she could call her mom or dad or a big brother or sister when she needed advice. Because although she had graduated from college and medical school with honors and she now worked as an obstetrician-gynecologist, she some-times needed advice and wisdom about plain old daily life. Sometimes she just needed to know what her mom or dad would have done about a certain problem or situation. Or again, what a big brother or sister would do.

But then the good news was that her mother-in-law had done all she could to become her mother in every way possi-ble, and Kenya loved her so much for that. Her father-in-law had also become a father to her, and in all honesty, they'd both begun treating Kenya as though she were their daughter from day one. They'd done so from the moment she and

Robert had first started dating, and since Kenya had heard more than enough monster-in-law/daughter-in-law stories to last a lifetime, she thanked God for Mr. and Mrs. Charles and Mary Griffin. Not to mention, they were the most loving grandparents they could be to Eli and Livvie.

Of course, Kenya was beyond grateful to have her three best friends in her life, too: Serena, Michelle, and Lynette. Her girls. Her ride-or-die companions. Her sister friends forever. They were always there for her, no matter what— through the good times, the bad, and the ugly—and the four of them had been the best of friends since they were small girls growing up in church. In fact, had it not been for their parents all joining the same church, there was a chance they might never have met one another. Not when they all lived in totally different neighborhoods: Serena on the far west end of town, Michelle on the far east, Lynette on the north side, and Kenya on the south. So even though Mitchell's population maxed out at around 150,000 residents and wasn't massive, all four of them had attended different elementary schools. They'd also done the same when it had come to attending junior high and high school, and interestingly enough, they had all attended different universities for undergrad, too. Serena had received a full academic scholarship to Yale, and since Michelle had always been just as interested in the medical field as Kenya was and wanted to become a nurse, her parents had insisted on sending her to Johns Hopkins. Then, as far as Lynette, she had received more than enough scholarship and grant money from Spelman, which had always been her school of choice anyway, and Kenya had attended Howard via scholarships, grants, and work-study, all of which had allowed her to graduate with no student loan debt. Of course, paying for medical school had been a very different story. but thankfully she had finished paying off the loans for that degree a few years ago.

Kenya lifted her insulated stainless steel mug from where it had been sitting next to her and drank the rest of her coffee, but when she heard the patio door opening, she turned and looked in that direction. She smiled when her husband, who still looked as good as he had the day she'd married him, walked toward her and sat down beside her. Next, he pecked her on the lips, but she could tell right away that something was troubling him.

"Honey, what's wrong?" she asked.

Robert sighed and shook his head. "Guess?"

Kenya's spirits plummeted because she knew whatever was going on had everything to do with Terri, Robert's ex-wife, who was also the mother of Robert's twelve-year-old son, Bobby.

"What happened?" she asked. "Because, I mean, it's not even seven a.m. yet."

Robert placed his phone in Kenya's hand. "Yeah, well, from the looks of this text message and how long it is, Terri has been up since before daylight."

Kenya scrolled through the message from beginning to end, seeing that it looked more like a full-length letter than it did a phone text.

Robert stood up. "I'm going back inside to get a cup of coffee, but prepare yourself, because she's really on one today. Big time."

When Robert disappeared through the patio door, Kenya scrolled back to the top of the message and began reading.

You know... it's bad enough that you walked off and left your wife and son, filed for divorce, and then had the nerve to get married barely a year after it was final. But now you have the audacity to be taking me to court about your so-called visitation rights? How dare you? Because it's not like Bobby is dying to spend time with you, your pathetic wife, or those other two kids, brats or whatever it is you have over there. Bobby can't stand any of you, and I don't blame him. Plus, Bobby has me, which is all he needs. I'm all he'll ever need, and the sooner you accept that truth, the better off everyone will be. And what's so pitiful, too, is that you know Bobby never wants to come to your house for even two hours, let alone spend an entire holiday weekend with you. So why in the world would you call and ask him if he wanted to spend Memorial Day weekend with you guys? Why, Robert? Why, when he's never spent a single holiday with you ever since you married that woman? And why should I have to spend ANY holiday all alone and without my son, when you have a whole wifey and two other children you can celebrate with anytime you want? And if you wanted to spend so much quality time with your son on the holidays, you should've thought about that before leaving him and me and filing for divorce. Yeah, I had an affair on you, and I have always been woman enough to own up to that indiscretion. But Robert, everybody makes mistakes, and you and I were supposed to stay married until death. Remember? Through everything. Remember? But no, you, the person who claims to love God so much, couldn't find it in your heart to forgive your own wife, Robert. And instead, you deserted Bobby and me and moved on. You moved on business as usual and acted as though your son and me didn't even exist. I mean, what a hypocrite you are. And I don't care what your little wifey does for a living or how much money she makes, she's still not smarter than me or better than me. And I also don't care how much money you make either, just as long as the two of you send me my child support payments every month. Still, though, if you force me to come see your evil behind in court, if I were you, I would prepare for the fight of my life because I'm not giving you my son. Not on holidays, in the summer, or on any weekends. Because it's like I said, he doesn't like any of you. And I don't like any of you. Actually, I can't stand the ground you walk on Robert, and I hate I ever met you, let alone married you. But that's okay because when I'm done fighting you in court about this visitation nonsense, we'll be heading right back there again about my increase in child support. Because for all I know, you might be earning a whole lot more money than you claimed you were earning two years ago. Because it's not like I have any proof of your salary. So maybe instead of letting you send these little three thousand dollar checks you send me every month, I should file a claim with child support. Because I definitely think it's time to reexamine those finances of yours again, so I can make sure my baby is getting everything he deserves. Don't you? He's just as important as your other two children, Robert. Actually, he's more important because he's your firstborn, and I'm your first wife. So make no mistake about it, I will always look out for my baby. For as long as I live. Actually, my child support should be based on both your incomes . . . meaning your income and the income of that witch you're so happily married to. But whatever. Oh and please know that there is no need for you to respond to this message. No need for you to contact me about anything. But there is one last thing I want to say. You have a nice day.

Kenya was speechless. She knew she shouldn't have been, not with Terri simply just being the same Terri she had always been. But now she was actually admitting via text message that she didn't want Bobby spending any time with Kenya, his eight-year-old brother, his six-year-old sister, and most of all, his own father? This woman was far too much, and while Kenya had always allowed Robert to deal with Terri on his own terms, even she knew that keeping his son away from him—on purpose—should never have been acceptable. Yes, it was true that Bobby seemingly didn't want to spend time with any of them, but it was only because his mother had poisoned his mind with so many lies about his dad. Terri had been doing this ever since she and Robert had divorced, but of course when Robert had begun dating Kenya, which hadn't started until their divorce was final, Terri had become even more bitter. Then, when Robert had informed Terri that he and Kenya were getting married, she had completely lost it. She had thrown a total fit, calling Robert every profane word she could think of, and from there, she had slowly but surely stopped Robert from seeing his son altogether.

At first, she began ignoring Robert's calls, but then eventually, she'd begun telling him what times he could and couldn't pick Bobby up. However, when Robert would arrive, she wouldn't answer the door. Or sometimes she would take Bobby and leave the house just before Robert was scheduled to come get him. She did this because she was angry and jealous of the relationship that Robert had with Kenya, and worse…she hated the fact that Robert also now had two other children. How did Kenya know this? Because she and Terri had once gone to the same hairstylist, and the stylist had told Kenya how she needed to watch out for Terri. She'd then shared all the horrible things Terri had been saying about Robert, Kenya, and their children. But the worst thing of all that Terri had admitted to Kenya's stylist was that not only did she hate Robert's other children, she also believed that had it not been for those "brats," Robert would have left Kenya and come back to her and Bobby a long time ago.

Kenya, of course, didn't like any of this, mainly because it was all so unfair to Bobby. That poor child had been forced to choose sides, and no matter what his dad or anyone else tried to tell him, including his paternal grandparents, he still believed everything his mother told him. He believed that his father had left and divorced his mom for no reason at all except that he had wanted to marry someone who made a lot more money than she did; never mind that even while Robert had still been married to Terri, he'd been a vice president at the same company he worked for now. So money certainly hadn't been an issue for Robert. Not back then or otherwise.

But sadly, Bobby also believed that his dad didn't love him, didn't want him, and that all he cared about were Livvie and Eli, something that couldn't have been further from the truth. Because if there was one thing Kenya knew about Robert, it was that he loved his eldest son with all his heart. So much so that had things gone Robert's way during his and Terri's divorce proceedings, he would have gained full custody of him. But Bobby didn't know any of this. He had no idea how much of a liar his mother was and how manipulative and deceptive she was. He also never would have imagined his mother sending this latest scathing text message to his dad, because Terri was very good at pretending to be someone else. She went to church every Sunday, smiled at everyone whom she came in contact with, and in public, she appeared to be one of the kindest women anyone could meet. That is, with the exception of those times she had frequented Kenya's hair salon. Still, what most people didn't know was that Terri was a master at being phony. She was sneaky and devious, and sadly, Kenya had a feeling that their interactions with Terri would become worse before they became better.

Much worse.

Kenya just knew it.

CHAPTER 4

Lynette

Lynette and her two daughters were now comfortably relaxing on their return flight home, and for the first time in a while, Lynette felt good—physically, mentally, and emotionally. At first, she hadn't been so sure that taking a trip was the right idea or if it would make any real difference for her. But it had, and she was truly happy about it. In fact, traveling down to Madison, Mississippi, the city her parents had returned to for their retirement, had ended up being one of the best decisions Lynette could have made. Because getting away to the South for an entire week had proven to be exactly what she, Chloe, and Tabitha had needed. Then, as it had turned out, Chloe and Tabitha had asked Lynette if they could fly home, pack more clothing, and then fly back to Mississippi to spend the summer with their grandparents. Actually, they hadn't even wanted to wait until summer, and instead, they wanted to leave as soon as possible.

But in all honesty, Lynette didn't blame them because she knew they needed a full break from the awfulness they had witnessed and experienced, thanks to Lynette and Julian's nasty and hurtful divorce proceedings. It had all been no joke, and although Tabitha and Chloe loved both

their parents, even they had begun asking Lynette why she allowed their dad to treat her so terribly. They were only fourteen and fifteen years old, but even when they'd first asked her this very question two years ago, Lynette had been stunned because she hadn't realized just how much they had been paying attention to her, their father, and the downfall of their marriage. Especially since Lynette had always tried her very best to hide the reality from them. She'd done all she could to protect their emotional well-being because it wasn't as though they had asked to be brought into this world, let alone trapped inside an unloving marital situation. It certainly wasn't their fault that their father had become one of the worst men Lynette knew, and sadly, one of the worst men Chloe and Tabitha knew, too.

But if Lynette was really being honest about who Julian was today and the fact that this was mostly how he had always been, she would also have to admit that he wasn't the man she should have married in the first place. Because while in the very beginning, when the two of them had first met, Julian had treated Lynette like a queen . . . once they'd gotten married, things had quickly begun to change. For one, he had totally dismissed the fact that just before meeting him, Lynette had received her bachelor's degree in psychology, and that she had been well on her way to building a career in human resources. She had even been hired by one of the largest corporations there in the city, but of course, after she fell in love with Julian and accepted his marriage proposal, everything had shifted. Not necessarily in the way she had wanted it to, but at the same time, Lynette had wanted to be a good wife, and she had also wanted to make her husband and his wishes her priority. She'd had no interest in losing herself as a woman or losing all her independence, but she had also wanted to honor God's Word as it related to a husband being the head of his household.

So as soon as Julian's construction company had secured a multimillion-dollar deal, which had happened only six months after they were married, Lynette had submitted her resignation to her boss. Not because she didn't love her job, but because Julian's company had taken off very quickly. Even the local and regional media outlets had already begun touting him as the youngest and one of the most successful construction business owners in the area. But even more so, Julian had sat her down and made it clear that he didn't want his wife working and that the wife of any successful CEO didn't need to work, anyway. He'd also insisted that it wasn't a good look for either of them status-wise, and that she belonged at home, raising their children on a full-time basis—children they didn't even have yet—but Lynette still had been fine with her husband's request. She'd been happy to support the husband she loved in any way she could and to become the best mother she could be to the two daughters they eventually had. That is, until all of Julian's late-night meetings and out-of-town "business" trips had become commonplace, and he had sometimes not found his way home until the very next morning.

Even on weekdays.

He had also never spent any real quality time with Chloe and Tabitha, and that bothered Lynette more than anything else. It had felt as though their daughters had been born to only one parent, but whenever Lynette had complained about this to Julian, all he would do was quickly remind her of the wealthy lifestyle he worked so hard to provide for her and the girls. Which meant that, besides his business and worldly possessions, he didn't care much about anything else.

Still, since Lynette had taken vows before God to stay married, for better or worse, and she hadn't wanted to cause her children any unnecessary pain, she had decided to grin and bear her loveless and pathetic marriage. She had made up her mind to do what she'd thought was the right thing to do. But then just under one year ago—on their sixteenth wedding anniversary, no less—Julian had arrived home, strolled into their first-floor master bedroom suite, just as nonchalant as he pleased, and announced that he was leaving her for another woman.

Even now, thirty thousand feet in the air, the thought of it all ignited every angry emotion Lynette could feel, and sadly, she couldn't help judging the beautiful young flight attendant who had just sashayed past her, smiling. Lynette knew she had no right assuming anything about a woman she didn't know, or anyone else for that matter. But after seeing the colossal diamond secured around the woman's ring finger, Lynette found herself wondering whose husband *this* woman might have met during some so-called business trip and had soon begun having an affair with. Because that was exactly what had happened to Lynette. Julian had boldly shared with her that from the moment he had walked onto the plane and seen "Crystal," the flight attendant who had been assigned to first class, he had fallen in love with her. And while hearing how much Julian loved another woman had been heartbreaking and devastating enough, what had hurt Lynette even more was when he had confessed the rest of the story: she was only twenty-five, three months pregnant with his twins, and as soon as his divorce from Lynette was final, he and Crystal were going to be married.

Lynette remembered how she had barely been able to breathe and how Julian had simply stood there staring at her with no emotion. He had acted as though he'd been telling her nothing out of the ordinary, and as if she should have been fine about all of it. But the thing was, she hadn't been fine at all. She hadn't been okay with any of what he had said—and it was at that very moment when she had made up her mind to take half of everything...including the seven-thousand-square-foot custom-built home they'd moved into just one year before. It had been his dream home, and not only had Lynette decided to take that from him, she had also decided to take anything else she believed she and her girls had coming to them.

She had promised Julian, too, that if he as much as *tried* to deny her anything she asked for in the divorce settlement, every company he did business with would learn very quickly that Julian Howard was a serial adulterer who had gotten his mistress pregnant, and that he was leaving his wife and daughters so he could marry her. Of course, to some men, none of those threats would have mattered one way or the other, but to men like Julian, who believed status and appearances meant everything, they did matter.

So just as Lynette had expected, Julian had quietly given her everything she had asked for without any hesitation. He hadn't been happy about it, of course, but his unhappiness had been the very least of her worries, and now Lynette was finally beginning to think about Lynette. The divorce had only been final for two months, but she was now ready to move on and begin thinking about how she was going to spend the rest of her life. She would certainly continue making her two girls her top priority, but she was also going to begin living. There was no doubt that the dating scene would be much different than it had been nearly twenty years earlier, but Lynette was more than willing to give it a try. Because no matter how terrible her life had been with Julian, she still believed in love, and she still believed that marriage could be a good thing. Especially if she could meet the right person.

And even better, her soul mate.

CHAPTER 5

Serena

It was Girls Day Out, and as always, Serena was beyond happy to see her three best friends. They'd been doing this for years, getting together for lunch the first Saturday of every month, and it was to the point now where they didn't just *want* to see each other, they *needed* to see each other. They looked forward to having some amazing girl time, and they also enjoyed being able to laugh and talk about everything—the good in their lives, the painful times, and everything else. They were also one another's emotional support system, which meant they could cry, complain, and share some of the most delicate parts of their realities in total confidence...and in four words: They could be themselves. Even better, the reason they could spend so much time together in person was because Serena, Michelle, Kenya, and Lynette had decided to make their hometown their permanent residence. This certainly wasn't the norm—four best friends graduating from college and all deciding to live in the same city. But they'd made a lifetime pact and vowed to remain in close proximity, both with their immediate family members and with one another.

As Joseph, the salt-and-pepper-haired, middle-aged, distinguished-looking restaurant owner, led them into the small, elegant, private dining room, all four women took their seats.

"It's so good to see you ladies," he said, smiling. "And how have you been?"

"We're doing well," Lynette answered, as did the others.

"I'm so glad to hear it. And did you ladies enjoy your holiday weekend?" Joseph asked.

Michelle, Kenya, and Lynette nodded yes, and then shared bits and pieces of their holiday activities with him, but since Serena had experienced one of the worst holidays in her adult life, she smiled but didn't say anything.

Joseph clasped his hands together in front of him. "So, are we doing the usual? Giving you an hour to chat with a glass of wine and then bringing out your favorite dishes? Unless maybe you're feeling a little adventurous and want to try something different for a change," he said, chuckling.

The women all laughed because it was no secret that they always ordered their same favorite meals, every time, and never veered away from them.

Kenya laughed. "Now, Joseph, you know it's definitely chicken fettucine for me."

"And broiled salmon for me," Serena said, smiling.

Lynette smiled at him, too. "And, of course, you know I can't imagine ordering anything except the best-tasting lasagna in the whole wide world."

"And I'll take my rib eye, medium to medium-rare," Michelle added.

Joseph raised his eyebrows. "Wow, really? So not just medium this time but a little medium-rare?"

"Yep, I'm doing what you said. I'm being adventurous," Michelle joked, and they all laughed again.

"Very well," he said. "And let me just say how much I

appreciate you ladies and the way you have supported my restaurant every single month for more than a decade. Not to mention, the many times you've also come here with your families for lunch or dinner. I mean, I know I've thanked you many times before, but for some reason I wanted to do it again today because your patronage means everything. It truly does, and I'm very grateful for it."

"You are quite welcome," Serena told him. "We love meeting and eating at Soriano's, and we love you, Joseph."

Kenya nodded. "We absolutely do, and we also appreciate the fact that you are kind enough to reserve our favorite room for us every single time we come. And you always take time out of your own schedule to personally seat us and take our orders, and that says everything."

"I wouldn't have it any other way, and please enjoy yourselves, ladies," he said, leaving the room and shutting the door behind him.

Michelle repositioned her body and relaxed further into her chair. "He's such a nice guy."

"He really is, and he always has been," Kenya said. Then she looked directly across the table at Serena. "Are you okay?"

Serena nodded. "I'm good."

"Are you sure? Because you don't seem fine, and that worries me."

Tears filled Serena's eyes, but she fought hard, making sure they didn't roll down her cheeks.

Michelle, who was sitting adjacent to Serena, rested her hand on top of her friend's. "Sis, what's wrong? What aren't you telling us?"

Serena felt genuine compassion from her girls, and although Lynette hadn't commented at all, her eyes showed just how concerned she was about Serena as well. So, while

Serena found herself debating back and forth whether she should tell them the entire story or not, she knew she needed to share at least some of it.

"Tim and I broke up."

"Oh no," Lynette said. "When? And why?"

"A week ago yesterday. I found out he was sleeping with another woman," she explained, but she couldn't find the courage to tell them about that salacious audio recording she had received via email. It was just too humiliating.

Still, Serena waited for some responses—but no one said a word. They each sat there in awkward silence, and Serena knew what they were thinking. Which was the reason that she decided to speak for them.

"I know you all never really liked Tim anyway."

Kenya leaned forward, placing her elbows on the table. "Well, that's not totally true. We just never liked him for you."

Serena slightly lowered her eyebrows. "Why?"

"Because he never seemed like the type of man who would ever fully commit to you," Lynette interrupted. "I mean, I'm sorry, sis, but I know the signs of a cheater better than anyone. I was married to one for years, remember? So I'll be honest, I never cared much for Tim at all."

Serena crossed her arms and then glanced over at Michelle. "And what about you? You never liked him, either?"

"Well, it wasn't like he was one of my favorite people in the world. And to me, on Valentine's Day when we all went out to dinner, he spent way too much time texting on his phone. All while the six of us were supposed to be enjoying a romantic couples' date," she said, referring to Serena and Tim, Kenya and Robert, and Michelle and Chris. "And again, he did this on *Valentine's Day*."

Serena wished she could deny everything Michelle was saying, but she couldn't. Not when Serena had been thinking the same thing herself. She even remembered how embarrassed she had felt that evening, and now she wondered if maybe Tim had been exchanging text messages then with the woman he was seeing now. But there was also something else she was ashamed of that had nothing to do with Valentine's Day. Because although Serena loved Michelle just as much as she loved Kenya and Lynette, she couldn't help feeling a little jealous of Michelle. The reason: Michelle was engaged to Chris. And now things were very different, because before Chris had proposed to Michelle, she and Serena had both still been looking for the right man, and eventually this had brought them even closer as friends than they already had been. So much so that Serena sometimes talked to Michelle much more than she did with Kenya and Lynette because she and Michelle had certain things in common. Particularly the fact that neither of them had ever been married. Now, though, with Michelle being engaged, Serena was the only one of them who fell into the true singles category. And not only was Serena unmarried, she was also forty...and before she knew it, she would be fifty. And then sixty. And so on.

The tall, thirtysomething waiter with coal-black hair rolled a cart into the room and placed a glass pitcher filled with ice water, four drinking glasses, a bottle of white wine chilling on ice, four wineglasses, and a basket of warm bread with butter onto the table. When he left, Lynette said, "So how did you find out he was cheating?"

Serena had so been hoping this question wouldn't come up, because while she didn't want to lie to her best friends, she also didn't want to share any shameful details with them. But since honesty and transparency were two of the main

34

reasons that they'd all been able to remain best friends for as long as they had, Serena knew she had to come clean.

"Some female sent me an audio recording," she said.

Michelle frowned. "Of what? Her and Tim's phone conversations?"

At first Serena paused, but then she said, "Of them having sex."

Michelle gasped and covered her mouth all at the same time.

Kenya raised her eyebrows. "Girl, you have got to be kidding."

Lynette shook her head in disgust. "I knew that clown was no good. I could tell from the first time we met him. He just had a certain look and attitude about him that didn't seem right to me."

Serena wasn't sure what to say except, "Well, it is what it is, and I'm done with him. So that's that."

Kenya drank some of her wine. "You deserve so much better, girl. You're a good person with a big heart, but unfortunately not every man can appreciate that."

"So true," Michelle said. "And even though some men will never settle down with just one woman, there are also a lot of men who will. You just have to meet the man who's right for you."

Lynette pursed her lips. "Yeah, but sometimes even the ones who do settle down will still mess around on you. Because here's the thing: If a man is going to cheat, he's going to cheat. And I don't care how beautiful you are, how intelligent you are, how well you cook, how great the sex is between you and him, or even if you're the kind of woman who will wait on a man hand and foot. None of that is going to stop him. Because if he wants to mess around, he will, and that's all there is to it."

"Exactly," Kenya agreed, and then turned her attention back to Serena. "So maybe it's time for you to become more prayerful about it. Because while I know you're a praying woman just like the rest of us, maybe it's also time for you to be much more specific. Meaning, maybe you should specifically ask God to bring you the man you're supposed to marry. The man He has designed for you and only you. Because so many times we don't do that. We pray, but we also have a tendency to still choose who *we* want and who we believe we should be with. And of course, that doesn't always work out too well."

"Maybe. But who knows," Serena said, sighing once again because while there had been a time when she had prayed faithfully for God to introduce her to her husband, over these last couple of years, she had sort of slacked off from doing so. She did believe in prayer and the fact that God could do anything, and she also prayed every single day of her life about other things. But then when God hadn't answered her prayers about marriage, she had stopped praying about that part of her life altogether. Because to her, it just hadn't been worth it to keep asking for something, over and over, and not receiving it. And then what if being single was all she could ever hope for? What if being unmarried was her destiny, and that it was simply just time for her to accept her fate?

"And while I know you may not want to hear this, either," Kenya said, "just because a man earns six figures doesn't mean he's going to treat you the way you ought to be treated. Because sometimes dating a man simply because he's a good man will make you so much happier. Regardless of what his income is."

"I agree," Michelle said. "Marrying someone with money can be great, but what good is any of that if he's awful to you?"

Serena laughed out loud. "This from a woman who's engaged to a cardiothoracic surgeon? And Kenya, don't even get me started on the fact that Robert is an executive vice president at one of the top companies in the city. And he was already a lower-level vice president when you met him."

Now Lynette looked at Serena. "And then there's me. I married a man who earned much more than Chris and Robert. He made seven figures every year throughout our entire marriage, yet he treated me like I was some worthless animal on the street. So, girl, moving forward, I hope you'll keep that in mind. I hope you'll somehow find peace with the fact that money and status will never guarantee you happiness. And another thing. While I'm not trying to be holier-than-thou, because everyone here knows I'm not, I had to learn the hard way just how true Hebrews thirteen, five actually is," she said, referring to the scripture that talked about how people should keep their lives free from the love of money and be content with what they have because God has promised that He will never leave them or forsake them, no matter what.

Serena heard everything her girls were saying, including Lynette's reference to the scripture in Hebrews. But she was also pretty tired of listening to all the unasked-for and unwanted advice they each seemed so dead set on giving her. She knew her friends meant well, but Serena quickly changed the subject to something that had nothing to do with her. "So are the girls still leaving next week?" she asked Lynette about her daughters.

"They are, and it feels really strange."

"I can only imagine," Serena said.

"And to be honest, I don't know if I'm ready to become a summertime empty nester. Because I'm sort of missing them already, and they're not even gone yet."

"That's so understandable," Michelle said, "but I also think you need this time alone so you can focus on your new normal. And well...just so you can focus on you and only you."

Kenya and Serena nodded in agreement.

"I know," Lynette said. "I've been thinking the same thing, and that's what I plan to do. But I'll still miss my girls. Although, I'm really glad they're excited about spending the summer with my parents, because it's not like their low-down father spends any real time with them at all."

"Wow," Kenya exclaimed. "That's so ironic because as you know with our situation, Robert wants more than anything to spend time with Bobby, but instead, he's having to fight for visitation—visitation, mind you, that the judge ordered a long time ago during Robert and Terri's divorce proceedings," she said, and then told them about some text message Terri had sent Robert four days ago.

Michelle pulled a dinner roll from the basket, buttered it, and tore it in two. "Well, we all know she's still in love with Robert, and that's why she's so bitter. And, of course, the reason she hates you is because she can't figure out why your marriage to Robert has worked out so well, but hers failed miserably."

"Well, all I know," Lynette said, "is that Julian will never have to worry about me trying to keep his kids from him. I mean, I just don't get that. And then there are some women who use their kids for any reason at all just so they can try to hurt their exes or try to stay in touch with them. I'll never understand that, either, because, to me, when the marriage is over, it's over, and everyone should move on accordingly."

"Exactly," Kenya said. "But the problem with Terri is the fact that she never remarried, and she also doesn't seem to date that much, either. Because maybe if she did, she wouldn't have time to focus on Robert one way or the other."

Michelle grinned. "Yeah, well, I don't think she's interested in dating or getting married to anyone because it's like I said. She's still in love with Robert. And she also still hasn't given up on the idea of them getting back together. Which is just plain sad and pitiful."

Serena listened to Kenya, Michelle, and Lynette conversing back and forth. She didn't join in, though, because for some reason, she couldn't stop thinking about Tim and the way he had betrayed her. It had been more than a week since she had learned about his affair, but her pain felt as fresh as it had when she'd first received the audio recording. Partly because she had truly loved Tim, and partly because she wanted to know who this *other* woman was and how she looked. Serena knew that neither question should matter to her in the least and that some might think she should actually be thanking the woman for exposing Tim the way she had, but Serena couldn't help wondering what was so special about her. What did she have that Serena *didn't* have? Most of all, Serena wondered why Tim hadn't as much as texted her ever since she'd called to confront him about the recording. Because in the past, whenever she had broken up with any man, he'd either lied, denied what he was being accused of, or he had simply apologized and begged for her forgiveness. But not Tim. Which was the reason that Serena's mind was made up: When she left the restaurant, she was heading straight over to his house. Because whether Tim believed he owed her an explanation or not, she wouldn't be leaving there until she got one.

CHAPTER 6

Serena

Serena pulled into Tim's driveway as planned and shut off her ignition, but now she felt a bit nervous and wondered if maybe she should start her vehicle back up and head home. Because the more she sat thinking, the more she realized how silly she was being. Pathetic, even. Especially since the one thing she had never done in the past was run after any man who didn't want her. She also never stalked her exes' Instagram pages the way she had been doing Tim's for a few days now. So she couldn't help wondering why this particular time felt so different. Although, maybe it was because of what she had been thinking earlier: that she was forty and had never been married.

Then, while she knew she shouldn't have as much as one word to say to Tim, she wanted him to tell her why: why he had decided to cheat on her...why he hadn't been man enough to simply just break up with her before starting a new relationship with someone else...and sadly, she wanted him to tell her why she hadn't been good enough for him. Because whenever a man dated any woman for nearly a year without making a single reference about marriage, it usually meant one of two things: He was holding out for someone better, or he wasn't all that interested in being married to anyone, ever.

Serena debated her decision one last time, and then opened the door and stepped out of her car. But as she walked along the brick pathway leading toward the front door, her heart beat just a little faster than usual. She also felt more nervous than she had only a few minutes ago, and she hoped she wasn't having an anxiety attack. She hadn't experienced one since earlier this year, but just in case she was, she inhaled and exhaled deeply. She did this five times, slowly and consecutively, and felt her body calming itself more and more. Then once she'd settled down completely, she rang the doorbell. Tim didn't answer right away, though, so she rang it again, and this time she heard him unlocking the door.

"Well," he said, "this is a surprise."

Serena showed no emotion. "Yeah, I'm sure it is."

Tim fanned his hand to the side of him, inviting her in, and then followed behind her. When they entered the family room, he said, "Please have a seat."

Serena did as he asked, but she could tell this was going to be harder than she had thought because just being there and seeing how cordial and nonchalant he was acting was infuriating her all over again.

Tim sat across from her on his other sofa. "So, what's up?"

Serena raised her eyebrows. "*What's up*? Tim, what do you think is up?"

"I don't know, that's why I'm asking."

"What's up is that you owe me an explanation."

Tim leaned his head back and exhaled loud enough for her to know he didn't want to have this conversation. But

Serena didn't care, because they were definitely discussing this—today. Whether he wanted to or not.

"So why did you do it, Tim?" she asked.

"Do you really think this is necessary? I mean, I know I messed up and that I maybe should have handled things a lot differently. But it's not like I can change what happened. What's done is done, and I'm sorry."

"Well, at the very least, why couldn't you just tell me that you wanted to end things between us? Why couldn't you just be honest about the way you felt?"

"Because I didn't want to hurt you."

"What? Hurt me *how*?" Serena said, raising her voice.

"See, this is the reason I didn't want to talk about this."

"Why?"

"Because I don't want to argue with you. I don't want to debate something that can't be corrected. I made a mistake, and I just told you I'm sorry."

"That's not good enough. Because if you weren't serious about me, then why did you pretend you were? Why did you keep dating me for all that time? And worse, why did you tell me you loved me?"

Tim stared at her. "Because I knew that's what you wanted to hear."

Serena's heart sank. It felt as though it had skipped several beats, and she was stunned at how easy it had been for Tim to look her straight in her face and lie about the feelings he had for her.

"So you were simply leading me on and using me?"

"Using you how?" he asked, frowning. "Because you and I *both* know that I certainly never used you for sex. You're celibate, remember?"

Serena wished she could argue her own point of view

about this, but she knew he was telling the truth. Still, none of what he had done justified the way he'd hurt her, and she wanted answers.

"Look, I just want to know why you did what you did when all you had to do was break up with me before doing it. And, anyway, how long have you been seeing this other woman?"

Now Tim dropped his face into the palms of his hands before finally looking back up at her. "Why can't we just leave things the way they are and move on?"

"Because you don't just date someone for almost a year, sleep around with some whore, and then walk away like nothing happened."

"Okay, fine," he said. "I did it because I was tired of dealing with all this celibacy nonsense. And yes, I should have just told you I wasn't okay with it, but for a while I sort of thought you'd come to your senses about it. I figured this was just some little temporary lifestyle you were trying out and that eventually, your feelings for me would change all that. But they never did, so I started looking elsewhere...a few months ago."

"A few months ago?" she yelled.

"Look, I told you, the reason I didn't say anything was because I didn't want to hurt your feelings. Especially when you were always telling me how much you loved me."

"And you were always telling me how much you loved *me*," she reminded him.

"Well, I shouldn't have, and I apologize for saying something I didn't mean."

"You apologize? Really, Tim? You apologize for lying to me and pretending that you loved me when you knew you didn't? Please. And I'll tell you something else. This is the very reason men like you usually end up regretting some of the stupid decisions they make. Because, sweetheart, eventually, we all have to reap what we sow."

Tim chuckled at her. "Wait, are you threatening me?"

"No, I'm just telling the truth. You deceived me and cheated on me for no reason, and now I wish I'd never met you, let alone gotten involved with you. Especially since it's not like you're the finest-looking man I've ever laid eyes on, anyway," she spat, purposely trying to hurt him, and then she stood up. "To be honest, you're not even close."

Tim got up from the sofa he was sitting on, too. "Oh, really? Well, since we're being so honest, you want to know the real reason why I was never completely serious about you?"

Serena folded her arms. "I do."

"It's because you're not the kind of woman I want to spend the rest of my life with. What I want is a woman who doesn't feel this obsessive need to have some hugely successful career. I want a woman who's looking forward to becoming a stay-at-home mom once our children are born and one who cooks, not just two or three times a week but *seven* days a week. And I just don't see any of that happening with you."

Serena shook her head because with the way he talked, he was sounding no differently than Lynette's ex-husband, Julian, had before they'd gotten married. "Well, if you're looking for a woman who's going to give up everything she's worked for, just so you can feel good about yourself, then you're right. I'm not the kind of woman you need. I'm also not the kind of woman who could ever be with a man who's as insecure and jealous as you are. Because I began noticing a while ago that whenever I talked about some of my speaking contracts or media interviews, you always changed the subject. Always. Every single time. So I should have known then that you weren't the kind of man I should be wasting my time with. But that's okay, though, because the good news is this: My life is going to be just fine without you, Tim, and I'm glad this relationship or whatever you want to call it is over," she said, strutting away from him and down the hallway toward the front entryway. Tim followed behind her in silence. But when she opened the door, she saw a medium-height, caramel-colored woman with a short, chic haircut, preparing to ring the doorbell. That is, until she saw Serena, and then she immediately jerked her hand away from it, looking startled.

Serena opened the door wider. "Oh, so I guess you're the trick who sent me that ratchet recording of you and Tim?"

The woman looked confused. "Excuse me? Who do you think you're talking to?"

"I'm talking to you because chances are, you knew all along about my relationship with Tim, but you couldn't have cared less. According to him, you guys have been dating for months, so it's very hard for me to believe that you didn't know he was seeing someone else. Not with how often he and I went out in public together."

"What?" the woman said. "Look, even though what I'm about to say is absolutely none of your business…for the record, I just met Tim yesterday. So, honey, whoever sent you some mysterious recording or otherwise, it wasn't me," she spat. Then she tossed an angry look at Tim.

"I'll explain everything later," Tim hurried to say to the woman. "I promise."

Serena walked outside, nearly brushing past the woman, went down the walkway, sat inside her car, and closed the door. She couldn't believe Tim was already seeing yet another woman, which also made Serena wonder just how many other women he was actually seeing in total. But what she mostly thought about now was how coming over there hadn't been as silly as she'd thought. Instead, it had been just plain stupid.

CHAPTER 7

Lynette

Lynette looked at her two beautiful daughters, first at Chloe and then at Tabitha, and smiled. Chloe was pulling clothing from her closet and debating what she should and shouldn't take on her summer vacation to her grandparents'. Tabitha, on the other hand, was sitting on the opposite end of the bed from Lynette, scrolling through her phone. Still, as much as Lynette smiled, the moment was also bittersweet because just as she'd been sharing with her girlfriends earlier, she was going to miss her daughters terribly.

"So what do you think, Mom?" Chloe asked, holding up three pairs of jeans. "Should I take this many? Because the last time we visited Granny and Grandpa in the summer, it was scorching hot every single day. And that's why I'm taking lots of shorts and sundresses, too."

"That's very true. But you never know, so I would take at least two pairs just to be safe."

Chloe nodded in agreement and hung one pair back inside her closet. "Now I just need to figure out what shoes to take."

"And don't forget to pull out some dresses for church on Sundays," Lynette reminded her.

"Oh yeah, that's right," Chloe agreed.

Lynette looked over at Tabitha, who glanced up at her sister but didn't say anything. Then she began scrolling through her phone again. This wasn't unusual, but Tabitha seemed a bit quieter than normal. Actually, when Chloe and Lynette had been helping Tabitha pack some of her own things a couple of hours ago, she'd been pretty quiet about everything then, too.

"Are you okay, honey?" Lynette asked her youngest daughter.

"I'm good."

"You do still want to go down to Mississippi, don't you?"

Tabitha never looked up from her phone, but said, "Yes."

Chloe grabbed a few pairs of sandals and lined them up on the floor near her largest piece of luggage. "What's up, baby sis? I mean, I know you're going to miss Mom, because I am, too. But what's wrong?"

"Nothing."

"I'm really going to miss you girls," Lynette said, swallowing tears. "More than you could possibly ever know."

"It's going to be hard on all of us, Mom," Chloe said, leaning against the glass top of her desk. "But while we're gone, I hope you'll have some fun for a change. I hope you enjoy yourself. Because, Mom, I'm really proud of you for finally standing up for yourself and ending things with Daddy."

Tabitha jerked her head up and frowned. "Chloe, you say that like you don't even love Daddy anymore."

"No, Tab. I'm not saying that at all. You know I love Daddy. But you and I also know that Daddy wasn't always kind to Mom. Sometimes he was just plain cruel, and you and I have talked about this like, how many times?"

Tabitha hunched her shoulders and looked back at her phone again.

Lynette knew her daughters hadn't been happy about the way their dad treated her, but she was a little shocked to learn that they'd been having what sounded to be quite a few private conversations about it.

Lynette stood up. "Chloe, come sit down next to your sister."

Once she had, Lynette continued. "Okay, look, girls. I know I've already apologized to both of you many times over this last year, but I really am so, so sorry about the divorce and all the pain it has caused both of you and because of what it has done to us as a family. I'm also very sorry that you won't have an opportunity to spend all of your high school years growing up in a two-parent household. I think that's one of my biggest regrets of all."

"I get it, Mom, but we'll be fine," Chloe insisted. "Right, Tab?"

"Do we have to talk about this?" Tabitha asked.

"Yes, we do," Lynette said, "because I can tell this is really bothering you. More now than it has been over these last few months."

"I just wish things could have turned out differently. Because even though Daddy was awful to you...and even though, at first, I wanted you and him to separate...it was only because you were so unhappy all the time. But now that he's gone for good and he has a whole new family, I really miss him...and Mom, it's almost like he doesn't even care about Chloe and me or about how we feel. We barely even see him anymore."

"I know, and I'm really sorry about that, too."

Chloe crossed her legs. "Well, I'm good with that. Because if Daddy doesn't want to see me, then I don't want to see him, either."

"Honey, you know you don't really mean that," Lynette told her.

"I do, Mom. Because Daddy did some really terrible things behind your back. He messed around with so many other women, and when Tab and I were little, he used to take us over to his secretary's house. Which back then I didn't think was a big deal, but when I got older, I started thinking back to how long the two of them would leave Tab and me in that woman's family room. She would turn on the TV and then give me the remote control so we could watch whatever we wanted. One time, we watched two whole movies on the Disney Channel."

Lynette couldn't believe what she was hearing. "Oh my Lord. Sweetheart, I am so sorry, and why didn't you tell me about this before?"

"Because I knew it would make you even madder, and I also didn't want you and Daddy to have yet one more thing to be arguing about. Then when I got older, I didn't tell you because I thought you would be mad because I hadn't told you a lot sooner."

Tabitha shook her head. "I can't believe you just told Mom that."

"Why not, Tab?" Chloe asked.

"Because we were little kids and for all we know, Daddy and his secretary could have been working. Daddy worked outside of his office all the time."

"On a Saturday? When he was supposed to be taking you and me to the movies and to get ice cream? Those Saturdays were supposed to be our daddy-and-daughter time because it was on the same Saturday every month that Mom got together with our aunties," she said, referring to Lynette's friends, whom Chloe and Tabitha loved like family. "And, anyway, if he was doing so much work, how come he never told Mom about taking us over there? Instead, he would tell her that we went all these other places because he knew if he lied and said we'd really gone to see a movie, Mom would want us to tell her all about it. And he knew we wouldn't be able to."

Lynette literally wanted to scream. How dare Julian expose his own daughters to his infidelity. And how could any man feel comfortable enough to take his children around some tramp he was sleeping with? But even worse, it sounded as though this had happened multiple times, and now Lynette wished she'd done a better job of protecting Chloe and Tabitha. She, of course, never would have imagined that Julian would stoop to such lowly measures, but in hindsight, she also thought back to some of those Saturday afternoons when Julian and the girls would return home, and Chloe had seemed quiet and distant, traits that had never been a part of her normal personality. Tabitha, however, had always seemed fine, but it was likely because as long as Tabitha could spend time with her dad, life had been good. She'd felt that way as a little girl, and she still felt that way now, even though Julian had gone an entire month without seeing them.

But enough was enough. Because while Lynette had made a pact with herself about not calling Julian for anything unless she absolutely had to, she knew she had to have a conversation with him about this. What he'd done was well in the past, but she still wanted to know why he would subject his girls to all his adulterous ways. Even more so, she wanted to ask him why he was acting as though Chloe and Tabitha no longer existed, and it was the reason she was going to schedule a face-to-face sit-down with him as soon as possible. Preferably tomorrow, because if Chloe and Tabitha didn't get to see their father before they left for

Mississippi, they wouldn't see him for the next two months, and that wasn't acceptable. Because unlike Robert's ex-wife, Terri, Lynette wanted her girls to have a great relationship with their father, and she wanted him to spend time with them. Quality time. The kind of time that included seeing their girls at least every other weekend, exactly the way he'd claimed he would do when the divorce was finalized. She wanted him to be a father to all of his children, and not just his new twin boys.

CHAPTER 8

Michelle

Full Faith Christian Center's adult choir had just finished singing John P. Kee's "Life and Favor," and Michelle, Chris, her parents, Aunt Jill, and the rest of their congregation applauded them for a job well done. Michelle loved her church. She always had, and as she sat in the fifth row in the middle section of pews, with her fiancé and aunt sitting on one side of her and her mom and dad sitting on the other, she felt grateful in many ways. Not to mention that no matter how old she got, every time she entered the sanctuary, she still thought about all the wonderful childhood church experiences that she, Serena, Kenya, and Lynette had shared. From joining the children's choir to participating in the church's annual Easter and Christmas plays to becoming members of the young adult choir when they'd become teenagers, the four of them had done everything together, and they'd enjoyed themselves in the process. They'd also learned so much about God, His Son Jesus, and the huge difference between right and wrong, and Michelle was thankful to her parents for making sure that so much of her upbringing had included reading and studying scriptures in the Bible because every bit of it had helped her become the woman she was today.

Pastor Rigsby, who had turned sixty-five years old a few days ago, left his front-row seat, strode up the red-carpeted steps and into the pulpit, and then set his iPad on the glass podium. Pastor Rigsby was a good man who loved God, his wife, his children, and his congregation, and while Michelle knew that no one was perfect, what she and most all the other members loved and respected about him was the fact that in the thirty years he'd been their senior pastor, there hadn't been a single scandal—something that wasn't the norm for so many other pastors who led churches in the Mitchell community.

Pastor Rigsby looked across the congregation. "It is of the Lord's mercies that we are not consumed, because His compassions fail not. They are new every morning, great is thy faithfulness," he said, quoting Lamentations 3:22–23. "And a beautiful good morning to all of you, Full Faith Christian Center."

"Good morning, Pastor," most everyone responded.

"So before I begin today's sermon, I just want to take a few moments to say thank you to all of you. From the bottom of my heart, thank you for all the cards, gifts, phone calls, and yes, all the many Facebook and Instagram well wishes I saw on the church's social media pages. You certainly know how to make a man feel special, and I sincerely appreciate it. I will say, though, turning sixty-five has me thinking a lot about my younger years and how I now have far more years *behind* me than I have in front of me. But then, at the same time, the good news is this: I'm doing all I can to take care of myself in every way possible. Physically, mentally, emotionally, and spiritually. I'm eating right, but I'm also still enjoying many of the foods I like in moderation; I work out five days per week, and although my wife and I will be celebrating our fortieth anniversary later this year, we're still having the time of our lives together."

The congregation applauded again, and said, "Amen."

"Also, one of the real reasons I wanted to share that with you is because I hope you're doing the same thing. And if you're not, I hope you'll begin taking better care of your-selves and living your life to the fullest. I hope you'll focus on what makes you happy and figure out what doesn't, so you can eliminate whatever that is completely from your life. Because my dear brothers and sisters, life is short. I know that's a clichéd statement that many of us have heard our parents and even our grandparents say for years, but I'm here to tell you that it's also one of the truest statements ever. So again, please live your life, and well...just be happy."

Michelle quietly took a deep breath and thought about every word Pastor Rigsby had just said, and she knew he was right. Life truly was short, and while she was in a good place physically, mentally, and spiritually, she knew her emotional well-being wasn't where it needed to be. Not with her constantly thinking about Steven when she knew she was engaged to this wonderful man sitting next to her. A gorgeous, successful, intelligent man. So why wasn't that enough for her? Why couldn't she just be happy with him and forget about what used to be, so she could fully focus on the present? Why?

Pastor Rigsby prepared to pray, the same as he always did before delivering any of his sermons. "Dear Heavenly Father, we come right now just thanking You for allowing us to see another day. We thank You for allowing us to wake up in good health and for giving us yet one more opportunity to praise You, worship You, and fellowship together as a con-gregation on this beautiful Sunday morning. Lord, we ask that You would heal those who are sick and that You would give strength, comfort, peace, and understanding to anyone, throughout the world, who has lost a loved one. Then, Lord, I ask that You provide me with the words, thoughts, and overall message that You want me to deliver to your children this morning and that those words, thoughts, and message will be a blessing to everyone here in the sanctuary, as well as to those who are viewing our service virtually. We thank You, Lord, for these and all other blessings in Your mighty and precious Son Jesus's name. Amen."

Pastor Rigsby opened his eyes and swiped his iPad a few times. "So today, if you will, please turn with me to Psalm sixteen, verse eleven."

Then once he'd given everyone a few seconds to find the scripture, he continued. "And it reads as follows: 'You will make known to me the path of life; in Your presence is fullness of joy; in Your right hand there are pleasures forever.'"

Many of the members agreed by saying, "Amen."

"This has always been one of my favorite scriptures. And the reason it's one of my favorite scriptures is because it promises us that God will always make our paths known to us. Meaning He will show us our purpose and our destiny. I also love this scripture because it confirms that if we stay close to God, His presence will provide for us the kind of joy that will allow us to live a happy and fulfilled life. So, having said that, my topic for today is: *Are you living the life God has designed for you, or are you living someone else's?*" And then he repeated it. "*Are you living the life God has designed for you, or are you living someone else's?*"

"Wow," a woman sitting over in another section said.

"All right now, Pastor," Michelle's dad said, nodding in agreement.

"There are so many times when many of us have found ourselves living a tremendous lie when we could be living a tremendous *life*."

There were more "Amens," and some of the members spoke among themselves, totally agreeing with Pastor Rigsby.

"But when we live in a way that we don't enjoy ... when we live the kind of life that we know wasn't designed for us, the only thing we can ever receive from living that kind of life is unhappiness. And when we live the kind of life that someone *else* wants us to live, or if we live in a way that we believe will be beneficial to someone else—yet at the same time it will be detrimental to our own lives and feelings—we do a great disservice to ourselves."

Michelle stared at Pastor Rigsby, and while she knew he had no idea what she was going through, he was still some-how speaking directly to her soul. He was also making her think long and hard about her entire situation.

Pastor Rigsby looked down at his notes. "And when I talk about living your life, I mean in all areas. For example, are you working in a career because your parents or some other family member convinced you to choose that line of work? Or are you following a career path that you've always been passionate about? And more important, does that career seamlessly coincide with the true and divine purpose God has assigned to your life? Or when it comes to dating and getting married to your significant other, are you with that person for all the right reasons? Or are you with them because it feels comfortable or because everyone around you believes you and this particular person make the perfect couple? Because let me tell you, there are some folks who have been married for years, yet they have never truly been in love. But the reason they got married anyway was because the relationship felt comfortable. Or they felt obligated to marry a certain someone for one reason or another...or everyone around them insisted that it was the right thing for them to do...or the person they married truly does love them, and they didn't want to hurt that person's feelings by saying no. But whatever the reason, when this happens, he or she soon comes to realize that they are not living the life God designed for them, and instead, they are living someone else's."

Tears streamed down Michelle's face, and Chris immediately wrapped his arm around her and pulled her closer. Her mom passed her a lace-trimmed handkerchief and caressed her arm, trying to comfort her, but now Michelle cried much more noticeably. She wept because not only had Pastor Rigsby spoken about what she was experiencing, but his profound words had caused her to become more confused than she already was. She also felt bad because while Chris and her mom were doing all they could to comfort her, she knew they had no clue as to why she was sitting in the middle of church service sobbing. They had no idea that she was reconsidering everything, and that it was all she could do not to call off the wedding and end things with Chris.

Right now.

For good.

Although, in her heart of hearts, she knew she didn't have the courage to do that. Which meant she would now have to spend the next few minutes trying to concoct a believable explanation—for Chris, her parents, her aunt Jill, and even for Serena, Kenya, and Lynette, because her friends were sitting in the same section of pews only a couple of rows behind her. So yes, as much as she hated to do it, she would have to tell them something. Even if what she told them was a lie.

CHAPTER 9

Lynette

Lynette walked inside what used to be her and Julian's favorite fine-dining restaurant and stepped closer to the wooden maître d' station. Actually, she still loved the food and the atmosphere at Tatum and Beck's the same as always, but because it reminded her so much of her marriage to Julian, she hadn't eaten there since the two of them had separated. But when she'd called Julian this morning and he had suggested it, she hadn't debated him because these days, she chose her battles with him very carefully. If she could help it, she would no longer battle with him about anything at all. Although, this thing about him taking Chloe and Tabitha over to some woman's house when they were just small girls did make her want to fight him to the death. But earlier today, after thinking more about confronting him, she had decided that it wasn't worth it.

George finished a phone call and looked up at her. "Oh my goodness. It's so great seeing you, Mrs. Howard." Then he walked around to where she was standing and hugged her.

"It's really great seeing you, too, George. It's been a long time."

"Yes, far too long if you ask me. Although I certainly

understand…you know, because of the…Well, I'm really sorry about that."

"Thank you, but I'm fine, George. Really I am."

"I'm glad, and if you'll follow me, I'll take you to your table. Mr. Howard has already been seated."

Lynette followed George through the dining area, and although Tatum and Beck's was pretty busy, when she spied Julian sitting in a booth toward the very back, she also noticed that no other customers were sitting in the booths directly in front of or behind him and that no one was sitting at the two tables to the sides of him, either. But this was classic Julian. Always making sure he stood out in a high-society, high-status sort of way, even if he had to pay to keep those booths and tables empty. Today, though, since Lynette did want to speak to him privately, she appreciated the gesture.

When Lynette arrived directly in front of the booth where Julian was sitting, the two of them locked eyes and then he looked her up and down from head to toe. She ignored him, though, and slid her body toward the center of the leather bench.

"Can I get you something to drink, Mrs. Howard?"

Lynette set her black handbag to the side of her. "Some sparkling water would be great, and thank you."

"Of course. And is there anything else I can get for you, Mr. Howard?"

Julian lifted what looked to be a glass filled with cognac or whiskey. "No, George, I think I'm good for now."

"Very well, sir."

Julian leaned back, smiled, and shook his head.

Lynette kept a straight face. "What?"

"Nothing. I was just admiring how good you look. But

then you've always been beautiful, so I guess I shouldn't be surprised."

"Julian, please. Because you and I both know that ship sailed a very long time ago."

"Oh, so now I can't even give you a compliment? The woman I was married to for more than sixteen years? The mother of my two daughters?"

Lynette folded her arms. "Well, I think the bigger question is, how would Crystal feel about all of this?"

"There you go," he said, sipping some of his drink.

"And not that I care, but what is that? And when did you start drinking hard liquor?"

"It's cognac, and I've been drinking it on and off for a while now. Even when you and I were still together. I just never drank it around you and the girls."

"Well, I guess that's yet one more thing I didn't know about you, huh?" she said. "But hey, that's neither here nor there, and it's also not the reason I asked for us to meet. I called you because we really need to talk about our girls."

"Okay, fine. What's going on?"

"What's going on is the fact that you're not spending any time with them, Julian. You're acting as though you don't even have any daughters."

"Well, it's not like I'm doing it on purpose. I just signed a new real estate development deal, and it has me working sunup to sundown. Even on weekends."

"Oh really? Well, when did you sign it?"

"About three months ago."

"Okay, then why weren't you spending time with them before that? Because it's not like you've even picked them up more than five times since we separated, and that was a year ago."

"I told you, I have a lot going on. But you're right, I haven't seen our girls as much as I should have, and I'll do better."

"Well, just so you know, they're leaving in a couple of days, and they'll be gone for two months."

"Why? Where are they going?"

"They wanted to spend the summer with my parents, and I told them they could."

"Well, that's good. I'm glad they're going, and I'll stop by to see and talk to them tomorrow evening. And by the way, how are your mom and dad doing? I know they don't have a lot to say to me anymore, but they were great in-laws and I still think about them from time to time."

"They're fine," Lynette said just as their waitress walked toward them.

"Good evening," she said, setting a bottle of sparking water on the table and pouring some of it in a glass goblet.

Julian and Lynette spoke back to her. "Good evening."

"Can I start the two of you with an appetizer?"

Lynette opened her menu and scanned it for a few seconds. "Sure, I'll have your house salad and an order of shrimp cocktail."

"I'll have the same," Julian said.

"Sounds good, and I'll be back to get your entrée order very soon."

"Thank you," Lynette told her, but when the woman left, she caught Julian staring at her again, so she quickly looked away from him.

"Can I ask you something?" he said.

"What is it?"

"How come you stopped calling me Jules? You always called me that, but now every time you address me, you say Julian."

"Are you serious?" Lynette said a little too loudly, and then looked away from the booth. Thankfully, each of the nearby tables and booths were still empty. "Do you really think I'm going to call you by your nickname? A nickname I gave you in the first place?"

"Why not?"

"You're really something else," she said.

"Look, Lyn, I know I messed up. I messed up badly, but that doesn't mean we have to be enemies, right? And anyway, you told me last month that you had forgiven me."

"I have forgiven you. For myself and for our daughters, but that's where our relationship ends. In fact, I'm not even sure why we needed to have dinner here."

"Well, it wasn't like we could talk in front of the girls."

Lynette couldn't deny what he was saying because as soon as he'd suggested coming to the house, she'd told him no, for the reason he had just mentioned.

"Well, I'm glad you've forgiven me," he finally said. "Because I know it wasn't easy."

"No, it wasn't, but I'm good now."

"Are you dating?"

Lynette glared at him like he was crazy, and while she wanted to tell him to mind his own business, she didn't. "I think it's best if we keep our personal lives private. Meaning, I won't ask you about your marriage to Crystal, and you don't ask me about any of my dating prospects."

"Prospects? Wow, that almost sounds like a yes to me."

"Well, here's the thing, Julian. What if I am dating? Because if I remember correctly, you had an affair—one of many affairs, I might add—you got your mistress pregnant, you deserted me and your daughters, and then you married that same mistress barely a week after we signed our divorce papers. You moved on, Julian, and so did I."

"I just don't want you to hate me, and I also don't want you to get hurt."

Lynette laughed out loud.

"Why is that funny to you? Because I'm very serious."

"It's funny because no one—and I do mean no one—has ever hurt me as badly as you have. Yet you have the nerve to say you don't want me to get hurt?"

"I know you don't understand it, and I also know I don't have any right asking you about anything you do, but I will always care about you, Lyn. Always."

"Well, you sure had a strange way of showing me that."

"Yeah, and there's not a day that goes by that I don't think about the way I treated you."

"Do you think about what you subjected our girls to?" Lynette asked.

The words had left her lips well before she could stop them because while their marriage was over and she had told herself she wouldn't bring it up, a part of her still wanted to question him about what Chloe had told her.

"What do you mean?"

"That witch that used to work for you."

"What witch?"

"Cindy. Your executive assistant."

Julian frowned. "What about her?"

"Chloe told me how you used to take her and Tabitha to that woman's house on the Saturdays I met with my girls for lunch."

Julian showed no emotion, but Lynette could tell how stunned he was to hear what she'd just told him.

"So is it true? Did you take them to Cindy's house and then leave them in some room watching television for hours?"

"Look, baby, I'm not—"

"Baby? Please don't call me that. Never, ever call me that again."

"Okay, fine. But as I was about to say, I'm not even going to try to deny what I did because it's true."

"Why, though, Julian? Why would you do something so awful and irresponsible?"

"I don't know. I don't know why I did half the things I did back then, and all I can do now is tell you how truly sorry I am. I mean that, Lyn. From the bottom of my heart."

"This was a bad idea," Lynette said, picking up her handbag. "I never should have agreed to meet you, and now I'm realizing that a phone call would have more than sufficed."

"Wait, are you leaving?"

"I am."

"What about the appetizers we ordered? And dinner?"

"Right now, that's the least of my worries, and all I want to know is when you plan on coming to see your daughters."

"I'll be by there tomorrow. Tomorrow evening."

"Fine, but just make sure you call ahead of time."

"I'm really sorry, Lyn. I'm sorry for everything, and for whatever it's worth, I still love you. And not just because you're the mother of my children."

Lynette looked at him, dumbfounded. She was also amazed at the amount of gall he had and how he clearly still didn't have any real understanding of just how much pain he'd caused her and their girls. After all these years even. But instead of wasting more time trying to explain things to him, she simply slid out of the booth and said, "Goodbye, Julian."

"Really? So you're just going to leave? Just like that?"

"Just like that," she said, turning and heading toward the front entrance of the restaurant. But as she exited the building, she couldn't help wondering why Julian had just told her he loved her. Because it wasn't so much about *what* he'd said as it was the seemingly genuine way he had spoken to her in that moment. It was strange to say the least, but more than anything, she wondered if maybe his two-month fairy-tale marriage to Crystal was already in trouble.

CHAPTER 10

Kenya

Eli and Livvie sat in the back seat of Kenya's SUV, and like most children who rode in vehicles with their parents, they had their eyes locked on their tablets. Their respective electronic devices held their undivided attention, and as Kenya glanced at them in her rearview mirror, all she could do was shake her head and smile. Because while they did take in a bit more screen time than she preferred, she couldn't deny that they were good children with big hearts, and that they both did exceptionally well in school. Which was the reason that while she did limit their overall usage when it came to playing games and watching movies through their apps between the months of September and May, she was a lot more lenient during their summer breaks and on weekends. She also didn't mind them using their tablets on the way to day camp either because she knew they couldn't take them into the facility. They could only bring in their smartphones, and even those could only be used at scheduled times or for emergency purposes.

When the light changed, Kenya adjusted her sunglasses on her face and drove through the intersection. She only had a short distance to go before dropping off the children at camp, and then she would be heading to work. Actually, with today being Monday, she would likely be seeing patients back-to-back because in addition to those who were already scheduled with appointments, there were always a good number of patients who experienced some sort of medical issue over the weekend and then called in first thing on Monday morning, asking to be seen. But it was all fine with Kenya because she truly loved the calling God had placed on her life. She loved delivering babies and helping women with various gynecological issues, and it just felt good to not only be able to earn a good living, but to also be able to serve others in a healing capacity. It was also a blessing to be living out her dream of becoming a doctor, something she'd begun hoping and praying for when she was a child. Even now, as she thought back to the way she would line up her dolls and stuffed animals on her bed and perform medical exams on them with the toy stethoscope her parents had given her one Christmas, she couldn't remember ever wanting to be any-thing else. She actually still had that stethoscope, along with the medical bag and all the other items that had come with it, and to this day, that same little medical bag and its contents sat on a bookshelf in her office at the private practice she had owned for nearly a decade.

Kenya drove into the parking lot of her children's day camp, and Livvie looked up.

"We're here, Eli," she said, nudging his arm because she knew with his headphones on, her brother couldn't hear her.

Eli looked up and out of the window, and after two other parents dropped off their children and drove away, Kenya rolled in front of the double doors and waved at one of the camp coordinators.

"You guys be good and have a wonderful day, okay?" Kenya told them.

"We will," Livvie said, grabbing her backpack, leaning between the two front seats, and hugging her mom. "Love you."

"I love you, too, sweetheart."

"See you later, Mom," Eli said, hugging her and opening the back door.

"I love you, sweetie, and I'll see you this evening."

"Love you, Mom," he said, securing his backpack onto his shoulders, jumping out of the SUV, and shutting the door behind him.

Kenya waited for them to walk inside and then pulled off. But as she did, her phone rang, and she smiled when she saw it was her mother-in-law calling. Then she pressed the large knob on her center console. "Hey, good morning, Mom. How are you?"

"I'm good, daughter. What about you?"

"Good. I just dropped off the little ones at camp, and now I'm on my way to work. And how's Dad doing?"

"He's fine, and he just went out for his morning walk around the subdivision."

"I can tell he's so happy to be retired."

"He really is, and now that I'm able to work from home, I can pretty much make my own hours, and then I think I'm going to retire next year, too. If not before."

Mary was a claims manager who had worked for an insurance company for more than thirty years, and Kenya was happy for her. "Good for you. I don't blame you. You and Dad have worked a lot of years, so it's time."

"It definitely is. But hey, on a different note, have you all heard anything else from Terri?"

Kenya had told her mother-in-law about the scathing text message Terri had sent to Robert. "No, we haven't, but I don't know if that's a good thing or a bad thing because you never know about Terri. You never know what she might be up to."

"Isn't that the truth? She's like a time bomb waiting to go off, and it's so unfortunate."

"I just don't understand her. I mean, I know she's bitter and angry, but I still don't get the way she thinks."

"Well, regardless of how bitter and angry she is, it doesn't give her the right to continue filling Bobby's head with so many lies," Mary said. "She's been doing that for years, and to be honest, I thought as time went on, she would get better. But she never has."

"I agree," Kenya said.

"She has always been the worst, though, because it's like I've told you before. When she and Robert were married, she was so jealous and possessive of him. It was so bad that she never even wanted him to spend time with me and his dad. Which, of course, always made me think something wasn't right with her mentally. Because what wife wouldn't want her husband spending time with his parents? It just never made any sense to me."

"I know, and now she's jealous and possessive when it comes to Bobby, and it's really bothering Robert a lot. But what can we really do?"

"Take her to court just like you're already doing. Because whether that woman wants to admit it or not, she knows Robert has always had specific visitation rights, yet she's done everything she could to keep Bobby away from all of us."

"You're right, but I have to say, I still don't understand what you and Dad have to do with any of this. I mean, why keep Bobby from seeing his own grandparents? Because it's not like either of you have ever done anything to her."

"No, we haven't, and even when she was married to Robert and she treated us like enemies, Charles and I never said a harsh word to her. Not one time. As parents, we stayed in our place and out of their business, and we treated her like family. But she still never really liked either one of us. And then, as you know, when she and Robert separated, things got worse because that's when she cut us off completely."

"Which is so ridiculous, and no matter how many times you tell me that, I'll never understand it."

"It's beyond ridiculous. Especially since when she got pregnant, Charles and I were the main ones encouraging Robert to marry her. We told him he should do the right thing, and he did. But sadly, the whole marriage ended up being a total nightmare for all of us."

"Well, I just keep hoping things will get better."

"I'm praying things will get better, too. For Bobby's sake and for yours and Robert's. I'm praying for that every day. But I also believe it's going to take a true miracle for any of that to happen. God is going to have to soften Terri's heart and change her whole way of thinking."

"I just wish she could find someone who really cares about her. Someone who can make her happy, because maybe then she wouldn't be so focused on Robert and how terribly their marriage turned out to be. My girlfriends and I were just talking about that again on Saturday, and Michelle swears that Terri is still in love with Robert."

"Hmmph," Mary said. "Well, as much as I don't like saying it, I'm with Michelle. Because any time a woman holds this much animosity against any man for this long, it can only be for one reason: She's still in love with him. I've even seen this happen with women who had awful marriages and have been divorced for thirty to forty years, yet they still can't accept that their ex-husbands have moved on with someone else, and they also still can't stand the women those men are now married to. And don't let those ex-husbands have a child or children with their new wives, because then it seems even harder for those women to let go of the past."

Kenya shook her head and continued driving. "Well, if that's the case, then I feel really sorry for her. Because what I can tell you is this: Even if Robert and I weren't married, he still wouldn't get back together with Terri. He just wouldn't. So, if I were her, I would make peace with all of it. I would forgive Robert for whatever she's upset with him about and move on."

"Yeah, well, that's what you and I would do. Or what most sensible people would do. But we're talking about Ms. Terri, and that's a whole different story. Still, though, I'm glad Robert has made up his mind to fight for visitation, because Bobby needs to spend time with all of you. He needs to have a relationship with his little brother and sister, and he's also missing out on all the love I know you have for him, too."

"I do love him. Because even though I've never been given a real chance to show him that or to even really get to know him the way a bonus mom should, I love him because he's Robert's son and because he's the big brother to my babies."

"Bobby is really missing out on a lot, and the poor thing doesn't even know it."

Kenya turned into the parking lot of her medical practice and rolled into her designated stall. "He really doesn't, Mom, but we'll keep hoping and praying for the best, no matter what."

"We will indeed, and hey, I need to get going. And you're probably pretty close to work, anyway, right?"

"I just pulled up, but I'm glad you called because you know how much I love our daily conversations. You make my morning."

"And you make mine."

"I'll talk to you later, Mom. Love you."

"I love you, too."

Kenya grabbed her briefcase and tote, but as soon as she glanced over toward the entrance of the building, she did a double take. Had this woman lost her mind? Because Kenya just knew Terri would never have the audacity to show up at her place of business. Not even someone as evil and as devious as her would resort to something so outrageous. Would she? But Kenya knew she was mostly just trying to convince herself that Terri had much better sense than she did because Terri was, in fact, standing at the front door and was now walking toward Kenya's SUV.

Kenya got out of her vehicle in a hurry. "What are you doing here, Terri?"

"I need to talk to you," she said, stepping closer to Kenya than Kenya wanted her to be. Because in today's times, it was hard to know just how crazy someone truly was or how violent they might be. Kenya also didn't like the fact that Terri's ponytail and the rest of her hair looked frazzled and as though she hadn't bothered combing it for the last couple of days.

"Talk to me about what, Terri?" Kenya asked.

"Your idiot husband and the way he's trying to take me back to court."

"You know," Kenya said, "I'm going to need you to leave."

"Not until I say what I came to say."

"Well, whatever it is, Terri, I don't want to hear it. And even if I did, it wouldn't be here. I mean, how dare you come to my practice," Kenya said, and then did another double take when she glanced over at Terri's red Volkswagen...and saw Bobby staring at them from the passenger seat, looking sad and ashamed of what his mother was doing. "And why on earth would you involve your own son in this kind of drama? Because Terri, you know Bobby doesn't deserve this."

"Don't you *ever* mention my son or ask me anything about him. You just need to worry about those so-called court proceedings, because if Robert doesn't cancel that court hearing, I'll make his life a living hell. And yours, too. I made it very clear a long time ago that I don't want Bobby spending time with either of you, and no judge, court, or anyone else is going to force me to let him."

Kenya shook her head. "So, does that also mean you no longer want all those monthly child support payments you talked about in that disgraceful text message of yours?"

"Don't try to change the subject," Terri exclaimed, clearly not wanting to discuss one of the things she cared about most, which was money. "This is about visitation and how it's not going to happen. How it's *never* going to happen."

Kenya stared at this madwoman like the lunatic she was, but instead of continuing this useless conversation, she grabbed her purse and briefcase from the front seat of her vehicle, shut the door, and strutted past Terri. She also glanced over again at poor Bobby, who still looked helpless and unhappy.

Terri, on the other hand, became more outraged. "You can ignore me all you want, but I meant what I said. And if you guys don't back off, you'll be sorry from now on. And sorrier than you've ever been."

Kenya never even looked back at Terri. Instead, she went inside the building and gave Terri thirty seconds to get into her car and leave the parking lot. And it was a good thing Terri did, because if she hadn't, Kenya had been ready to call the police. She'd already pulled out her phone just in case, and if Terri ever showed up back there again, Kenya would be calling them immediately. And then waiting patiently for them to come and arrest her.

CHAPTER 11

Serena

Serena pedaled faster and faster, easily keeping up with the female virtual trainer who was leading her morning cycling class, and with her endorphins kicking in more and more by the second. She loved this feeling, and it was the reason she looked forward to working out not just three to five times per week but six to seven times. She did this even if there were days when she could only get in twenty to thirty minutes of HIIT, which stood for high-intensity interval training.

Sometimes she walked on the treadmill, sometimes she rode her bike the way she was doing right now, and sometimes she strength trained with hand weights or by using her own body weight to do squats, lunges, and push-ups. She worked out not only because she wanted to remain in good physical health but also because it helped her mental well-being. She also loved the fact that working out on a consistent basis kept her weight under control, something she had struggled with during her childhood years until she'd met her college roommate, Samantha. Of course, when it had come to personality, familial stability, financial status, and most everything else, Serena and Samantha couldn't have been more different. Yet from the moment they'd met, the two of them had connected and loved each other, and it hadn't been long at all before Samantha's healthy eating habits and workout regimen had become Serena's. It was true that Serena still enjoyed every kind of food imaginable, but thanks to Samantha, she was good about eating whatever she wanted in moderation on weekends and then eating clean on most other days of the week.

Serena finished her cycling session, wiped the sweat from her face with a towel, and drank lots of water from her plastic water bottle. Then once she cooled down and her heart rate settled, she slid off the bike, left her exercise room, and strolled down the hall to her home office. Her first thought was to head upstairs to shower, but at the same time, she wanted to take a quick peek at her email just to make sure she didn't have any urgent messages. However, when she sat down and opened her mailbox window, she didn't see anything out of the ordinary. Still, what she did see were three different messages from Nicole, her assistant, each with the words *Speaking engagement inquiry* in the subject line.

The first one she opened was from a large local corporation that she'd spoken at three months ago for Women's History Month, but this time they were looking for a keynote speaker for a company-wide event that would include all employees. They also wanted to know if she could do a special breakout session later in the day with their project managers. So Serena responded to Nicole with both the keynote and breakout session fee amounts she would need to request. After that, Serena read and responded to the other two email messages, one from a university in Texas that wanted her to speak to their incoming business students this fall, and the other from a women's organization that had just learned that their luncheon keynote speaker would no longer be able to attend. The luncheon was this coming Saturday, so this actually was an urgent email and last-minute request, but thankfully, Serena was available. And unlike most inquiries, the organization had already included what fee amount they could offer, which conveniently was the same amount Serena would have been requesting.

Serena scanned through a few more miscellaneous messages and thought about how tremendously God had blessed her career, and most important, her purpose, which was to speak to women in business. There were definitely times when she spoke to both men and women, but for the most part, she spoke to large groups of women. This was a dream come true for her, and she was grateful for all the many opportunities God continued to provide for her, although she did wonder why she couldn't find the same satisfaction and happiness when it came to her personal life. Because Lord knew it was so challenging and problematic. It always had been, which was the reason that while she was more than confident when it came to her purpose and career, she was now becoming more and more self-conscious about her looks, her personality, and who she was as a woman. She, of course, knew that having a man or a husband didn't define her, but as of late, this was mostly what she thought about every single day. She woke up with it on her mind, and she went to bed the exact same way, and this recent breakup with Tim had made things that much worse for her.

Serena closed out her email window, but just as she did, her phone rang and she saw it was her mother. So Serena answered the call and pressed the speaker icon on her phone. "Hey, Mom. Good morning."

"Hey yourself," Juanita said with a smile in her voice. "And good morning to you, too. Are you up?"

"Yep. Just finished my workout not too long ago."

"I need to be working out myself," she said. "But, of course, you know that's not my thing."

"Uh-huh, but you also know what your doctor said, Mom. He wants you to start walking at least thirty minutes per day."

"Yeah, he does, but lately I've been getting much better glucose readings."

"Only because you're taking medication for it. But if you lost the twenty to thirty pounds that he wants you to lose, you probably wouldn't have to take anything. And you also wouldn't be at risk for becoming diabetic. And while I know you don't think so, being prediabetic isn't a good thing. Plus, your A1C is slightly elevated."

"I just need to watch what I eat, and I'm doing that."

Serena loved her mom, but she also wished Juanita would take better care of herself and that she would realize how important listening to her doctor truly was. But Serena knew this wasn't a debate she was going to win, so she changed the subject.

"So, what do you have planned for today?" Serena asked.

"Not a whole lot. I'm just glad to have the day off."

Juanita worked full-time at one of the local DMV facilities, and in Illinois, they were closed on Sundays and Mondays, which she loved.

"What about you?"

"I need to work on a couple of speeches, and then I have a Zoom meeting this afternoon with a literary agent who's interested in my book idea."

"The idea you told me about a few weeks ago?"

"Yep."

"I knew you would eventually write a book someday, and

I'm so proud of you, Serena. You've done very well for yourself, and you should be proud, too."

"I'm grateful, Mom. I really am."

"Oh, and by the way, Diane said she tried to call you yesterday right after church and then again last night, but she couldn't get in touch with you."

Serena knew she had purposely not answered her sister's calls, the same as always, but she chose her words very carefully because the last thing she wanted was to hear her mom lecturing her about it. "Yeah, I saw that she called, but I was really busy yesterday."

"On a Sunday?" she asked, and Serena could tell she didn't believe her.

"Yeah, I had some work I needed to catch up on before today." she said.

"Well, you should call your sister. You sometimes go weeks without talking to her, and you know I don't like that. You know it makes me sad."

Serena wished she could tell her mother the truth: that she still resented her sister because of the relationship Diane had had with her father when they were children. But she knew her mother wouldn't understand—and to some degree, Serena felt guilty about holding on to the past, as well as about feeling somewhat jealous of her sister and the loving relationship she shared with her boyfriend. Still, Serena told her mother what she wanted to hear. Even if she wasn't going to make good on it.

"I'll call her later."

"Good, and how are things going with Tim?"

Serena hesitated before responding because not only was Tim the last person she wanted to talk about, she also wasn't ready to tell her mother about their breakup. And she certainly didn't want her sister to know about it, either, so she finally said, "Everything's fine."

"Did you two go out this weekend? I meant to ask you that yesterday when we were at church."

Serena leaned forward in her chair and lied again. "No, we stayed in and watched movies."

"Oh, okay. And what about marriage? Is he still not talking about that?"

"No, not yet."

"Well, as you already know, I don't get that. I also don't like it because while I do admire Tim as a person, in today's times, it's never a good sign when a man dates you for more than six months and doesn't at least mention the subject of marriage. He might not be ready to buy a woman a ring yet, but if a man is truly in love with you, he'll at least mention how he feels about marriage. And if it gets to be a year or more, and a man hasn't proposed, well honey, that says everything."

Serena would never tell her mom that she'd been having the exact same thoughts just this past weekend, particularly when she'd gone by Tim's house to confront him about that audio recording. So instead she said, "I know, Mom, but every couple isn't the same. Some people get married only weeks or months after they meet, and some get married two or more years later. It just depends."

"I guess, but all I'm saying is that if a man truly loves you and wants to marry you, he knows very quickly. He knows right away, and it doesn't take him years to figure it out."

Serena rolled her eyes toward the ceiling, but right after she did, her throat tightened and she took deeper breaths, in and out. Her heart raced, too, and she felt nervous. Which meant this wasn't a false alarm this time. It wasn't the same as the way she'd felt on Saturday just before walking inside Tim's house. This current episode was a full-blown anxiety attack, but thankfully Serena was able to close her eyes and begin her usual breathing exercises without her mother realizing it, because if her mother learned that she was having attacks again, she would worry about her nonstop.

So, Serena steadily breathed in and out as quietly as she could until she had finally gotten her attack completely under control. But then she thought about her breakup with Tim and how there was no denying that this was the reason she was struggling with her anxiety again in the first place. She was hurt and lost to some degree, and it was the reason she knew she had to get over him. Not next week or next month. She had to get over him immediately because, so help her, it was time to move on.

It was time to pull herself together and do whatever else it took to protect her mental health, even if it meant focusing only on her career and being successful.

Even if it meant giving up on love and marriage altogether.

CHAPTER 12

Michelle

Michelle signed on to the computer in her office to review the history of her next patient, who had just checked in for her annual physical. She smiled when she saw the name Hattie Michaels, because Ms. Hattie, as Michelle so affectionately called her, was one of her favorite people, personally and professionally. She was one of the best women Michelle knew, and Michelle always looked forward to seeing her and talking to her.

Michelle scanned the charting notes for Ms. Hattie's last office visit, and although she was ready to begin her patient's annual physical, she decided to give her medical assistant a few more minutes to finish updating Ms. Hattie's digital record with today's vital readings and any new information that needed to be added. In the meantime, though, Michelle took a look at the rest of her schedule for the day and then thought about church service yesterday and how deeply Pastor Rigsby's words had affected her. Then, to make matters worse, as planned, she had lied to everyone about the reason she'd become so emotional, and she could still hear herself now, explaining things to Chris as soon as Pastor Rigsby had given the benediction.

"Are you okay, baby?" Chris had asked right away.

"I'm fine."

"You seemed so upset during service. More than I've ever seen you before."

"I know. I'm not sure what came over me except for some reason, when Pastor Rigsby started talking about people who get married, even though they're not in love with each other…I don't know, it just made me think about how blessed I am to have you in my life rather than ending up with someone I wouldn't have been happy with. So, my tears were really tears of joy, more than they were anything else. And then I thought about women who can't find their soul mate the way I have and also about women who are just like the people Pastor Rigsby spoke about in his sermon. Women who have been married for decades, yet they've been miserable the entire time."

It was then that Chris had hugged her, and when she'd noticed her parents and aunt standing behind Chris, smiling because of the conversation they had just overheard. Then, Michelle was ashamed to say, she had repeated a similar version of that lie to Lynette, Kenya, and Serena. Although, there was no denying that the three of them had looked skeptical, and Michelle wasn't surprised because they all knew each other better than anyone else, and hiding things from even one of them was nearly impossible. But thankfully, none of them had called and questioned her about it.

Michelle signed out of the scheduling system, left her office, and went strolling down the hallway.

Trina, her medical assistant, passed by her. "Mrs. Michaels is in room three."

"Sounds good, and thank you," Michelle said, knocking on the door, opening it, and walking inside, smiling. "Good morning, Ms. Hattie."

Ms. Hattie smiled brightly, and while she was eighty-two years old, she didn't look to be any more than seventy. "Good morning, beautiful girl. How are you?"

"I'm doing well," Michelle told her, sitting down at the small desk where her laptop was. Then, for some reason, Michelle thought about how, from the very first time they'd met, Ms. Hattie had made Michelle feel as though she was more of a surrogate grandmother to her than she was a patient.

"I'm glad to hear it," Ms. Hattie said.

"And how are you?"

"Well, I'm doing pretty good for an old lady, and I'll tell you what else, honey. I'm alive. The good Lord saw fit to wake me up yet one more time this morning, and I'm just grateful to see another day. Which is the reason I don't complain about much of anything if I can help it. And especially when it comes to some of the minor aches and pains any eighty-two-year-old woman might feel from time to time."

Michelle chuckled. "Amen to that, Ms. Hattie. You've got the right way of thinking, and I love it."

"And then, even though I'm here for my yearly physical today, I'm mostly just happy to come spend a little time with you."

"Well, you know the feeling is mutual, and I'm also glad to know that your blood pressure looks great this morning," Michelle said, reviewing her assistant's notes.

"That's good to hear, and my gout hasn't been bothering me much anymore, either."

"Wonderful."

"But enough about me," Ms. Hattie said. "I know you must be getting more and more excited by the day about marrying that handsome young doctor of yours."

Michelle forced a smile onto her face. "Yes, I really am."

Ms. Hattie eyed her with no emotion. "Hmm, well, you don't look too excited to me. So, what's wrong?"

"Nothing. I'm just a little tired is all."

"Tired? No, sweetheart, it's much more than that. Because believe me, I know when a woman is head-over-heels in love and can't wait to get married. And that's not what I'm feeling from you right now. You wanna talk about it?"

Michelle knew she needed to get on with performing Ms. Hattie's physical, but before she could stop herself, she said, "You know me well."

"Talk to me, sweetheart. Tell me what's wrong."

"I'm having second thoughts about everything, and I feel awful about it."

"And how long have you felt this way? Because the last couple of times I was here, you seemed so happy about getting married. You were thrilled."

"For a couple of weeks or so."

"Well, whenever any of us have second thoughts about anything, there's always a good reason for it. And what I can also tell you is this: Marriage is a lot easier to get into than it is to get out of. Which is the reason it's so important to marry a man you feel you would never want to live without. A man you love in a way that comes second only to the love you have for God."

Michelle didn't know what was wrong with her, because just like yesterday when Pastor Rigsby had been delivering his sermon, tears filled her eyes. They didn't roll down her cheeks this time, but she was still far more emotional than she should be in her work environment.

"Because take it from me," Ms. Hattie continued, "I know what I'm talking about, and the reason I know what I'm talking about is because I got married for the wrong reasons, too. My husband is one of the kindest, most thoughtful, and most caring men you'll ever meet, so the next thing I knew, I went from dating him to accepting his marriage proposal to ending up in a very pleasant marriage that was also a loveless one. And we're still married today. Nearly sixty years later."

Michelle shook her head in disbelief. "I am so sorry."

"Honey, there's no need to apologize at all. Because when I say we have a loveless marriage, I don't mean we don't love each other, because we do. I'm just saying, we were never truly in love the way a husband and wife should be. Instead, we've always loved and cared about each other the way family members and best friends love and care about each other."

"Then why didn't you just get a divorce?"

"Well, at first, I stayed for the children, and then once they'd all become adults, I stayed because my relationship with my husband was comfortable. But, sweetheart," she said, touching the side of Michelle's face, "you don't have to be like me. You still have a chance to marry someone you love with every part of your being."

Now Michelle's tears flowed slowly and freely, and she gently wiped her face with both hands. She also wondered why this Steven fiasco was happening. Why she had suddenly run into him the way she had just three months before her wedding. Because if it had to happen, why couldn't she have connected with him well before she'd become engaged to Chris, or even better, months before she'd ever begun dating him? Then today, Ms. Hattie had shared what the future might hold for Michelle if she married someone she wasn't fully in love with. But while Michelle understood and agreed with everything Ms. Hattie had just told her, as well as with everything Pastor Rigsby had spoken about yesterday in church, she also didn't want to hurt Chris. She didn't want to disappoint her parents, either. But on the other hand, no matter how hard she had tried over the last few days, she hadn't been able to stop thinking about Steven. In fact, she now thought about *him* more than she thought about her own fiancé, and that worried her. It also made her sad, and it was the reason she knew she had to do something. She wasn't sure what it was exactly, but she knew she had to do whatever it took to forget about Steven so she could move on and be happy with Chris.

CHAPTER 13

Lynette

Lynette readjusted her phone, which was clipped at her waist, and tapped her right earbud to increase the volume of the audiobook she was listening to. She was taking her usual evening stroll through her neighborhood, a quiet, gated community, and enjoying a great romance story from one of her favorite authors. She was also trying her best to look as good as she could, what with the fitted orange-and-hot-pink matching sleeveless workout top and pants she was wearing. Normally, she saved her best workout clothing for the fitness club she belonged to, but ever since Emmett, the most gorgeous and well-built man she'd seen in a while, had complimented her on the way she looked two weeks ago, she'd begun paying a lot more attention to what she wore when she went walking. That had been her first time ever seeing him, and once he'd introduced himself and mentioned what street he lived on, she hadn't been able to forget about him. Which was the reason that even though Lynette lived quite a few blocks away from Emmett and it usually took her about fifteen minutes to arrive in front of his house, she now walked in that very direction every single day. She also made sure to do it around the same time—every single day—because what she'd quickly come to realize was that

Emmett seemed to always be standing near his front lawn or in his driveway right on schedule. In fact, this was how she had discovered which house he lived in, too, even though he hadn't told her his exact address.

Lynette turned the corner and as soon as she did, she saw Emmett leaning against the back of his black convertible sports car. But as she walked down the sidewalk and closer to where he was, her stomach churned, which could only mean one thing: She was as nervous as a sixteen-year-old schoolgirl. Still, she muted her audiobook, smiled, and pretended this ridiculously handsome man was no big deal to her. Not even in the slightest.

Emmett casually folded his arms and gazed at her from head to toe. "You're looking as good as always, I see."

Lynette stopped in front of his driveway, and it was all she could do not to blush. "Thank you."

"So, have you been walking for a while this evening?" he asked.

"Not really. Only about fifteen or twenty minutes," she said.

"Maybe one of these evenings we can walk together," he added.

"Maybe we can."

"Actually, if you're up for it, I'd love to take you to dinner. Or we could just meet for coffee. But only if you want to."

Lynette had been hoping he would eventually ask her out, but now that he had, she wasn't sure what to say. But finally, she told him, "Let me think about it, and I'll let you know. Is that okay?"

"Of course, and there's no pressure at all."

"So did you have a pretty busy day today?" she asked, switching the subject.

"I did. But it was mostly because of all the IT specialists I interviewed. My firm was just hired by a pretty large company to handle all of their IT consulting projects, so I need to hire a few more independent contractors to help out with that."

"That's wonderful, and congratulations," she said.

"Thank you," he said.

Not long after Lynette and Emmett had met, he had told her about the IT consulting firm he owned, and it sounded as though it was doing very well for him. Actually, from the looks of the house he lived in, which was much larger than hers and easily ten thousand square feet, his company must have been doing *exceptionally* well. She had also seen him driving three other vehicles: a Lexus sedan, a Range Rover, and a Ford pickup.

Lynette glanced at her watch and realized it was almost time for Julian to drop by for his visit with the girls, so she took a couple of steps backward, preparing to leave. "Well, I guess I should get going. But it was great talking to you."

"Same here, and hey," he said, walking toward her and passing her his business card, "my cell number is written on the back, and if you do decide you want to have dinner or meet for coffee, just call me."

"I will. See you later."

"See ya."

Lynette started down the sidewalk, but the farther she walked away from Emmett, the more she knew they had a strong connection and a high level of chemistry between them. So she would definitely be calling him. Then, if she began seeing him on a regular basis, she would also have to break some important news about him to Kenya, Michelle, and Serena. They would, of course, be happy to know that she was finally seeing someone, but she wasn't sure how they were going to react—once they learned that her new love interest was ten years her junior. Something that made Lynette both hesitant and excited all at the same time.

When Lynette had arrived back home and walked up the long, winding driveway, she'd seen Julian parking his vehicle in front of the garage and then stepping out of it. Now the two of them were sitting with their daughters at the kitchen island, preparing to have a family discussion.

"So," Julian said, "I know I've apologized to you girls before, but I also feel like I need to apologize to you again because as much as it hurts me to have to say this, I was never a good father to either of you. There is no doubt that part of the reason I didn't spend any real time with you is because I was so caught up with trying to build a successful life for all of us, but I still could have done better. I could have been a better father to both of you and a better husband to your mom, and I'm so sorry I wasn't who I needed to be for any of you. I'm also sorry for not spending much of any time at all with you since your mom and I separated. But going forward, things are going to be very different."

Tabitha smiled at her father and was clearly happy about all that he was saying, but Chloe examined her perfectly manicured fingernails, which needed no attention whatsoever, and she never as much as looked at him.

"I know I will never be able to make up for all the pain I've caused you girls, but I'm still going to do the best I can."

Tabitha smiled again. "We'll be fine, Daddy, and we're just glad you're here now."

Chloe lowered her eyebrows, pursed her lips, and looked at her baby sister as though she were crazy. "I don't believe you."

Tabitha frowned. "You don't believe what?"

"Nothing, just forget it," Chloe said, and went back to inspecting her fingernails.

Julian looked at her. "I know you're upset, but I promise you, sweetheart, I'm really going to be the dad I'm supposed to be, and when you and your sister get back from your vacation, I'm going to work out a schedule with your mom so you can start spending a couple of weekends per month with me."

Now Chloe stared directly at him. "But what if that's not what we want? What if we don't want to spend any weekends with you and your new wife? Or should I say you and your new family?"

Lynette knew how angry Chloe was at her dad, but her words still shocked Lynette. She also knew they were some-what disrespectful, but she didn't say anything because she completely understood why Chloe felt the way she did.

On the other hand, though, Tabitha seemed elated about what her father was saying. "I can't wait to spend some weekends with all of you, Daddy, and I also want to see my baby brothers," she said, but she didn't mention her new stepmom.

"Well, you can do whatever you want," Chloe told her.

Julian gazed at his oldest daughter again with a look of sadness, and Lynette almost felt sorry for him.

"Sweetheart," he finally said. "I know it's going to take some time, but I'm really hoping that you'll eventually be able to forgive me. I hope you'll give me a chance to make things right."

Chloe ignored him and hopped down from the counter chair. "Mom, I have some more things I need to pack, so can I be excused?"

"Yes, that's fine, and Tabitha, you should probably finish getting the last of your things together, too."

"Okay, Mom," Tabitha said, standing up and walking over to hug her father. "I love you, Daddy."

"I love you, too, sweetheart, and I'll come upstairs to see you before I leave."

"Okay," Tabitha told him, but as she and her sister went up the back staircase, she said, "Chloe, why did you have to be so mean to Daddy?"

"Because he deserves it, that's why."

"Well, I wish you wouldn't treat Daddy like that. He made some mistakes, but he's really sorry. He's sorry for all of it."

"Yeah, whatever," Lynette heard Chloe say before shutting her bedroom door. Then they heard Tabitha shutting her door a couple of seconds later.

"I hate this," Julian said. "But it's all my fault, and now I just have to deal with it the best way I can."

Lynette gazed at him, but she wasn't sure what he wanted her to say.

"And Lyn, I just want to tell you again how sorry I am. Especially about what you mentioned yesterday at dinner. I never should have involved our girls in my outside affairs, and I will always regret subjecting them to something so inappropriate. I was wrong, and there's just no other way to explain it."

Lynette still wasn't sure what he wanted her to say, so she just kept listening.

"And I'll tell you something else. When I told you last night that I still loved you, I meant what I said."

Lynette had no idea where all of this was coming from, so she finally said, "Look, Julian. Let's not do this. What we had is over, and you have a whole new wife and two new children living in a whole different household."

"I know that, but Lyn, if I could do things over, I would do them very differently. I would be totally and completely faithful to you, and I would be the kind of husband you always wanted me to be," he said, gazing around the kitchen, up at the tall tray ceiling, and then toward the massive family room. "We had everything, and we had each other."

"Yeah, you're right. We did. But where is all this coming from, Julian? Because I'm pretty sure Crystal wouldn't be happy about any of what you're sitting here saying to me. Actually, my guess is that she would be outraged."

"Maybe. But I'm just being honest."

This conversation was way too deep for Lynette, so she stood up and decided to end it. "Well, I think you need to keep your honesty to yourself and go home to your wife. Because that's where you belong. You made your choice, I accepted it, and now I'm good, Julian. I'm over you, and I'm happy."

"Well, if I said your words didn't hurt, I'd be lying. But I guess I deserve them."

"You do. And then some. But it's like I said, I'm over you, and I'm happy."

Now Julian got up from his seat. "Then I guess there's nothing else to say."

"There isn't," she said matter-of-factly. "And since your real reason for coming by here was to see your daughters, that's who you should be talking to, anyway."

"Point taken," he said, turning and heading upstairs to see their daughters but then looking back at her with no particular expression whatsoever. Still, the way he spoke to her and looked at her was very strange, and when he was out of sight, Lynette wondered why he was acting even more loving toward her than he had yesterday. The whole idea of it all was so bizarre, and again, she wondered what was going on with his marriage. She wanted to know why he didn't seem as happy as he usually did about the new life he was living. Although, when it came to Julian, there was just no telling.

CHAPTER 14

Kenya

Kenya slipped on an ankle-length, summer-floral lounging dress and sat on the edge of the king-size bed. She'd just changed out of her work clothing and taken a shower, and now Robert walked into the bedroom and shut the door behind him.

"Hey, babe," he said, loosening his tie, removing his suit jacket, and pecking her on the lips.

"Hey, how was your day?"

"Well, it was going fine until you called me this morning about Terri. I'm still stunned about all of it, and for the life of me, I can't believe she brought Bobby with her."

"Yeah, well, I'm still upset, too, and the whole thing makes me want to get an order of protection against her. And at the very least, if she shows up there again, I'm having her arrested. I'm not saying a single word to her, and I won't be hesitating. I'm just doing it."

Robert unbuttoned his shirt but didn't say anything, and Kenya wondered why. Especially since they were always on the same page when it came to Terri and all her foolishness.

"Is something wrong?" she asked.

"No, not really. I mean, I definitely understand how you feel and why you feel the way you do...and that if Terri continues to harass you, she certainly deserves to be locked up. But I also don't want to hurt Bobby."

Kenya stared at him for a couple of seconds. "Hurt him how?"

"By taking his mother away from him. He's already dealing with a lot, but if Terri goes to jail, it'll completely traumatize him."

"I get what you're saying, but surely you don't expect me to let Terri show up at my practice anytime she wants to."

"No, but maybe I can talk to her. To make sure she doesn't do that again."

Kenya laughed.

"What's so funny?"

"I'm laughing because you know just as well as I do that you're the *last* person Terri is going to listen to. You've never been able to get her to do anything. And to be honest, I don't think anyone can, because that woman won't even do what a judge has ordered her to do."

Robert sat down in the high-back chair that was right near their bed and took off his shoes. "I'm so tired of all of this. I'm tired of fighting with Terri and tired of not seeing my son."

"I'm tired, too. And even more so after what happened this morning. I'm sick of her."

"The worst thing I could have ever done was have sex with that woman. Because had I not done that, she wouldn't have gotten pregnant, I never would have married her, and we wouldn't be dealing with all the drama we're dealing with now."

"Well, what's done is done, and there's no changing the past. It's just not possible."

"I know, but I still regret it because it wasn't like I was

some young kid. I don't regret having my son—not for one second. Because I have always loved him with all my heart. But I still knew better. I knew how important it was to use protection, and it wasn't like Terri and I had been dating all that long, anyway."

Kenya didn't say out loud what she was thinking, but she regretted it, too, because not in her wildest imagination had she ever dreamed she'd have to deal with such a difficult ex-wife who was also an envious and narcissistic one. Kenya had never even considered that Terri could cause so much trouble, and it was because of this that Kenya didn't wish this chaos on anyone. So she finally just reiterated something similar to what she had told her mother-in-law this morning. "I guess all we can do is hope and pray for the best."

"Yeah, you're right, but with Terri I just don't know, and that's why I'm thinking I need to take more drastic measures."

"Like what?"

"Well, I'm not sure how you'll feel about this, but ever since Terri sent me that text message, I've come to the realization that she's always going to be a problem. She's always going to try to keep my son away from me. And then after the stunt she pulled today, she's confirmed my thinking even more. Which is why I don't see where I have any other choice but to file for full custody."

This wasn't what Kenya had been expecting to hear, and while she understood how Robert felt, she also knew that if he did this, Terri would act an even bigger fool than she already was. "I hear you, but the only thing is, by the time you finish fighting Terri in court, Bobby will likely be grown and in college."

"Yeah, I know it won't be easy, but baby, she's not a good

mother. I mean, look at what she involved him in today. She's also not even making Bobby study or do his homework the way he's supposed to, and his grades are really suffering from it."

"How do you know?" Kenya asked, because there was no way Terri would ever tell Robert that kind of information. Especially the kind that would make her look bad as a mother.

"I called the school to see if Bobby's counselor was working during the summer session, and thankfully, he was. So the receptionist left a message for him, and he called me back this afternoon. He also told me that Bobby missed ten days of school this past semester, and they were all for unexplained reasons. But worse than that, he said Bobby barely passed to the seventh grade."

"Gosh, that's really sad, and how terrible that this is happening. I feel so bad for Bobby. But I have to admit, too, honey, that I have some real concerns about him moving in with us."

"Why?" Robert asked.

"Because of how uncomfortable he seems around all of us. Not to mention, the few times we have seen him, he refused to even speak to Eli and Livvie. He looked at them like he wanted nothing to do with them, the same as he wants nothing to do with you or me. I know it's because Terri has likely said so many terrible things to Bobby about Eli and Livvie, but we still have a responsibility to protect them, too."

Robert glared at her in a way that told Kenya he wasn't happy about what she'd just said. "You're not saying Bobby would try to hurt his own brother and sister?"

"No, but I'm not saying he wouldn't, either."

"I don't see that happening. Not at all."

"Maybe not, but even though Bobby is Eli and Livvie's brother, I'm afraid that if you force him to come live here, it won't go well. Not with Bobby or his mother."

"Of course, Terri won't be happy, but I also can't spend the next few years not being a father to my son. Because as it is, I've already missed far too many years of his life, and I can't do that anymore."

Kenya hated this. Because while her heart went out to her husband and she was proud of him for wanting to be the great father his son needed him to be, she still worried about Terri and what the fallout from all of this would be. She also worried about Eli and Livvie and how this potential new living arrangement would affect them mentally and emotionally. Because as much as she wished things could work out wonderfully for everyone involved, she didn't see Bobby willingly packing up his things, moving in with them, and being thrilled out of this world about it. Not when he didn't seem to like them all that much, and he barely even knew them. So how could he ever be okay with moving in and seeing them on a full-time, everyday basis? Kenya just didn't see that happening. Although, no matter how hesitant and concerned she was, there was still something else she knew for sure: She would never try to talk Robert out of seeking full custody of his firstborn child. She wouldn't even consider something so selfish, which meant she had no choice but to woman up, prepare for the huge battle that was sure to come, and support her husband in any way she could.

CHAPTER 15

Lynette

Lynette had just picked up her phone and called Kenya so she could tell her about Julian, but before she could, Kenya had dropped this Terri bomb on her, and Lynette couldn't believe what she was hearing.

"She showed up where?" Lynette asked, raising her voice.

"At my job, girl. When I pulled up, she was literally waiting for me. And get this. She had Bobby in the car with her. Can you believe that?"

"She what?"

"You heard me."

"Why? Or actually, why was she even there in the first place?"

"Remember when I was telling you guys at the restaurant about the text message she sent? Well, she's still upset about Robert taking her back to court for visitation, and somehow she thought threatening me was going to change that."

"Well, I know you had her arrested, right?"

"No. But I wish I had. Although Robert thinks having her arrested will make things worse for Bobby."

"That might be true, but when you're dealing with a woman like Terri, you sometimes need to get the law involved."

"Tell me about it."

"This is really something," Lynette said.

"I know, and girl, I'm so tired of it. I've *been* tired of Terri for a while, but now things are getting to the point where she's doing and saying anything she wants, and I'm not okay with that."

"I don't blame you, and what did Robert say about her showing up, harassing you?"

"He was livid, but it's like I just told you, he doesn't want her going to jail because of Bobby."

"Well, at some point, that woman is going to have to be stopped. Before she does something even worse."

"I agree, but what I didn't tell you, too, is that now Robert wants to file for sole custody of Bobby."

"And he thinks Terri is going to allow that? Because I don't see it."

"I don't, either, but he's very serious about it," Kenya said.

"This is crazy, and why do baby mamas do this? Why can't they just co-parent and get along with their exes for the sake of their children?"

"You tell me because I have no idea why. I mean, if I was some awful stepmother who had treated her or Bobby badly, then I could see her acting the way she does. But there's not a single thing Terri can say that I've said or done except marry Robert."

"And have kids with him," Lynette reminded Kenya.

"Yeah, you're right. That part, too."

"So where is Robert now?"

"He and the kids ran by his parents' house so he could set up a new television they just purchased."

"Well, let me just say this now. Whatever happens, girl, please don't let Terri come between you and Robert. Don't let that miserable woman cause problems in your marriage, because she's so not worth it. I've seen this kind of thing happen before, and what you and Robert have to do is stand together through all of this, no matter what."

"I agree, but I won't lie. When Robert said he didn't think arresting her was a good idea, I wasn't happy about it. But because I quickly tried to place myself in his position, I didn't debate him on it."

"I'm glad because, again, it's just not worth it."

"You're right, and hey, that's enough about me. What's going on with you? Were you just calling just to be calling, or were you calling for a reason?"

"Girl, Julian came by earlier this evening to see the girls, but it didn't go too well. At least not with him and Chloe, anyway."

"Oh no. Why?"

"She's still really mad at him for leaving us. She hates the fact that he's gotten remarried, and that he's basically forgotten about them."

"Well, it's not like any of us can blame her. Because what child is going to be okay with having her father walk out and then immediately move on with a whole new family?"

"I know, and while I do believe Julian really is sorry and wants to do better, it's going to take Chloe some time to forgive him. Tab, on the other hand, though, is just happy to be seeing him again, so she's fine."

"Every child is different. Some children will love their fathers and will forgive them for anything they do, and others will want nothing to do with them for years to come."

"That's very true," Lynette said. "So, all Julian can do is continue showing up and proving to Chloe that he really wants to be a good father to her. But that's only part of the Julian story because, girl, not only did he tell me last night at dinner that he still loves me, he had nerve enough to say it again this evening. And get this: He said he regrets the mistakes he made and that if he could do things over, he would."

"And you're surprised about that?" Kenya asked.

"I sort of was."

"Well, I'm not. Julian is like a lot of men who believe the grass is greener somewhere else. That is, until the honeymoon phase is over with the tramp they left you for, and reality sets in."

"Yeah, but he almost sounds like something's not right between him and Crystal. He seems unhappy."

"That's because he probably is."

"He did a lot of dirt, though, Kenya. More than you ever really knew about, and then this weekend I found out from Chloe that he would sometimes take her and Tabitha with him when he visited one of his women. They were little girls then, but remember Cindy? The executive assistant he had a few years ago?"

"Noooo. Julian should be ashamed of himself. I mean, talk about being low down."

"I knew he was having affairs, but not once did I think he would take our girls around any of those whores at their own houses. I mean, I'm sorry to vent like this, girl, but that's the part that really sends me into a rage."

"Please. You don't have to apologize to me because I wouldn't have thought that about Julian, either. And I also don't understand what happened to him, period. Because when you guys first got together, he seemed so different. And so in love with you."

"Yeah, well, I know it may have seemed that way, but it's like I just told you. There's so much you never really knew because I was too embarrassed to even tell *you* about all that went on," she said, because while she hadn't felt comfortable telling anyone about some of the awful things Julian had done to her over the years, if she had, she would have told Kenya because Kenya confided in her about most everything, too. It was true that she and Kenya did tend to share quite a bit of their personal business with Michelle and Serena, but Lynette also knew that Michelle and Serena didn't always tell her and Kenya everything they were feeling or dealing with. The four of them loved and trusted one another with their lives, but when it came to sharing everything, including the worst of the worst, Lynette and Kenya sometimes conversed privately about their issues the way they were doing now, and Serena and Michelle did the same thing.

"Like what?" Kenya wanted to know.

"Like the time when Chloe was two and Tab was just a newborn, and Julian went on one of his so-called business trips, which was really a vacation with one of his colleagues he was having an affair with. She owned a construction company about an hour from here."

"What? And how did you find out?"

"I hired a private investigator."

"Gosh, Lyn. I am so sorry."

"He was awful right from the start, but I kept telling myself that things would get better, and then I was stupid enough to believe that when it came to being married to powerful, wealthy men, this was just the way things were."

"But you didn't deserve any of what you went through, and now I'm almost afraid to ask how many affairs Julian actually had."

"A lot. And it was all the time."

"I can't believe you never told me any of this. I mean,

I knew about the affairs he was having toward the last few years of your marriage, but..."

"I just couldn't tell you. I was too ashamed, and I knew how stupid it was for me to keep putting up with Julian and the way he was treating me. Then, there came a time when I simply couldn't fathom having my girls grow up in a single-parent household. I didn't want that for them, but when he told me Crystal was pregnant and that he was leaving me for her, something rose up in me and I found more courage than I've ever had. And that's when I knew I was taking him for everything I could get financially. I decided that very day that me and his girls would never have to worry about money, where we were going to live, or anything else."

"And I'm so proud of you for standing up for yourself the way you did."

"Yeah, but now he's sniffing around like some pitiful-looking puppy, and while I don't care about Julian the way I used to when we were married, I do wonder what's going on."

"Shoot, you've got me wondering, too," Kenya said, and they both laughed.

"Well, when I find out, you know I'll be calling you fast, quick, and in a hurry. But there's also something else I need to tell you."

"What's that?"

"You know how you and the girls keep saying I need to start dating again?"

"Yep."

"Well, I think I met someone."

"Really? When? And where? And what's his name?"

Lynette laughed again. "Wow, you sound more excited about it than I am."

"Because it's time, girl, and you know we just want you to be happy. We want you to live your life."

"His name is Emmett, and he's one of my neighbors. Well, he's sort of my neighbor, but he lives quite a few blocks away from me."

"And?"

"I met him during one of my evening walks."

"When?"

"A couple of weeks ago."

"And you're just now telling me about it?"

"I wasn't sure where things were going to go with us. So I didn't say anything."

"Have you been out?"

"No, but earlier this evening, he gave me his number, and he asked me if we could."

"And what did you say?"

"That I would think about it."

"What is there to think about? Unless he's not what you're looking for."

"He's everything I'm looking for. He looks good, and he owns what seems to be a really successful IT business."

"Well, good for you, girl, but I still can't believe you didn't tell me you met someone."

"There's actually another reason... there's a little more to the story."

"Like what? Wait, please don't tell me he has kids with five different women."

Lynette laughed out loud, and Kenya laughed with her.

"Girl, no. Or at least I don't think he does."

"Well then, what is it?"

"He just turned thirty."

"Yikes."

"Now you see why I didn't want to tell you."

Kenya chuckled a bit. "No, actually it's fine. Because if you're compatible in lots of other ways, age doesn't matter."

"Yeah, but I will admit that doing the cougar thing is a little scary."

"Maybe, but in today's times, a ten-year difference isn't a lot."

"No, and especially when the conversation is mature and interesting, and that's the sort of vibe I get when I'm talking to Emmett."

"So when are you going out with him?" Kenya asked.

"I think I'm going to call him after I drop the girls off at the airport tomorrow."

"Well, I'm happy for you, and I'm also glad you're over Julian. I was always glad, but after hearing all this other stuff about the way he treated you, I'm even happier to know you're done with him for good. Because it sounds like being with Julian was a nightmare."

"It was, but you know what's so good about being hurt in such an extreme way?"

"What?"

"No one—and I do mean no one—will ever be able to hurt me that way again. Because when this kind of thing happens, it's almost as if you become immune to certain kinds of pain."

"I believe you're right about that."

"Well, I guess I should go so I can make sure Chloe and Tab have everything all packed up for tomorrow."

"Please tell them I said to have a wonderful time, and that their Auntie Kenya loves them."

"I will."

"Oh, and hey, so when are you planning to tell Serena and Michelle about this new man in your life?"

"Soon. And speaking of Michelle, did you see how hard she was crying at church yesterday?"

"I did, and something's not right."

"I thought the same thing and when I got home, I almost called her. But then I decided not to."

"Hopefully it wasn't anything serious, and she was just having a moment like she told us."

"Yeah, maybe so. Maybe it really was nothing at all," Lynette agreed out loud, but deep down, she had a feeling there was much more to Michelle's story. Much more than Michelle was willing to tell any of them.

CHAPTER 16

Michelle

Michelle had never been so unsure about doing anything as she was right now, and she hoped with all she had in her that she was making the right decision. Although, at this point, she wasn't sure what else she could do to fix her dilemma: being in love with one man and preparing to marry another. Because as it was, she was so tired of thinking about him and the past they'd shared together and feeling as though she was mentally cheating on Chris behind his back. So yes, she had to make things right by any means necessary.

Michelle tossed the fresh-looking, crisp mixed greens with bamboo salad tongs and then added in pecans and sliced onion. She loved mixing together huge salads and serving them with her specialty, homemade ranch dressing, which had more of a sweet taste to it, and she especially enjoyed making them for Chris. She also loved cooking his favorite dish, Creole shrimp and grits, which she would be finishing up just as soon as her shrimp, sausage, vegetables, and other ingredients had simmered. But then, as she pushed the wooden salad bowl to the side so she could check on them, she heard Chris unlocking the front door and walking inside. They still didn't live together, but they had given each other keys to their respective houses many months ago, and soon Michelle would be moving in with Chris. She would then be turning the home she owned into a rental property.

"Hey, babe," he said, kissing her and giving her what looked to be two dozen red roses.

"Hey, yourself, and what are these for?"

"They're just because."

"Thank you," she said, smiling, kissing him again, and pulling a large glass vase from one of her lower cabinets. Then she filled it with lukewarm water and placed the flowers inside it.

Chris walked over to the stove. "Wow, I see you're making my favorite. And on a Monday night, too, so what's the occasion?"

"I just wanted to do something special for you. And have a romantic dinner."

"I see," he said, looking over at the glass table near Michelle's patio doors, which she had covered with a beautiful white linen tablecloth and set with her best china, silverware, napkins, and wineglasses. "Do you need any help?" he asked.

"No, I'm good, and you can just relax."

Chris stepped closer to her and hugged her from behind. "I love you so much, and thank you."

Michelle leaned her head back and rested her cheek against his. "I love you, too, and you're quite welcome."

Chris kissed her on the cheek and then strolled over to the open-style family room, which was only a couple of feet away from the kitchen. When he took a seat on the sofa, he turned on the television and immediately switched the channel to CNN, something Michelle wasn't surprised about because Chris loved watching anything news related.

After another half hour or so, though, Michelle set two candles on the table, lit them, and placed their salad and food dishes in the center of it. Then once they sat down, they held hands and Chris said grace.

"Father God, thank You for my beautiful fiancée and for this wonderful meal she has prepared for us. Thank You for blessing us time and time again, and we also ask that You would please bless this food and that You would allow it to serve as great nourishment for our bodies. We ask You for these and all other blessings in Your Son Jesus's name. Amen."

"Amen," Michelle said, and opened her eyes.

Chris lifted the bowl of salad from the table and removed a sizable helping of it for Michelle, and then one for himself. "Everything really looks good, baby, and it smells delicious."

"Thank you, and I hope it tastes good, too."

"So how was your day?" he asked.

"It was great. I had a full schedule, but the day went by pretty quickly. What about yours?"

"It was busy, but you know my procedure days always are. Although, I was really happy about the angiogram results for one of my patients who I thought might have blockages. But as it turned out, he didn't have any large enough to require any stents. He does have hypertrophic cardiomyopathy, but it's nothing a couple of medications and a healthy lifestyle won't take care of. Because if he takes his medication consistently and makes those changes in his diet, he could live a very normal life from now on."

"That's really good to hear. And how old is he?"

"Well, that's the thing. He's only forty-five, but he's never really taken good care of himself. If he had, some of what he's dealing with could have been prevented."

"I see the same thing with some of my patients. Especially when it comes to high blood pressure, high cholesterol, and type two diabetes. But lately, I've been seeing way too many people coming in with diabetes or prediabetic numbers, and it's mostly because they won't try to lose at least a little weight."

"That's an ongoing issue in my office, too."

Michelle lifted some of her salad onto her fork. "And you know Serena is worried about the same thing with her mom. She's been prediabetic for a while, and her fasting glucose numbers are steadily rising all the time."

"I'm really sorry to hear that, and I hope things get better for her."

"I do, too, but according to Serena, her mom doesn't seem all that worried about it."

Chris and Michelle continued chatting, finished eating their salads and the rest of their dinner, and then they each enjoyed a glass of chardonnay.

"Baby, that was the best. It always is, but as they say, you really put your foot in that meal this evening."

Michelle smiled. "I'm glad you enjoyed it."

"And hey, isn't our next pre-marital counseling session tomorrow evening?"

"It is," she said, already dreading having to face Pastor Rigsby because of what she'd been thinking and how negatively she had been feeling about the wedding and everything else. Although, after tonight, she was hoping things would return to normal, so she could get back to being excited about marrying Chris and all their future plans.

"So you want to watch a movie?" Chris asked.

"No," she said, staring at him with serious eyes. "I want to do something else."

"Like what?"

Michelle sighed and grabbed Chris's hand. "So...I've been doing a lot of thinking...and I don't want to wait any longer."

"For what? Because I know you're not talking about what I think you're talking about."

"I am."

"Why?"

"Because I really want to," she lied. "I know you've been waiting for a very long time, and while I also know making love before we get married is not the Christian thing to do, I can't help that I want what I want. And let's just be honest, it's not like either of us are virgins. We've both had sex before with other people, and we're not perfect."

"No, we're not. But from the time we started dating, you were very clear about wanting to remain celibate. In fact, I specifically remember you telling me how you and Serena had gone to a women's conference somewhere outside of Chicago and how moved both of you had been by one of the speakers who had been celibate for a few years."

"Yeah, and that's definitely what made us both decide that from then on we were going to wait until we got married. But I don't feel that way anymore. Because it's like I said, I want what I want."

At first Chris didn't say anything, but then he laughed. "Look, if this is some kind of joke you're playing, it's not funny."

"I'm not joking at all. I would never joke about something like this. And I've also never been more serious about anything. I want to make love to you, Chris. Tonight. Right now."

"I still don't see what changed your mind and why you

changed it so suddenly. Because it was just on Memorial Day when we were at your parents' that you were still saying we had to wait."

"I know, because I was trying to do the right thing. But I also thought about how we'll be married three months from now, anyway."

"Yeah, I know that, but are you sure about this?"

"I am, but if you have a problem with it, we can still wait," she said, secretly hoping that this wasn't the case.

"Remaining celibate was your thing, and I was only going along with it because I loved and respected you enough *to* go along with it."

"And I appreciate you for doing that. But Chris, I really want this," she said, squeezing his hand. "I need you. Tonight."

Chris paused for a few seconds but then stood up and pulled her toward him. "Come here."

Then when Michelle got up and moved closer to him, he wrapped his arms around her waist, Michelle clasped her hands behind his neck, and Chris gazed into her eyes. "So you're really sure about this?"

"I told you I am," she said, and Chris kissed her forcefully and passionately.

Finally, Michelle led him upstairs to her bedroom. But when she closed the door, she hoped with every fiber of her being that making love to Chris would seal the deal. That it would help her forget about Steven and all that he meant to her—for good. Then she prayed that God would forgive her for the sin she was willingly about to commit. She prayed He would understand and have mercy on her.

CHAPTER 17

Serena

So I'm not even sure how to tell you this because when I do, you're not going to be happy about it," Michelle said to Serena, who was sitting at the back of her favorite coffee shop, working. Michelle had called Serena a few minutes ago, but now Serena wondered how they'd gone from talking about today's weather to discussing whatever bad news Michelle was getting ready to share with her.

"What happened?" Serena asked. "What's wrong?"

"I broke our pact. I slept with Chris."

"You did what?" Serena nearly shouted and was glad very few people seemed to notice.

"I know, and I'm sorry," Michelle said. "But it just happened."

Serena frowned as though her best friend could see her through the phone. "Michelle, how does something like that just *happen*?"

"It did. Chris came over, we ate dinner, and one thing led to another."

"I don't believe I'm hearing this. I mean, wow. Just wow."

"I'm sorry."

"And you should be. Especially since every time I felt myself becoming weak and wanting to give in to Tim, you talked

117

me out of it. You made me see how important it was to wait. You said it was the godly thing to do, remember?"

"That's because it *is* the godly thing to do. But I messed up."

Serena was too angry to speak, so she didn't say anything else. She just sat there, and so did Michelle, who obviously didn't know what else to say, either. But then she finally said, "I really am sorry, girl, and I'll call you later to explain more. Once I leave work. Okay?"

"Whatever," Serena said, and pressed her earbud to end the call.

Still, she was stunned by what Michelle had just told her, and more than anything she wanted to know the real reason why this had happened. Because, as her best friend, Serena knew who Michelle was as a person, and she also knew that Michelle almost never did anything on a whim. She wasn't the impulsive type, not when it came to any area of her life, and she tended to plan almost everything. So this sleeping-with-Chris thing wasn't something that had caught Michelle by surprise. No, it was something she had thought long and hard about, weighed the consequences of, and then gone ahead with doing it anyway. So again, Serena wanted to know what had brought about such a major change of heart, and she also wondered if all that crying Michelle had been doing at church on Sunday had anything to do with it.

Serena shook her head and then returned her attention to her laptop, where she had been working on the speech for the women's luncheon that was now confirmed.

She scanned through what she had written prior to answering Michelle's phone call.

One of the most important things women can do is support other women. And while this is something that should happen automatically—and it is something that should never have to be stated—sadly, support from some women can sometimes be nonexistent. Of course, it is true that none of us will ever be able to directly support every single woman alive, but what we *can* do is celebrate *all* women in our hearts—whether we know them personally or not. Which is the reason why, before I begin my keynote this afternoon, I want to ask you four questions and I want you to think about them very carefully...Number one: Are you your sister's keeper? Number two: Are you always happy about the success of other women? Number three: Does another woman's success cause you to struggle with feelings of anxiety, hurt, or jealousy? And number four: When other women have great news to share, is it hard for you to compliment or congratulate them?

Serena clicked her mouse at the end of what she had written, but before she continued writing more, she sipped some of her chai tea. She had already drunk some Colombian roast coffee before leaving home, but she also rarely missed having a cup of tea during the late morning hours or early afternoon. She sometimes even enjoyed a hot cup of chamomile and vanilla tea just before bedtime as well, which truly did help her sleep better. This, of course, didn't work for everyone, but it had always made a noticeable difference for her in terms of the way she rested.

Serena took another few sips, glanced down at an incoming call from her sister, Diane, pursed her lips, and declined it. But right after she did, she saw a tall, handsome, forty-something guy walk in, and he smiled at her. Serena smiled back, but the first thing she thought was how she'd never seen him in there before, even though for the most part, she frequented this particular coffee shop nearly every weekday. Then, since it was well after nine a.m., she knew most of the people who came in for coffee or tea during this time of the morning were either self-employed or on vacation, or they didn't work at all. Actually, a good number of them were easily over sixty and retired.

Still, this man looked good, and while Serena tried her best not to stare at him, she couldn't help taking a couple of other glimpses in his direction when he wasn't looking. Then when he'd placed his order and walked around the counter to wait for it, she noticed how well his polo shirt and jeans fit his muscular body. But after she'd admired him for a little too long, he caught her staring at him, and she cast her eyes back toward her laptop as quickly as she could. Now, of course, she felt desperate and embarrassed, so she began typing any words she could think of—words that had absolutely nothing to do with the speech she was working on. But she knew she had to do something. Anything at all, so that he would think she wasn't paying a single bit of attention to him.

So much for that, though, because when Serena looked up again, she saw him strolling toward her table.

"So how are you?" he asked, smiling.

"I'm doing well. And you?"

"I'm doing great. Even more so since I'm on vacation this week."

Serena smiled because it was just as she had been think-ing earlier: Most people who came in after nine o'clock were either self-employed or on vacation, or they didn't work at all. "Good for you. There's nothing like taking some time off and enjoying a nice long break."

"That's for sure. Although, if I hadn't wanted to get some painting done inside my home, I would have likely gone to visit my parents. They live in Florida, and I haven't seen them since Christmas."

Serena knew it shouldn't matter, but she loved hearing that he owned a home.

"It sounds like you have your work cut out for you this week, then," she said.

"Well, not really, because I did most of it yesterday, so now I only have a little more to finish. Which I'll do maybe tomorrow or Thursday," he said, eyeing her laptop screen. "But it looks like you're definitely *not* on vacation, so I'd better let you get back to what you were doing. I didn't mean to interrupt you, and I mostly just wanted to say hello."

Serena smiled and wanted to invite him to have a seat with her, but she didn't. "It was no problem, and I'm glad you did."

"Well, you take care, and please enjoy the rest of your day, all right?"

"I will, and you, too," she said.

But as the man walked out of the door and into the parking lot, Serena watched his every move and wished she had at least told him her name and then asked him what his was. But she also hadn't wanted to seem too forthcoming or like she was way too interested in him, even though she knew she was *more* than interested. So instead, she leaned her head to the side as far as she could, peering through the window and waiting for him to sit inside his black BMW 750i. When he did, she smiled because most of the men she knew who drove this kind of a luxury vehicle had great jobs or owned successful businesses. She was trying so hard to not focus on the material aspects of men any longer, but she also wouldn't be sorry to learn that this man right here held an executive position of some kind and was doing very well for himself.

Now Serena wished even more that she'd gotten to know him a little better, and since he was currently stepping back out of his vehicle and closing the door, she wondered if maybe she might be getting her opportunity. But she didn't have to wonder long, because when he reentered the coffee shop, he headed directly back toward her table.

"So, while this isn't the norm for me," he said, "I wondered if we could maybe chat by phone sometime."

"I would love that," Serena told him.

"Good. And by the way, my name is Jake. Jake Matthews."

"I'm Serena, and it's great meeting you."

"Same here," he said, passing her a piece of folded paper with his phone number written on it.

The fact that he hadn't given Serena a business card made her a bit hesitant and nervous, but she still smiled and gave him hers.

"Okay, I'm leaving for real this time," he said, chuckling a little. "See ya."

"You take care," she said, and while she was no longer sure about what he did for a living, she still felt better than she had in nearly two weeks, and she couldn't wait to talk to him again. Because for some reason, she felt good about this. She'd only chatted with Jake for a few minutes, but he seemed so nice, down to earth, and genuine, and those three aspects alone gave her a strong sense of peace. So instead of worrying about whether or not he held some sort of C-suite position, she was going to keep an open mind about everything. Most of all, though, she prayed he was nothing like Tim.

CHAPTER 18

Lynette

Lynette waved goodbye to her girls one final time. But as they boarded their flight from Chicago's O'Hare airport to Jackson, Mississippi, which was only about twenty minutes from her parents' home in Madison, it was all she could do to keep from crying. Even during the nearly one-hour drive from their home, heading down I-90 east, Lynette had wanted to break into tears, and the only reason she hadn't was because she hadn't wanted to upset Chloe and Tabitha. Especially when they were so excited and happy about their trip, and they couldn't wait to see their grandparents again.

But that was then, because now that the two of them had stepped into the Jetway and Lynette could no longer see them, tears fully flowed down both her cheeks. She knew her daughters were intelligent, independent teenagers who were going to be fine, but she couldn't help missing them already. She also couldn't help thinking about all the emotional pain they'd had to endure over the last year or so, not to mention some of the hurt and disappointment they were still struggling with, specifically as it related to the absence of their father—even if Chloe did work hard at trying to pretend otherwise.

But as Lynette took a seat near the windows facing the airplane, she pulled a soft white, cotton handkerchief from her leather tote, gently wiped her face with it, and breathed deeply. She told herself that Chloe and Tabitha's trip was a good thing, both for them and for her, and that if there was one place her girls could go without Lynette having to worry about their safety, it was with her parents.

So now she sat, waiting patiently for the last of the passengers to board the plane and then for it to back away from the jet bridge. This was also when she thought about how drastically airline rules and FAA protocols had changed since the country's catastrophic 9/11 tragedy and how had it not been for the fact that her daughters were minors, she wouldn't have been able to accompany them to their gate the way she had today. Something that she wasn't sure she would have been okay with, mostly because of all of the sex trafficking that now took place worldwide on a daily basis.

Lynette crossed her legs, but just as she did, her phone signaled to her that she had a video call coming in. When she saw that it was Chloe, she pulled it from her purse.

"Are you girls okay?" Lynette asked, somewhat concerned.

"We're fine, Mom," Chloe said, smiling with Tabitha leaning in and smiling, too. "We just wanted to see you one more time before we have to turn off our phones."

"Oh, that's very sweet of you girls, and I'm really going to miss you."

Tabitha frowned a bit. "Have you been crying, Mom?"

"I'd rather not answer that," Lynette said, laughing.

"We're really going to be okay, Mom," Tabitha told her.

"We really are," Chloe added. "We're gonna have a great time, and remember, we want you to do the same thing."

"I know, and I will. I promise," Lynette told them, but

then she heard one of the flight attendants making final announcements in the background.

"Okay, I guess we have to go," Chloe said. "But we love you, Mom."

Tabitha smiled again. "Yep, we love you dearly, Mom, and we'll call you when we land."

"I love you both, and please be safe."

"We will," Chloe assured her, and they both waved at Lynette.

Then moments later, the plane slowly backed away from the jet bridge and headed toward the runway, and when it was no longer in sight, Lynette silently said a prayer for her daughters and left the gate area.

Now, she strolled through the terminal and back toward the front of the airport. Then, she took an escalator down to the lower level and went through a long corridor to an elevator that was near the section she had parked her vehicle in. She pushed the elevator button, and while she stood waiting for it to arrive, a gorgeous man who looked to be fiftysomething and maybe six feet, three inches tall walked toward her, smiled, and greeted her with a nod.

Lynette smiled back at him and then moved closer to the elevator, which was opening, and they, along with two other men, stepped onto it.

They rode up to level two in silence, which was where the other two men stepped off, and then once they made it to level three, Lynette exited the elevator and so did the handsome man who had smiled at her.

"Well, you sure do travel lightly," he said as they left the elevator lobby and were now walking side by side in the parking ramp.

"Excuse me?" Lynette said, although she certainly knew

what he meant and that he was purposely trying to make conversation with her.

"You're leaving the airport, but you don't have any luggage. So, I was just saying how lightly you were traveling."

"No, actually, I just dropped off my two daughters, who are on their way to see my parents."

"Oh, okay."

"And what about you?" she asked. "Where are you traveling from?"

"New York. I work for a hydraulics company not far from here, but I had a business conference to attend over the weekend through yesterday."

"I see," Lynette said, wondering if they were parked near each other or if he was simply just walking in her direction so they could continue their conversation. Either way, she was happy to be chatting with him.

But then he slowed his gait.

"Well, it was really great talking with you, but I'm just a few cars down from here."

"It was great meeting you, too," she said.

"Oh, and by the way, my name is Pierce," he said reaching out his hand to shake hers.

"I'm Lynette," she told him.

"Well, again, it was nice to meet you, and hey . . . if I'm not being too forward, I'd love to talk to you again. But only if you're okay with that."

"Sure. Why not?"

Pierce pulled a pen and a business card from his briefcase and wrote something on the back of the card. "Here's my cell number, but you can also call me at my office number. Either is fine."

"Sounds good, and I will."

"Oh, and although I don't see a wedding ring on your finger, I guess I should have at least had the decency to ask if you were married."

"No, I'm divorced," she said, wondering why she'd shared this much information with a total stranger when all she'd actually needed to do was answer him with a simple no. But then, she knew part of the reason she had responded the way she had was because this meeting-new-men thing still felt a bit awkward to her.

"Good...well, I don't mean it's good that you're divorced. I just mean 'good' in the respect that you're not married."

"Not a problem," Lynette said. "I knew what you meant, and I also appreciate your being thoughtful enough to ask."

"Well, again, it really was great seeing you, and I look forward to hearing from you soon."

"Take care," she said.

"You, too, and be safe driving home."

"I will," she said, continuing through the parking lot and then heading down the aisle where she had parked her vehicle. Once there, she sat inside of it, started the ignition, then headed down to the main level and out of the parking garage. As she approached the self-service pay booth, she pulled on her sunglasses, and after inserting her credit card and waiting for a receipt, she drove out of the airport and onto I-90 west toward home. But as she did, she couldn't help thinking about Pierce and how wonderfully handsome he was. She also thought about how quickly she'd gone from meeting no one to now meeting two gorgeous, intelligent men who seemed noticeably interested in her—and she was certainly interested in them. Although, how in the world would she choose between them? But then, maybe she wouldn't have to. Maybe once she spoke to both Emmett and Pierce and got a chance to know the two of them a little better, she would find that she had much more in common with one of them than she did with the other. Or maybe she would discover that she was compatible with *both* men, and if so, what was wrong with her dating Emmett *and* Pierce? Because it wasn't as though men didn't do this kind of thing all the time. It also wasn't as though she was planning to sleep with multiple men, either, so in truth, she could do whatever she wanted. She was grown, divorced, and free. Which meant she no longer had to answer to anyone. Not on any day she could think of.

CHAPTER 19

Michelle

Michelle's guilty conscience was nearly suffocating her, and if there were some miraculous way that she could take back the terrible thing she had done, she would have. Especially since making love with Chris hadn't been the best. It hadn't been awful or unbearable, but it hadn't been great, either—not even close. And sadly, it had seemed more like she and Chris had been merely having sex...just to be having sex. In fact, the entire evening had felt average at best, and to make matters worse, Michelle had spent most of her time thinking about Steven. At one point, she had even found herself daydreaming about him, because what she now knew was that there likely wasn't anyone—Chris or otherwise—who would ever be able to make her feel the way Steven once had. Not physically or emotionally. These were simply the kinds of truths that couldn't be denied, not when Steven had always satisfied her in ways she still couldn't explain today. Yes, having sex before marriage was wrong and it was something she had made a conscious decision to stop doing, but she'd be lying if she said she didn't miss being with Steven in that way. And she would also be lying if she said she could learn to live with being unhappy in her bedroom—the way she now knew she would certainly be if she married Chris.

Michelle sighed deeply and shook her head in confusion. She then sat on her sofa, waiting for Chris to pick her up for their pre-marital counseling session with Pastor Rigsby, and just the thought of seeing either of them made Michelle's heart race faster and faster. Because how in the world would she keep a straight face? How would she be able to sit in a room with both her pastor and her fiancé, all while knowing that she was in love with another man? And worse, how much longer would she be able to keep up such a horrible façade?

Michelle sighed and shook her head again and then thought about Chris's overall reaction to their having sex, which had been totally opposite from the way she'd been feeling. He had seemed as though he couldn't have been happier or more content with the way things had turned out, and in all honesty, Michelle couldn't understand it. Although, maybe what the two of them had experienced last night had been the norm for him. Maybe Chris was one of those men who didn't require anything spectacular and was mostly just happy to share an evening of intimacy with the woman he loved. Or maybe Michelle's dissatisfaction had more to do with the fact that she had immediately begun comparing him to Steven, because from that point on, she hadn't been able to enjoy her time with Chris even a little.

Steven, Steven, Steven.

No matter how hard she tried to think about something else, her thoughts always settled back on him, and the whole idea of it was beginning to unnerve her.

Michelle took yet another deep breath, but when she saw the Facebook Messenger notification at the top of her phone screen, she clicked on it. And it was then that her emotions overtook her completely.

Michelle,

I hope you're doing well, and I also hope it's okay that I'm contacting you here on Facebook. I've actually wanted to do so ever since seeing you that day at the store, but I didn't want to cause any problems for you or your engagement. But the more I tried to move on with my life and the more I told myself I needed to let you do the same, the more miserable and anxious I became. Because you see, Michelle, I'm still so very much in love with you. I knew this well before I saw you again, but after seeing you, this was when I realized right away that I could never love anyone the way I love you. And if you want to know just how much I really mean that...just know that as much as I loved my ex-wife, I still never loved her as much as I have always loved you. What you and I had was special. What we had was true love. We depended on each other, and we had this amazing level of compatibility. We had what most people spend their entire lives searching for, and I just couldn't allow you to marry someone else without sharing my true feelings with you. I also couldn't let you marry someone else when I know for sure that you still love me, too. I saw it in your eyes that day at the store. So please, will you call me?

Michelle wasn't sure what to say or do, and as her heart raced even faster, she knew it was partly because she feared what might happen if she called Steven and partly because of the excitement she felt about being able to talk to him again. She knew her feelings were wrong on every level, but she also couldn't help wanting to at least hear him out. She wanted to hear what he had to say by phone, even though she knew having anything to do with him might lead to disaster. But she also couldn't ignore everything he'd just said to her in his message. He'd told the truth about so much, and there was no way she could pretend otherwise. There was no way on earth she could act as though Steven didn't exist and that...she wasn't in love with him. Not when, in reality, she loved him dearly.

For the most part, Michelle and Chris had been quiet on the ride to the church. Not because they didn't like talking while driving, but because they always enjoyed listening to SiriusXM radio's Heart & Soul channel. Sometimes they even sang the lyrics together, especially if they heard a song they both loved. Although, what Chris didn't know today was that Michelle had been so occupied with her thoughts that she hadn't paid much attention to any of the music they'd heard. Because for one, she couldn't stop thinking about the Facebook message Steven had sent her earlier and how she now couldn't wait to call him. Then, if that hadn't already been terrible enough, Michelle had spent much of the drive replaying the night before over and over, and regretting the way she had ended her vow of celibacy. She also felt a great sense of shame about the reason she had decided to sleep with Chris in the first place, which was the fact that she'd been hoping it would make her forget about Steven—once and for all.

But it hadn't.

If anything, it had made things worse, because although she and Chris were now sitting in front of Pastor Rigsby, Michelle realized that not only did she want to talk to Steven, she also wanted to see him. She was even starting to feel as though she *needed* to see him, and that wasn't good.

Pastor Rigsby leaned halfway back in his black leather high-back chair and clasped his hands together on the top of his desk. "Well, let me just begin by saying that I am so very proud of the two of you."

Michelle and Chris smiled, but Michelle also wondered what Pastor Rigsby was referring to.

"Because let me just tell you," he continued, "being Christian or not, remaining abstinent for such a long period of time isn't easy. Especially when two people are deeply attracted to each other and they're in love. But the two of you have kept your faith strong, even when I'm sure you've had moments where you had to fight major temptation."

Michelle smiled again and while she didn't turn to look at Chris, she was sure he was just as ashamed as she was. Not so much because they'd had sex, but because they weren't being honest with Pastor Rigsby. They certainly hadn't lied to their pastor directly, but they also hadn't told him the truth about what they'd done last night, and to Michelle, that was the same as being dishonest.

"I do want to ask both of you a very important question, though," Pastor Rigsby said. "And I also want to warn you ahead of time that this question might make you a bit uncomfortable."

"Okay," Chris said.

"Have you thought about what your marital sexual expectations will be? Because while the two of you haven't been intimate in that way, I remember both of you admitting that you'd had sex in some of your other relationships."

Chris repositioned himself in his chair. "You mean in terms of frequency?"

Pastor Rigsby nodded. "Yes, and also what's allowed and what will be off-limits. And please know, I'm certainly not asking you to share any specific details because I believe these kinds of preferences should remain private between a husband and wife. But I do want to make sure you discuss this subject because when couples don't, problems can arise months or even years down the road."

Michelle wasn't even sure what to say. Not when the sex between them last night hadn't gone too well. Not when she wasn't even looking forward to having sex with her fiancé ever again. So instead of responding to Pastor Rigsby, she waited for Chris to share his opinion.

"To be honest, I hadn't even thought about either of those questions," Chris said.

"Most people don't," Pastor Rigsby acknowledged. "Most husbands just assume that their wives will want to have sex every single night from now on. When in reality, their wives might be preparing for something totally different. Or if their wives do start out this way, later on things can change. Especially once you begin having children, taking care of the entire household, and well...just dealing with life on life's terms."

Chris nodded, but Michelle still didn't say anything. That is, until Pastor Rigsby asked her directly what her thoughts were.

"I really hadn't thought about any of this, either," she said.

"Well, just make sure you sit down very soon to discuss this. Preferably this week. That way you can make sure you're on the same page. You can talk about what you both like, as well as what you don't like, and you should also begin talking about your plan for having children. Because another thing that sometimes causes problems is when one spouse wants to have children right away, but the other wants to wait a year or two or sometimes even longer. There is nothing wrong with either preference, but again, it's important to make sure you're in agreement about all of this before your wedding day."

Chris nodded. "Actually, we have talked about that a little. Because while neither of us is getting any younger, we still both agree that we want to enjoy at least some time together alone as a married couple. For at least a year and then move forward with starting a family."

"Good," Pastor Rigsby said, and then he looked at Michelle. "Is everything okay?"

"Yes, I'm fine."

"You seem a little on the quiet side this evening, so I just wanted to make sure."

Michelle didn't look at Chris, but she could see in her peripheral vision that he'd turned to look at her, and it was all she could do to keep her composure—it was all she could do to stop herself from telling him everything. Specifically, that she was having second thoughts about marrying him. But instead, she kept her eyes on Pastor Rigsby and prayed he would move on to the next topic. She prayed that this pre-marital counseling session would end much sooner rather than later and that when Chris drove her home, he wouldn't want to come in for a visit. Because, right now, she just didn't want to have to face him or take a chance on having him realize that she wasn't herself this evening— just as Pastor Rigsby was already suspecting. She didn't want Chris figuring out that something was very much wrong with her, and that their relationship was in trouble. But more than anything, she wanted to call Steven. She wanted to hear his voice and reminisce about old times. She wanted to catch up on every aspect of his life—a life her parents had forced her to miss out on completely.

CHAPTER 20

Lynette

C hloe and Tabitha had arrived safe and sound, and now that Lynette had spoken to them on three separate occasions, she knew it was time to stop worrying about them. Especially since, to some degree, Lynette knew her parents were going to be just a bit more cautious and stricter than she was, because the last thing they wanted was for something bad to happen to either of their granddaughters on their watch.

So now Lynette sat on the plush sofa in her family room, preparing to call Emmett. And to her surprise, she felt a little uneasy about it. Which didn't make a whole lot of sense because it wasn't as though she'd never spoken with him before. Sure, she'd only chatted with him for a few moments during her nightly walks, but there was still nothing for her to be nervous about. But then, maybe the real reason she felt a little anxious about all of this was because having an official phone conversation meant their relationship was moving to a new level.

Still, Lynette took a deep breath, curled her legs under her bottom, and dialed Emmett's phone number.

He answered on the third ring. "Hello?"

"Hey, this is Lynette. How are you?"

"I'm doing well, and what about you?"

"I'm doing great."

"Wonderful."

"Is this a good time for you?" she asked.

"It is. And even if it weren't, I would make time."

"Is that right?" Lynette said with a smile in her voice.

"Absolutely."

"So did you have a pretty busy day?"

"Actually, I did. But it was a good day, though, so I'm not complaining. How about you?"

"Well, earlier I dropped my daughters off at the airport. They're going to visit my parents."

"Here in Mitchell or over at O'Hare?"

"O'Hare."

"Oh, okay. How long will they be gone?"

"Most of the summer."

"That's a long time."

"Tell me about it. But they really wanted to go, and my parents really wanted them to come, so I know they'll be fine."

"Is this your first time being away from them this long?"

"Yes, so I won't lie, I'm definitely missing them."

"That's so understandable, though. And you said your divorce was just finalized not long ago, right?"

"It was," she said, remembering that she'd purposely mentioned that to him a couple of weeks ago when he'd asked if she was dating anyone.

"How long were you married?"

"Seventeen years, but we separated right after our sixteenth wedding anniversary."

"Wow, that was a long time."

"Yeah, a long time indeed."

"I was married once, too. But it was very short-lived."

Lynette was a little shocked to hear this. "Really? How long ago?"

"It's been maybe five years now, but we were only together for three. Well, actually, we were together for four years but only married for three."

"I'm very sorry to hear that."

"Don't be. Our separation was mutual. At least for the most part, anyway."

"So were you just not compatible? Or not in love with each other?"

"We loved each other just fine, and we also had a lot in common. We were really good together. That is, except when it came to having children. She wanted at least three, and so did I. But after trying for two whole years, I learned that I would likely never be able to have any, and that's just not something my ex-wife could live with."

"I'm so sorry."

"At first, it was really tough for me to accept, and then when my ex told me that she couldn't spend the rest of her life without children, I was devastated. I was also angry because my first thought was 'What happened to for better or worse?' But at the same time, I also knew that if we stayed together against her wishes, she would be miserable, and our marriage would never be what it should be. So, I eventually agreed to sign the divorce papers."

Lynette felt so bad for Emmett. "I don't even know what to say."

"I'm sure, because it's a lot. But I really am good, though, and I've moved on from all of that. And anyway, enough about me. Because I'm sure your life is a lot more interesting."

"Not really. I mean, I sort of gave up most of my dreams

of having a successful career so I could devote my time to my husband and daughters. And that was all fine with me until my marriage began falling apart."

"Can I ask what happened?"

"My husband was a serial cheater. He slept with a lot of women, and eventually he got one of them pregnant."

"Man, that's heavy, and I'm sorry you had to experience something like that."

"Yeah, it was a lot to bear, and to add insult to injury, he married her."

"The woman he got pregnant?" Emmett asked, and Lynette could hear the shock in his voice.

"Yes. And not only did he get her pregnant, they had twins."

"Wow."

"Yeah, wow is right. But like you, I've moved on with my life."

"I'm glad to hear that because I know it couldn't have been easy."

"No, it wasn't, and it also wasn't easy for my girls, which made things that much more painful."

"How are they doing overall?"

"As well as can be expected, given the situation."

"Divorces are never easy for anyone, and especially not for children," Emmett said. "I know it wasn't for me, anyway."

"Your parents divorced when you were young?"

"They did. When I was only seven. And my brothers were ten and twelve."

"Oh my."

"It was really hard for me, and to make things worse, my mom invited her boyfriend to move in, and he never liked my brothers and me. I mean, don't get me wrong, he was a great provider and he's also the reason we never went without anything, but he also didn't say very much to any of us. And he never took us anywhere as a family. He would only take my mom out, and if we wanted to go somewhere, only our mom went with us."

"Did they ever get married?"

"Yeah, once I left for college. And since I was the youngest, I guess he'd just been waiting until no one else was living in the house but the two of them."

"That's awful."

"It was the worst, and for a long time my brothers and I didn't have a lot to do with our mom or him. But then a few years ago, he died, and slowly but surely we let bygones be bygones and we became close with our mom again."

"I could never do that."

"What?"

"Put a man or anyone else before my children. My girls and I are a package deal, and before I even think about introducing them to anyone, I would have to be dating them for a very long time."

"I understand, and I don't blame you. Not at all."

"They've already been through a lot, so they need to be my priority."

"Of course. And just so you know, I would never try to compromise that. I would never expect you to do anything you don't feel comfortable with. Not when it comes to your girls or anything else."

"I appreciate that."

"I do have a question for you, though," he said. "And it's sort of an elephant-in-the-room kind of inquiry."

"What is it?"

"Well, I'm assuming that if our age difference was a

problem, you wouldn't be calling me, but I still have to ask. Is it?"

"Sort of. But not really. Does that make sense?" she said, and they both laughed.

"Actually, it does. It makes perfect sense."

"I mean, because let's face it," Lynette said. "Older men date younger women all the time, but you don't see as many older women dating younger men. You do see it more now than, say, twenty years ago, but it's still not the norm."

"No, but that has never bothered me, and to tell you the truth I've always been attracted to older women. In fact, even the last woman I dated was five years older than me. And I've also dated other women who were around the same age as you."

"Really? And why do you think that is?"

"Well, you know how most people believe that women mature much earlier than men?"

"I do."

"Well, in my case that's not true. I've always been much more mature than my friends, and mostly, whenever I dated women who were my age or younger, they seemed a bit on the immature side to *me*. And some of them seemed downright irresponsible."

Lynette loved that Emmett was being so transparent about his feelings, and his words made her feel somewhat better about being older than him. She knew nothing was guaranteed, though, and that even if things did work out between them and they began dating exclusively, it would still be a good while before she fully believed he wasn't interested in women who were younger than her. She wasn't calling him a liar, but she also knew that not all women in their twenties and thirties were immature, and that maybe Emmett just hadn't met the right one. That was neither here nor there, though, because what she knew now, even more so than she had before calling him, was that she liked him. A lot. So, while she was going to be as careful as she possibly could when it came to trusting him and growing closer to him, she wasn't going to pass on getting to know him better. Instead, she was going to date him and see what happened. She was willingly going to take a chance because not only did she like *him*, she could tell he liked her, too. And she hoped that was a good thing.

CHAPTER 21

Serena

I t was early evening and while Serena still hadn't heard back from Michelle, she wasn't all that surprised. Not when she knew Michelle didn't like confrontation. Michelle also didn't like going back on her word, not since childhood. Yet this was exactly what she was doing now, what with this whole breach-of-celibacy drama. Serena was so disappointed in her, and to tell the truth, she was angry about all of it. Why? Because deep down, Serena knew that part of the reason Tim had begun seeing and sleeping with other women was because Serena wouldn't sleep with him herself. Yes, she knew becoming celibate had been her own choice and that no one had forced her to make that decision, but she also couldn't stop thinking about all the times she'd wanted to give in to Tim. Yet Michelle had always stopped her before she had.

Over this last year, Serena would call Michelle, explain to her how hard staying celibate was becoming for her, but then Michelle would quickly remind Serena that committing such an unnecessary sin wasn't worth it, and that if Tim truly loved her, he would gladly wait until they were married. Which had all been fine and well for Serena.

Until today.

Because just hearing Michelle confess this morning about what she had done with Chris had been enough to make Serena cringe. Especially since Michelle had committed the very sin she had regularly discouraged Serena from committing.

But as much as Serena had gotten herself all worked up and now wanted to call Michelle to tell her exactly how she was feeling, she didn't. Instead, she calmed her racing thoughts and decided she would simply wait until Michelle found the decency to call her instead. Because no matter what well-thought-out explanation Michelle was surely trying to conjure up, her story wouldn't likely make Serena feel much better about the situation anyhow. Not when Michelle had already proven that she was a total hypocrite.

Serena called and chatted with her mom for a few minutes, and then she browsed through Instagram, Facebook, and Twitter—checking to see if the Jake guy she'd met had any social media pages set up. But strangely, he didn't. Although, as popular as social media was, Serena also knew that not everyone was interested in having a social media page, so Jake not having one didn't mean much of anything. But now, since she couldn't find him online, she sat debating whether she should just go ahead and call him. Of course, she was definitely going to contact him at some point. But what she debated was whether she should call him right away this evening or wait until tomorrow. Or possibly the next day, even. She pondered what to do because it was just as she had been thinking earlier: She didn't want Jake believing she was desperate. Even though technically, she sort of was, because in all honesty, she was hoping with everything in her that *he* was the one. She prayed he was the man of her dreams, and that he was the man she would soon be marrying. She knew it was silly to be thinking so optimistically about a man she barely knew, but she couldn't help the way she felt. She also couldn't help wanting what she wanted, which was to find a good man, marry him as soon as possible, and begin living the kind of amazing life she believed she deserved.

Serena continued debating what to do, but when she couldn't take it anymore, she picked up her phone, dialed Jake's number, inhaled, exhaled, and waited for him to answer.

"Hello?" he said after the fourth ring and just before Serena was about to end the call.

"Hey, how are you?"

"I'm good. Is this Serena?"

"Yes. Did I catch you at a bad time?"

"No, not at all, and I'm glad you called. So did you finish what you were working on?" he said, obviously making small talk.

"I did, and actually, I was working on a speech that I'll be delivering this weekend."

"Oh, wow. Well, you may as well know that I already Googled you and saw that you have a blog and that you speak for a living. And I was really impressed."

"Thank you."

"So, did you always want to be a speaker and a writer? Or did all of that evolve once you became an adult?"

"I guess you could say it was a little of both. When I was a child, I loved talking all the time and I even got in trouble for it. Both at home with my mom and at school. I loved writing, too, though, and by fourth grade it became my favorite pastime."

"That's awesome."

"And what about you?" she asked, happy Jake had brought up the subject of work and what she did career-wise.

"Me? Well, my work certainly isn't as glamorous as yours, but I love what I do."

"I wouldn't call mine glamorous, either, because while I really enjoy what I do, my work is like any other work. There are advantages and disadvantages. Things I love about it, as well as things I wish I didn't have to deal with at all."

"I hear you. Believe me I do, and to answer your question, I work for Klein-Wagner Corporation."

Serena had known he likely didn't work in an office environment, but at the same time, she hadn't expected to hear that he worked for one of their local factories. Nonetheless, though, she was going to keep an open mind about everything Jake was sharing with her.

"Really?" she said. "And what do you do there?"

"I work in skilled trades. Pipe fitting, to be exact."

"Oh, okay."

"Now, this certainly wasn't the plan my parents had for me, but after graduating high school, I just couldn't see myself going to college. I also couldn't imagine having any job that would require me to sit inside an office building every day. I mean, I know there's nothing wrong with doing that. Nothing wrong with it at all. But I just knew it wasn't for me, and that's the reason I decided to do something different."

"You still had to go back to school, though, right?"

"I did. But instead of taking classes in a traditional way, I took a test for an apprenticeship program, passed it, and began working and going to school at the same time. Then, after three years, I became a journeyman. And after that, a master pipe fitter, which is what I am now. So my love for math and science really paid off, even though I chose not to attend a four-year university. And that's also the reason I earn six figures. I'm not sharing that to be boastful. I'm just stating a fact because a lot of people don't realize what a great living skilled-trades professionals earn. Most people don't even think it's possible."

"Wow, you've really done well for yourself, and now I'm the one who's impressed."

Jake laughed, and so did Serena because he was right. She'd had no idea that any factory job paid that kind of money. That is, unless it was maybe a supervisory or management position of some sort.

"But I do want to ask you a couple of things up front, though," he said. "If that's okay with you."

"Of course."

"Are you dating anyone?"

"No. I'm not. Are you?"

"Nope. I've been single for a while now."

"That's good to hear," Serena said.

"And what about the conversation we just had? Does it bother you?"

Serena slightly lowered her eyebrows. "Does what bother me?"

"What I do for a living."

"No," she said, even though she wasn't sure how she actually felt about it.

"Are you sure?"

"Well, I guess the bigger question is, why do you ask?"

"Because I've dated professional women who have degrees before, and it rarely works out."

"Why?"

"Because they want a man who also has a degree. Someone sitting on the top floor of some huge corporate building

147

in a corner office. So now, I just think it's best to ask up front so that neither of us ends up wasting our time."

"No, it doesn't bother me at all," Serena hurried to say, because the last thing she wanted was to scare him off. She was, for sure, the exact kind of woman he was referring to, but she wanted to give him a chance. She also thought about the conversation she'd had with Kenya, Lynette, and Michelle at their last girls' get-together, and how they'd insisted that it was time for her to date better men—even if they might not have a college degree or earn the kind of money Serena was hoping for.

"Are you sure?" Jake asked.

"I'm positive."

"I'm glad to hear that, because while I may not have a bachelor's degree or a master's degree, I still handle my money very responsibly. I'm also a good man with a big heart, and I'll always try to treat you the way I want to be treated."

"I appreciate hearing that, and I will treat you the same."

"Good, and now that we have that out of the way, let's talk about something a lot more interesting."

"Which is what?"

"Why a beautiful, intelligent, successful woman like you isn't dating anyone."

"Well, thank you for the compliment. But that's a long story, and telling it might take all night."

"Then it's a good thing I have all night, isn't it?" he said, and they both laughed again.

"You are too funny," Serena told him, and then realized she hadn't felt this happy in a very long time.

She hadn't felt this hopeful in years, and she prayed she wouldn't lose interest. Because even though Jake didn't earn the $250,000-plus salary that Tim earned and he didn't have a degree, Serena could tell he was a good guy. He seemed like such a respectable man, and she wouldn't mess things up this time. Instead, she would ignore his shortcomings and focus on all his great qualities. She would keep an open mind and give him a fair chance. The way any decent woman should.

CHAPTER 22

Michelle

Chris pulled into Michelle's driveway and parked, but he left his engine running. "Is everything okay?"

"I'm fine," she said, finally looking at him. "Just tired."

"Well, you hardly said anything on the way to the church, and the most you just did on the way home was answer my questions with one- or two-word answers."

"I'm so sorry," she said, speaking as genuinely as possible. "I had a really long day at work. But once I get some rest tonight, I know I'll be fine."

"Well, I truly hope so. And I also hope you know that you can tell me anything. Anything at all."

"I do, and now that you mention it, there is something I need to be honest about."

"Okay. What is it?"

"I sort of regret not remaining celibate."

"Oh, really? Why?"

"Because it was something I truly believed in."

"Then why did you make such a big deal about us making love last night?"

"Because I really wanted to. But if you're okay with it, I'd rather we not do so again until we're married."

At first, Chris paused, and Michelle knew he was disappointed. She also hated all the lying she was doing.

"Fine," he said. "I don't really understand this, but fine."

"Baby, I'm sorry."

"I am, too, but we only have three months to go. So, I'm good."

Michelle reached over and caressed the side of Chris's cheek. "I love you."

"I love you, too," he said. "I'm also really sorry I can't come in for a visit, but I have a super-early surgery scheduled for tomorrow morning. So I need to get home, wind down, and get to bed."

"I understand, and no worries. We'll get together tomorrow, though, for sure."

"Sounds good," he said, leaning over and kissing her on the lips. "You have a good night, baby, okay?"

"I will, and you, too," she said, opening the door and exiting his vehicle.

Then once she walked up to her front door and opened it, she turned and waved goodbye to Chris as he drove away. He headed down the street and out of her subdivision, and Michelle had never felt more relieved. Because the last thing she'd wanted to do was sit with Chris for the next two to three hours, pretending that she was just as in love with him as he was with her. As it was, she'd had to ride in the same car with him to the church, sit through their counseling session, and ride back home with him, all while lying about the way she felt about their relationship, engagement, and impending marriage. She was being so unfair to Chris, and it wouldn't be long before she would have to tell him the truth. It was also only a matter of time before she would have to come clean to her parents, aunt, and girlfriends, none of which she was looking forward to doing.

Michelle removed her heeled sandals, silk sundress, earrings, and bracelets, and slipped into her summer pajama set. Then she climbed into her bed and curled up with her phone, rereading Steven's message. But as much as she wanted to dial the number he'd included at the end of it, she couldn't stop thinking about Chris and the way she'd flat-out lied to him. She also thought about how wonderful of a man Chris was and that maybe she was giving up on him too quickly. Maybe it was simply best to leave the past in the past and to move forward with the awesome life God had already given her. Maybe it was wrong to focus only on what she wanted, when that would also mean hurting Chris to his core.

Michelle didn't know what to do, so instead of calling Steven, she thought about Serena and the conversation they'd had this morning. It had been clear from the start that Serena wasn't happy about the news Michelle had told her, but as much as Michelle wished she could avoid her for at least another couple of days, she knew that would only make things worse. Which meant it was better to call Serena now and get it over with. And it also might be best to just tell her the truth.

Serena answered on the first ring. "Hello?"

"Hey," Michelle said.

But then there was silence.

"So, I know you're upset," Michelle told her.

"And you don't think I should be?"

"No, I do. I completely understand, and that's why I want to explain what happened."

"I'm listening," Serena said.

"So...I didn't have sex with Chris because of the reason you're thinking."

"Yeah, okay, Michelle. Whatever you say."

"I'm serious. And although I hate admitting this to anyone—even you—I'm to the point now where I really need to confide in someone pretty badly."

"About what?"

"I saw Steven a couple of weeks ago," she said, already feeling somewhat relieved.

"Steven? The guy you dated umpteen years ago?"

"Yes."

"Okay, but what does he have to do with you sleeping with Chris last night?"

Michelle opened her mouth to speak and then burst into tears.

"Girl, what's the matter?" Serena asked. "What's wrong?"

Michelle sniffled a few times and wiped away most of her tears. "Serena, everything is so messed up right now. I mean, really, really messed up, and I'm so lost and confused."

"Why? What happened?"

Michelle took a few seconds to settle herself down. "I'm still in love with him, girl...and I'm not in love with Chris."

"What?" Serena exclaimed. "What do you mean, you're still in love with him? And that you're not in love with Chris? You've been in love with Chris ever since you met him, and you're getting married to him three months from now, remember?"

"I know that. And yes, I do love him, but I'm not *in* love with him."

"And you just figured that out? After being engaged to him all these months and making all those wedding plans?"

"I didn't know. Not until I saw Steven again. I saw him at the grocery store, and that changed everything."

"Wow, girl. I don't even know what to say. Or how to feel about any of this."

"Yeah, well, then just try to imagine how I'm feeling. And then on top of all of it, I thought maybe if Chris and I made love, I would forget about Steven. I thought it would solidify my relationship with him. I thought it would fix everything. But it all backfired."

"How?"

"Because it wasn't worth it."

"Meaning what? You didn't enjoy it?"

"Not even a little."

"Oh no," Michelle heard Serena nearly whispering, which meant she was as shocked as Michelle had been.

"Yeah, exactly, and now I don't know whether to keep my commitment to Chris or tell him the truth."

"Well, of course, you have to tell him the truth," Serena quickly insisted. "Right?"

"I want to. I really do. But it's just not that easy. He'll be devastated. And then there's the whole thing with my parents. Because you know they never thought Steven was good enough for me. My father basically told me that if I married him, Steven would never be welcome in their home. Then Daddy claimed that Steven was only marrying me because he and Mom had money. Which couldn't have been further from the truth."

"I remember that," Serena said, now sounding less angry and bit more empathetic toward Michelle. "I remember it well."

"And then he threatened to remove me from his and Mom's will, claiming that all Steven would end up doing was leaving me for another woman and taking me for everything I had. It was so ridiculous because the only reason Mom and Dad didn't like Steven was because instead of going to college, he became an assistant manager at a fast-food restaurant."

Michelle waited for Serena to comment, but when she didn't, Michelle knew why.

"Are you still there?" Michelle asked.

"I'm here," Serena said.

"So I guess you think my parents were right. Because you sure are quiet."

"No, to be honest, I was thinking about my own situation."

"Which is what?"

"I met someone today."

"Oh, really?"

"Yeah, but he doesn't have a degree, either."

"Does he seem nice?"

"He really does, and I ended up talking to him tonight for three hours."

"Then his educational background shouldn't matter to you in the least," Michelle said in a not-so-nice tone. "It should be the last thing you're even thinking about."

"Well, you don't have to get so upset about it."

"I'm sorry. I didn't mean to. But treating people differently just because they don't have some doggone degree or they don't earn some massive salary is just plain ridiculous. It's awful."

"Well, I can't help who I am or how I feel, Michelle. You know it's the way I've always been, and you know why. I just don't ever want to be broke again. Not the way I was back when I was growing up. But the good news is that I'm really trying to do better. I want to be better, and that's why I'm going to keep talking to Jake. That's his name."

"Well, good for you, and please don't mess this up, Serena.

Give this Jake guy a chance. Do the right thing before you end up like me."

"I hear you, but what are you going to do? Because it's like I said earlier, you're getting married three months from now."

"I don't know. Part of me wants to call Steven to see what else he has to say, and part of me wants to end all communication with him."

"Excuse me? Are you saying he's already contacted you? Since you saw him at the store?"

"He sent me a private message on social media."

"Wow, girl."

"Yeah, tell me about it."

"Well, if I were you, I would get this handled as soon as possible because Chris doesn't deserve this. He also doesn't deserve to be left at the altar. I mean, girl, you know I love you with all my heart, and I'll always be here for you. But I'm not okay with seeing Chris get hurt. And I think you know Kenya and Lynette will feel the same."

"I'm sure they will, but please don't say anything to them. It was hard enough telling you, but it's like I said before, I really needed to confide in someone about all of this."

"I won't say a word. But again, you really need to take care of this."

"I will. I don't know how, but I will. I have to."

CHAPTER 23

Kenya

Kenya and Robert sat together in silence, waiting for their attorney to call them into his office. Actually, William Lockhart was a longtime friend and college buddy of Robert's, and as a result, Kenya and William's wife had become friendly over the years as well. But now, for the second time, they were here to retain his legal services. His specialty was family law, and while Robert and Kenya had consulted with him in the past and he'd also filed a motion for contempt regarding Robert's visitation enforcement, not once had they ever imagined they would need to retain his services regarding custody. They'd also never considered the possibility that things would become as hostile as they had with Terri. But here they were, preparing to tell William everything he needed to know about Terri, Bobby, and Robert's desire to gain full custody of his son.

"Mr. Lockhart will see you now," William's twenty-five-year-old legal assistant told them. Kenya knew her age because, coincidentally, she was celebrating her birthday today.

"Thank you," Robert told her, and he and Kenya walked inside William's office.

"Good morning," William said, standing up behind his desk.

"Good morning," they both responded.

"Please have a seat," he told them, and he sat back down as well. "So how are the kids?"

"They're doing well," Robert said. "What about your three?"

"They're doing well, too."

"And Cynthia?" Kenya said, asking about his wife.

"She's doing great."

"We haven't spoken in a while, but please tell her that I'll be calling her very soon to catch up," Kenya told him.

"Will do," he said, and then he turned his attention to Robert. "So based on our brief conversation yesterday, it sounds like you're really going through it. Especially if you now want to proceed with filing for full custody."

"Hmmph," Robert said. "Man, you don't know the half of it."

"I'm really sorry to hear that, because I know this can't be easy. But to begin, why don't you give me a little more background. Of course, I certainly know how ugly your divorce was and that Terri has never really allowed you to spend time with Bobby, but take me back over these last couple of weeks. Tell me what happened since we filed the visitation motion. That way, I can begin reevaluating everything."

Robert pulled out his phone, opened his text messaging app, clicked on Terri's name, and passed his phone to William. "Here's what she sent me the day after Memorial Day."

William read through the message and then returned Robert's phone to him. "Well, she's definitely not a happy woman, and she absolutely doesn't want you to have a relationship with your son. Let alone see him."

"No, she doesn't, and that's why I've decided to file for full custody. Meaning, I don't just want visitation anymore, which she isn't allowing me to have, anyway. I now want full custody and nothing less."

Robert nodded and then looked at Kenya. "And you're completely on board with this, too? Because as we move forward, maintaining a united front as husband and wife is going to make all the difference."

"Yes, if this is what Robert wants, then I'm all in," she told him.

"But is this what *you* want? Because again, having the two of you of one accord will be crucial."

"I would love nothing more than to have Bobby come live with us. But I'll be honest...and Robert already knows my feelings about this...my concern is what crazy thing Terri might do if she loses custody of him. Because just three days ago, she showed up at my place of business, going completely off on me. And she had Bobby in the car with her."

William raised his eyebrows. "Really?"

Kenya nodded.

"And why? I mean, why was she there at all?"

"Because Robert is taking her back to court about his visitation rights."

"And what did she say exactly?"

"The question is, what didn't she say?"

"Did she threaten you?"

"She told me that if we followed through with the court proceedings, we would be sorry."

"Did you call the police?"

"No."

"Well, as much as I hate saying this, you probably should have. Especially if we want to begin building a case against Terri."

Kenya wanted so badly to tell William how, even though

she agreed with him, Robert didn't think it was a good idea. But just as she finished that particular thought, Robert shared that information himself.

"I'm not sure calling the police would have been the right thing to do. Not when Terri has already been acting so ridiculously. I also don't want to hurt Bobby any more than we have to."

"I hear you," William said, "and believe me, I understand. But unfortunately, if we're going to win custody, we're going to need all the ammunition we can get. I know it may sound cruel, but you're going to need every piece of evidence you can find that will prove Terri to be an unfit mother. Which brings me to my next question. Do you have anything that will help us in this area now? Do you know how their living conditions are?"

"Not really, because Terri has never allowed me to come inside her home. And there were also times when she would move and not even give me their new address. I did speak to Bobby's school counselor the other day, though," Robert said, and then shared those particular details with William.

"That's all important to know, but we're going to need more," William explained. "Which means it wouldn't hurt for us to hire a private investigator. That way we can keep tabs on when Terri comes and goes. Who comes to her house and how long they stay. What she buys from the grocery store. It would also be good to keep an eye on your son, so we can see just how well he's actually being taken care of. And of course, you'll need to begin recording dates and times of visitation order violations, such as keeping you from seeing Bobby, preventing you from video-chatting with him or talking to him on the phone, and badmouthing you to him. It would also be good if you can write down things like this that have happened in the past, along with dates and times, and I'll need to see all text message exchanges between the two of you."

Robert sighed and looked over at Kenya.

"Well, we knew this wouldn't be easy," she said.

"Yeah, we did. But I just hate that things have gotten so bad between Terri and me. They were never good, but now they're at their worst."

"Divorces and custody battles are rarely friendly," William said. "But when you have an ex who hates you as much as Terri seems to hate you, things can become pretty ugly. Very quickly. And you have to do whatever it takes to prove why you're the most fit parent."

Robert nodded in agreement.

"You should also know that while winning custody isn't impossible, you'll need to prepare for the fight of your life. Both you and Kenya will need to prepare."

Robert sighed again, and Kenya knew it was because he wasn't comfortable hearing all that William was telling him. But she could also tell he knew that if he truly wanted custody of his son, he didn't have a choice.

"So if you give me the go-ahead, I'll cancel the visitation hearing and file for a custody hearing instead. I'll also contact one of the best private investigators I know so he can get started on your case right away."

Robert clasped his hands together. "Fine. Yes, let's move forward."

"Good, and if Terri shows up at your home or work or anywhere else, threatening either one of you, please call the police. I know you're not comfortable with that, Rob, but it's like I was saying before, we really do need all the ammunition we can get. Because if we don't get the ammunition we need, it won't be worth pursuing this at all."

Robert nodded, but Kenya could tell that this was still the very last thing he wanted to do. And to be honest, she didn't want to have to call the police on Terri, either. Because Kenya was a mother, too. But if Terri showed up threatening her again, Kenya wouldn't hesitate. She would call the authorities as quickly as her fingers could dial the numbers 911.

CHAPTER 24

Kenya

Kenya glanced at her fitness watch and looked over at Robert. "The kids still have another two hours before summer camp is over, so we might as well head home for a while."

"I was thinking the same thing," Robert said, driving out of their attorney's parking lot.

"So that was a lot, huh?" Kenya asked him.

"Yeah, it was, and it's also exhausting."

"I know, but if you definitely want to file for custody, I think we have to do everything William is asking us to do."

"I agree, but it's still a lot, and it's not something I'm looking forward to. Especially when I know things are likely going to get worse before they get better."

"That's probably true, but we'll get through it."

"Yeah, I believe we will, but I guess my biggest concern is you."

"Meaning what?"

"As in, are you really on board with all of this? I know you told William you are, but I just want to be sure because once we move forward with this, there won't be any turning back."

"Yes, I'm definitely on board. But it's also like I've told you before, my concern is about Terri and how she's going to react. Because dealing with her could end up being a nightmare."

"Well, I'm just hoping that won't happen."

"Yeah, but we can't count on that. So, I guess I need you to know how serious I am about calling the police. Because if Terri even thinks about coming near our children or me, that's exactly what's going to happen."

Robert glanced at her for a second and then returned his attention to the street they were heading down. "I know we've already been over this, but I still need to ask you this again. You would really have her arrested? Even though we've talked about how badly that could hurt Bobby?"

Kenya loved her husband with all her heart, but now she realized maybe it was time for her to stop glossing over the way she truly felt. "Look, Robert, I'm not sure what you're thinking or why you feel the way you do, but as much as I know how deeply you love your son and that you have a right to fight for custody of him, you also have a responsibility to me and our other two children."

"I know that, but I just don't want to make things worse."

Kenya stared at him. "So then what are you saying, Robert? That Terri can do anything she wants to me, Eli, or Livvie, just as long as you get custody of Bobby? Because if the court rules in your favor, that woman is going to go ballistic. She's going to become worse than she's ever been, and no matter how you think all of this is going to play out, she will never accept having her son taken away from her."

"She won't have a choice," he said.

"Yeah, well, if you believe that, then you're living in a fantasy world."

"Oh, so now just because I want custody of my son, you think I'm not dealing with reality?"

"That's not what I said."

"Well, that's what it sounded like."

Kenya didn't like where this conversation was going, so she pulled her sunglasses out of her purse, placed them over her eyes, and gazed out of the passenger window. Robert didn't say anything else, either, and now Kenya understood why Lynette had given her forewarning about Terri and not letting her come between them. Because before today, Kenya couldn't remember the last time she and Robert had disagreed so intensely and then suddenly stopped speaking to each other in the middle of a conversation. They hadn't done something like this in years, and it bothered Kenya. Although, nonetheless, she still meant what she'd told Robert. Because if Terri showed up anywhere near her or her children, Kenya was calling the police. And there wasn't a single thing Robert or anyone else could say to stop her.

When they arrived home, Robert pulled into the garage, and he and Kenya both got out of the SUV and went inside. They still hadn't said anything else to one another, but now as Kenya set her purse on a chair in the kitchen, Robert gently drew her into his arms and gazed into her eyes.

"Baby, I'm sorry," he said.

"I'm sorry, too," she admitted, and Robert kissed her.

Then they both sat across from each other in the kitchen.

"And there's something else I want you to know as well," he said. "It's not that I don't get why you feel the way you do, because I understand completely. But the other reason I don't want to have Terri arrested is because if that happens and Bobby finds out, he will hate you and me both for the rest of our lives."

"Well, you know that's not what I want, but when you're dealing with someone who's as bitter as Terri, you can't pretend it's no big deal. You have to take her threats very seriously."

"I know, and I agree with you one hundred percent, but because of Bobby, I'm hoping it doesn't come to that. And to be honest, I'm wondering if maybe I should call her to let her know that I'm filing for full custody."

Kenya was somewhat taken aback. "Why?"

"Because maybe if she realizes what's about to happen, she'll decide that cooperating with the judge's visitation order is far more in her best interests."

"And you would be okay with that?"

"I would if she agrees to let Bobby spend every other weekend with us, every other holiday, as well as every other Christmas, no matter what the holiday schedule looks like for Terri and me in a given year. And of course, half of the summer. What I want is for her to agree to everything the judge ordered her to do from the very beginning."

"I don't know. I still don't see her saying yes to that, but you do have a point about her possibly agreeing to visitation versus taking a chance on losing custody altogether."

"Well, even if she doesn't, I think it's worth a try. So, I'm going to call William to ask him to hold off on filing the custody motion. At least until we find out one way or the other what Terri is going to do," he said.

"I agree."

"And baby," he said, reaching across the island and grabbing Kenya's hand, "I also want to say this. From this day forward, let's not argue about Terri ever again. Not for any reason. Because no matter what happens, you and I are Team Griffin, and nothing will ever change that."

"You're right, and yes, let's not ever do that again," she told him, all while hoping Terri would come to her senses. Although, the more Kenya sat thinking about everything, something dawned on her. Actually, it was more of an idea she had—an idea that would likely get Terri's attention much more quickly than the subject of custody.

CHAPTER 25

Serena

It had been twenty-four hours since Serena had spoken to Jake, but she still couldn't stop thinking about him. Which was a good thing because without her even realizing it before now, she'd gone a full day without thinking about Tim and the fact that he had moved on without her. There was, of course, a part of her that wondered how any man could be so cruel, but if she was going to continue asking herself that particular question, then she would also have to ask herself why any of the men she'd dated had either begun seeing other women behind her back, or they had simply just stopped calling her and coming around for no reason.

But the good news was that Jake seemed very different, and he made her feel special. It was true that she had met him only recently, but even after one phone call—which she still couldn't believe had lasted for three whole hours—she felt unusually optimistic. He seemed so genuine, and it had been a very long time since she had felt this way about any man. While she was embarrassed to admit it, in the past, she hadn't focused all that much on any man's character or any other important human qualities. Why? Because, sadly, all she had cared about was the kind of upper-class lifestyle she thought they could give her. But now, after being dumped

168

time and time again and meeting someone like Jake, she was starting to see the error of her ways. She also saw just how right her best friends had been all along, and that fixating only on a man's income level and what kind of home he lived in wasn't a good idea. It was shallow at best, and this whole Tim fiasco had opened her eyes in ways she hadn't counted on. Plus, she truly couldn't stop thinking about Jake—even though he didn't fit her usual standards. And that had to mean something.

Serena studied the speech she would be giving two days from now and added a few more sentences here and there. But in all honesty, she was mostly sitting there waiting for Jake to call her once he left work. So she kept busy until about a half hour later, when her doorbell rang. She wasn't expecting anyone, but when she went toward the front of her house and opened the door, she saw her sister.

"Hey," Diane said.

"Hey," Serena said, wondering why her sister had dropped by unannounced, but more important, why she had come there at all.

"Can I come in?" Diane asked.

"Sure," Serena said, and they headed down the hallway and into the kitchen. "Please have a seat."

Diane sat down and then dropped her purse in the chair next to her.

"Can I get you anything?" Serena asked.

"No, I'm fine," she said.

Serena then sat down across from her. "So, what's up?"

"Well, since you haven't been answering any of my phone calls, including yesterday morning and the day before, I decided it was time to come talk to you in person."

"Okay, talk."

Diane took a deep breath. "Look, sis. So here's the thing. There's something I've been wanting to talk to you about for a very long time."

"Really? What?"

"Us and our relationship."

Serena stared at her sister for a few seconds, but then said, "I'm not sure what you mean exactly."

"What I mean is that we really don't even have a relationship. And it's mostly because of the way you treat me as a sister. You act like you hate me. You've always acted that way, and I've never understood why."

Serena didn't respond because in all honesty, this whole do-drop-in visit had caught her completely off guard, and she didn't appreciate the way her sister was invading her space.

"So you don't have anything to say?" Diane asked.

"I do, but I'm not sure this is a conversation we should be having."

"Well, not only do I think we should have it, I believe we should've had it decades ago. Because at least then, I wouldn't have gone all these years trying to figure out what I did to you."

"Maybe. But before we continue any of this, I want you to know that I definitely don't hate you. I could never hate you. You're my sister, and I'm sorry you thought that."

"Then what is it, Serena? You just don't like me? You can't stand being around me? What?"

"The reason I don't like talking to you or seeing you is because it brings back too many painful memories for me."

Diane frowned. "Why?"

"Because of your dad and the way he would always pick you up and take you places. But even worse, he bought you brand-new clothing all the time. Your entire childhood."

"And you blame me for all the stuff my dad bought for me? Are you kidding, Serena?"

"Diane, you knew my father never came around and that I didn't even know who he was. Yet all you ever did was brag about your dad and how great he was. Then, you would go on all those shopping trips with him, come home, and brag some more. You bragged about everything, even though you knew I basically had nothing. You also knew Mom didn't have a lot of money, and that she couldn't buy me the same things your father got for you. But you never cared about any of that. You only cared about yourself, and I resented you for it."

Diane shook her head. "Gosh, I don't even know how to process any of this. I mean, really, sis? I'm thirty-eight, and you're forty. So that was like . . . how long ago?"

"Some wounds take a very long time to heal, and some *never* heal at all."

"Yeah, but only when they're not dealt with. So why haven't you ever said anything to me about this before? And even if you didn't feel comfortable talking about it with me, you could have gone to Mom about it. Or you even could have gone to one of your *girls*. Although, maybe you already have. Because you've always trusted your friends way more than you trusted me, anyway. Always. And you cared about them a whole lot more, too. I've known that ever since we were kids."

"That's not true. I do care about you, and I love you as my sister. It's just that I get along with my friends a lot better. And they've never hurt me the way you have, either."

Diane chuckled with sarcasm in her voice. "I can't believe you feel this way."

"Well, I do," Serena said, crossing her arms. "I know you may not understand why I feel the way I do, or you may not even want to hear the truth. But you're the one who stopped by *here*. And you're also the one who wanted to have this conversation."

"Yeah, I did. But it never dawned on me that your hateful feelings toward me had anything to do with my dad. Because anything he did for me wasn't my fault, Serena."

"I told you I don't hate you. I just don't prefer to be around you."

"Well, to me that's basically the same thing. Because when your own sister wants nothing to do with you, it still feels like she hates you. And even more so, Serena, because as siblings, you and I are all we have. And yeah, I know you have your three *girls*, but I don't have any friends that I love more than I love you."

"Yeah, but you have Darryl," Serena said, realizing for the first time that Diane truly believed Serena loved Michelle, Kenya, and Lynette more than she loved her. Which just wasn't true.

"But what does having Darryl in my life have to do with anything?" Diane asked.

"I was just making a point because you said you didn't love anyone more than you love me. But I know that you definitely love Darryl more than you love me because he's all you ever talk about."

"I do love him, but that's not the same thing, Serena. And actually, since we're on the subject, you don't seem all that fond of him. Even though he's never been anything but nice to you."

Serena sighed and looked away from her sister.

"You really don't, do you?" Diane asked.

Serena looked at her again. "I really don't what?"

"Like Darryl."

"I barely even know the man, Diane. So why would I dislike him?"

"I don't know. You tell me. Because whenever he's around, it's very obvious."

Serena laughed. "Well, how about this. The next time I see him I'll make sure to plaster a huge smile across my face before I speak to him."

"You think this is funny?"

"Not really."

Diane shook her head. "You honestly have no idea, sis. You have no idea at all, and you should be very careful about what you resent or what you become jealous of."

"Jealous? Honey, I'm not jealous of you or of your little relationship with your boyfriend," Serena told her, even though she knew a part of her truly was jealous. And it wasn't because she didn't want her sister to be happy, either. It was more because Serena hadn't found someone to love her the way Darryl loved Diane.

"But you were jealous of my relationship with my dad, and it's like I said, you have no idea."

"I have no idea about what?" Serena asked.

"That you were Mom's smart little golden child."

"Huh?" Serena said, frowning. "Girl, please. What in the world are you talking about?"

"You always got straight As. Every single year and every single school quarter. And I spent my entire childhood listening to Mom brag to everyone about her genius daughter. Her daughter who was going to get her out of the projects someday. Her daughter who was going to make her proud."

"So you're saying that Mom wasn't supposed to be proud of my accomplishments? And that I shouldn't have dreamed about moving her into a better neighborhood?"

"No, I'm not saying that at all. Because I'm glad you did exactly what you always said you were going to do for her. But what I am saying is that because I was a C student, even in elementary school, Mom would always tell me I should be more like my big sister."

"I don't think so," Serena said, dismissing what Diane was telling her. "Because I don't remember Mom saying anything like that to you."

"Yeah, well, that just means you have selective memory, then. Because not only did she constantly compare me to you, when you left for Yale, it got even worse."

"How?"

"She spent my entire junior and senior years of high school telling me that if I had applied myself more, I could have gotten straight As and gone to Yale just like you. But I think the most hurtful thing she ever said to me was 'Instead of your daddy spending all that money to buy expensive clothes for you, he should have been spending it on a tutor. Because maybe then you would have cared a lot more about your schoolwork, and you wouldn't have gotten all those Cs in every subject.'"

Now Serena felt bad, both about what she was hearing and about the sad look she saw on her sister's face, but she didn't comment. Mostly because, for the first time in her life, she was ashamed of the way she had treated Diane since childhood.

"So you see," Diane said, "I may have had a great dad, but Mom has always made me feel as though I'm not as good as you. Yet I forgave her for that a long time ago. And I've also never even told her about any of this."

"But Mom loves you. She loves both of us."

"She absolutely does, but I don't think she realizes how damaging her words were. How damaging it was for me whenever she compared me to you. I also don't think she was trying to be hurtful. But she always made such a big deal about you and your Ivy League degrees. She bragged on you for years to anyone who would listen, and during your last year of undergrad, she used to tell people that if she couldn't save enough money to buy a plane ticket to your graduation, she would hitchhike. That she would literally hitchhike to Connecticut with strangers if she had to."

Serena remembered her mother saying that once, but as it had turned out, Michelle's parents had been kind enough to purchase her mother a round-trip airline ticket. Still, Serena hated how much all of this had affected Diane.

"So just like you got tired of me bragging all the time about my dad and the clothes he bought me," Diane continued, "I got tired of hearing Mom brag about you and all your accomplishments...all the time. But more important, Serena, when I bragged about my dad to you, I was only a child. I was a child who bragged mostly so I could get back at my big sister for being smarter than me. But still, even though Mom made me feel that way, I was never jealous of you, and I always loved you. With all my heart. And I have always been so very proud of you."

Tears filled Serena's eyes. "Sis, I am so, so sorry. I had no idea."

"I'm sorry, too, and I really wish you would have told me a long time ago how you felt. Because maybe if we'd talked back then, it would have saved us both a lot of heartache."

"You're right, and for whatever it's worth, you have *always* been smart, Diane. You just never liked school the way I did, and you absolutely hated doing homework. Sometimes you would even hide your assignments and tell Mom you didn't have any homework."

Diane laughed. "Yeah, I know. But I did finally get it to-gether, and not only did I graduate from college, I graduated with honors."

"Exactly, and I'm so proud of you. And I can also tell how much you love being a dental hygienist."

"I do. I love everything about my job, and I wouldn't change anything."

Serena smiled. "Well, again, sis, I am so sorry about the way I behaved all these years. It was very childish of me."

"And that's where you're wrong. Because I can't even imagine how hard it must have been growing up without a father. And then after all this time, still not knowing where he is. I also know it couldn't have been easy watching me wear brand-new clothing all the time when you sometimes had to get yours from the Salvation Army and Goodwill."

"No, it wasn't, but that's also the reason—to this very day—I send monetary donations to both the Salvation Army and Goodwill a few times a year. Every year. I also donate any clothes or shoes I'm no longer wearing."

"I didn't know that, but that's really wonderful, sis, and good for you."

Serena smiled at her sister. "I really do love you, Diane, and I hope you can forgive me for all the years I kept my distance from you."

"I love you, too, and I hope you can forgive me as well."

"I already have, and I promise you, I won't ever let some-thing like this happen again. Not ever," Serena said, getting up and walking around to where her sister was sitting.

Then they hugged and cried and spent the next four hours laughing and talking about everything. They enjoyed their time together the way any two sisters should.

CHAPTER 26

Michelle

Michelle had just arrived home from work, changed into more comfortable clothing, and now she was heading down to her kitchen to prepare for an evening with Chris. He'd called earlier to say he would be over around seven, and although he had told her that he'd already had an early dinner with a couple of his colleagues in the hospital cafeteria, she knew he would still want at least something to snack on. So she began pulling out everything she needed to make a charcuterie board for them. Chris loved eating cured meats, fruit, olives, nuts, crackers, various cheeses, and more, and when Chris was happy, Michelle was happy. Which was even more the reason she knew she needed to forget about this whole Steven business. She needed to get over what used to be so that she and Chris could continue living the incredible life they had been enjoying together for months now.

Michelle placed purple and green grapes side by side, but then her phone rang. When she saw that it was Chris, she reached over and pressed the speaker button. "Hey, babe. You on your way?"

"I wish I was, but unfortunately, I have bad news."

"Oh no, what happened?"

"A couple of hours ago, a seventy-five-year-old man was brought into the ER by ambulance, and he needs a triple bypass."

"Oh my. I am so sorry to hear that, and I hope he's going to be fine."

"I believe he will be, but I also don't think it's a good idea to go with my original plan, which was to wait until tomorrow morning. I think it's best for us to get him into the OR right away this evening, so they're prepping him now for surgery."

"Well, of course, I hate you won't be able to come by, but you know I understand completely."

"But I know you're still disappointed, and if it's not too late when we finish up, I'll call you on my way home."

"Okay, well know that I'm praying all the best for your patient and for a successful procedure."

"Thank you, baby. I appreciate that, and I'll talk to you later."

"Love you."

"I love you more," he said, ending the call.

Michelle set her phone back on the counter, covered the food with Saran wrap, and placed it in her stainless steel refrigerator. She truly had been looking forward to spending the evening with Chris, but now that he wouldn't be able to make it, she wondered if maybe watching a movie would keep her mind occupied. Or maybe she should call her mom to see what she was doing. She hadn't chatted with Kenya or Lynette this week, either. Instead, though, as Michelle made her way into her family room and dropped down on her love seat, she found herself clicking the Facebook Messenger icon on her phone and opening the message Steven had sent her two days ago. She knew rereading it was a mistake and that the best thing she could do for herself was to delete it, but she just couldn't. So instead, she read the message again. But the only thing that rereading it did was tempt her to click on Steven's profile page to view his latest posts. However, after reading what were mostly human-interest stories, Michelle reopened his message and reread it—yet again. And it was then that she began telling herself that maybe it was okay to call Steven just this one time. Because maybe if she spoke to him, it would give her an opportunity to tell him once and for all that the two of them couldn't be together. Ever again.

But then she thought, maybe it was best to do as she had been thinking before.

Just delete his message.

Delete it and move on was what she knew she needed to do, but God forgive her, she just couldn't see herself going another day without talking to him. So, with no further hesitation, she dialed the number Steven had sent to her.

"Hello?" he said.

"Hey, how are you?" she asked, nestling farther into her love seat and making herself more comfortable.

"It's good to hear your voice. Especially since I didn't think you were going to call. I was afraid you'd decided against it."

"Why?"

"Because right after I sent you the message, I saw that you'd read it almost immediately."

Michelle didn't say anything, and to be honest, she hadn't even thought about the fact that once you received a communication on Messenger, the sender could see what time you saw it.

"So did you have to work today?" he asked, sounding as though he wasn't sure what to say next.

To tell the truth, Michelle didn't know what to say either. "I did. What about you?"

"Yes, and actually, I just got home about an hour ago," he said.

"Oh, okay," she said.

"Well, I guess I should just begin by saying that I know seeing you again didn't happen at the best time for you. Nor is my asking you to call me. But, baby, I couldn't help myself. I couldn't spend the rest of my life pretending that I don't still love you. I just couldn't do that."

"I hear you, and I get that, but unfortunately, this really is bad timing. To be honest, the timing couldn't be worse."

"But, baby, do you love him?"

Michelle hated that Steven kept calling her "baby," because she knew it was beyond disrespectful to Chris. But she also couldn't deny how good it felt. And she had to admit, whether she wanted to or not, that the way Steven was talking to her felt normal and nostalgic. Comfortable, even.

"Well?" Steven said when Michelle still hadn't responded to his question.

"I do love him," she said.

"But you're not *in* love with him. I know you're not."

"How?"

"I can tell, and let's face it, had it not been for your parents, we would still be together. Had it not been for your dad giving both of us such awful ultimatums, I never would have stopped calling you or being with you. But most of all, I never would have married someone else."

Michelle knew in her heart he was telling the truth, and she was sorry she had allowed her parents to decide what was best for her. She was sorry that she and Steven had lost so many wonderful years. "So what happened between you and your wife?"

"We were way too different personality-wise, and while opposites definitely attract, we argued about everything. And we did so all the time. But one of the biggest problems we had was something I never told her about."

"And what was that?"

"She wasn't you."

Michelle swallowed a bit harder than usual because hearing this was a lot. But then she gathered her thoughts and composure. "I hate that things turned out for us the way they did, but Steven, you know I'm engaged now. I'm engaged, and I'm about to be married."

"I know that, but baby, with everything in me, I'm begging you not to do that. I'm asking you to please call off your wedding. I'll do anything you want, but please don't marry someone else."

"I have to because I don't want to hurt Chris. I know you might not understand, but sometimes we have to make certain sacrifices that we don't necessarily want to make, just so we don't hurt other people."

"I do understand that, but just answer me this: Do you still love me?"

Michelle paused and then said, "Yes."

"Are you *in* love with me?"

She paused again, but finally told him, "Yes."

"Well, then, you have to tell him. You have to do the right thing."

Tears rolled down Michelle's face, and neither of them spoke for a few seconds.

"I'm sorry, but you really do have to tell him...and then you have to tell your parents. You have to tell them the truth about us and how in love we still are with each other."

Michelle's heart sank because no matter how much she did love Steven or how much she knew she wanted to be with him for the rest of her life, she just couldn't disappoint Chris like that. She was also afraid of what an unpopular familial decision like this could do to her relationship with her parents, what with Steven telling her that day at the grocery store that he was still in the fast-food business. Although, if being happy with the man she loved meant having to live without the emotional support of her parents, she was more than willing to accept that. Which meant her sole dilemma centered almost entirely around the fact that she just couldn't see hurting Chris. Not when he loved her as much as he did. Not when, until now, she'd been completely happy with him and excited about becoming his wife.

Michelle shook her head no, even though no one could see her. "I'm sorry, Steven, but I just can't. I really wish things were different, but they're not, so you're going to have to move on with your life. We're both going to have to move on and forget we ever knew each other."

CHAPTER 27

Lynette

M om, we are having the best time with Granny and Grandpa," Chloe exclaimed. "The best time ever!"

Lynette placed her phone on speaker and smiled. "Well, that's really good to hear, sweetie, and I knew you would."

"Yeah, Mom," Tabitha said, "she's having the best time all right, but it's mostly because of Joeyyyyy."

"Who's Joey?" Lynette asked.

"Her little boyfriend," Tabitha said, tattling on her big sister and laughing about it. Something she always did whenever boys were involved.

"Shut up, Tab," Chloe hurried to say. "He's not."

"Oh yes he is," Tabitha sang. "When we were still outside, I heard him ask you to be his girlfriend."

Lynette didn't like the sound of any of this. "Who is this boy, Chloe?"

"His grandparents live right across the street, and he and his parents are here visiting until this Sunday," Tabitha said.

"Is your name Chloe?" her big sister asked her.

"Nope, but I answered anyway," Tabitha said, still laughing.

"Do Mom and Dad know these people?" Lynette wanted to know.

"Yes," Chloe said. "They know them very well, and Granny and Grandpa even go to dinner with them sometimes."

Hearing this part of the story made Lynette feel somewhat relieved, but not much because she always worried about her girls. And she especially worried about them now that they were both in high school. Actually, this would be Tabitha's first year, but Lynette still knew it was only a matter of time before Tabitha became a lot more interested in boys, too. She and Julian had allowed both girls to talk to boys on the phone during their junior high years, but they'd also decided that neither of them would begin dating until they turned sixteen. So Lynette was very glad to hear that this Joey kid would be heading back home this weekend.

"Well, you be careful," Lynette told Chloe.

"She will, Mom," Tabitha chimed in. "Granny and Grandpa will make sure of it. Especially Grandpa," Tabitha said, giggling.

"Whatever, Tab," Chloe said, and then asked Lynette, "So what have you been doing today, Mom?"

"Not a whole lot."

"Well, I hope you're going to have some fun like you said you were."

"I am. I promise."

"Have you talked to Daddy again?" Tabitha wanted to know.

"No, I haven't. Have you?"

"Yes, he called us yesterday."

"He called you," Chloe hurried to correct her sister.

"Whatever, Chloe. Anyway, Mom, I talked to him, and he can't wait for us to get back so he can see us."

"That's good, honey. I know you're looking forward to that."

"I am, but I'm also really glad to be down here with Granny and Grandpa because they have so many fun things

184

planned for us. We're even going to a water park next week for a whole day."

Lynette wasn't surprised to hear this, because if there was one thing she would always be grateful for, it was all the quality time her parents had spent with her and her older brother. From Disney World to Disneyland to Niagara Falls to Washington, DC, to Jamaica and Cancún and even to London, her parents had taken them on one vacation after another. Then, every Sunday after church, they had gone to dinner at their favorite family restaurant, and sometimes they went to the park on Saturdays for picnics.

"Well, Mom," Chloe said, "Tab and I are getting ready to watch *Black Panther*, so you wanna speak to Granny?"

Lynette shook her head because her girls had already watched this movie too many times to count. Although Lynette loved it, too, so she didn't blame them.

"Yes, put her on, and I love you both. And I'll call you tomorrow."

"Love you, Mom," they both told her, and after one of them brought the phone to Lynette's mother, she heard her mom say, "Take this off speaker." CeCe had never liked talking to *anyone* on speakerphone, and she had no problem reminding folks about it.

"Hello?" she finally said.

"Hey, Mom," Lynette said.

"Hey, dear."

"So how's everything going?"

"Fine. Everything is going well, and how are you?"

"I'm good," Lynette told her. "Missing my girls, though."

"I can imagine, but you know your daddy and I are taking good care of them."

"Yeah, I know. But I still miss them, and then Tab just

informed me that Chloe calls herself having some little boy-friend down there already."

CeCe laughed out loud. "Well, she's definitely been talking to him outside and on the phone, but that's about it. And you know we would never allow any private visiting. So, if he comes over here or the girls go over there, it will always be completely supervised. Plus, we already told Chloe that anywhere she goes, Tab goes, and vice versa."

"Good. I'm sure Chloe didn't like hearing that, though."

"I don't think she did, but she didn't say anything. But then that's one thing about your girls, they don't do a lot of talking back. You've raised them to be very respectful, and I'm really proud of you for that."

"Thank you, Mom. I appreciate that, but I do feel like I failed them in an area that mattered most."

"How?"

"Getting divorced."

"Well, it wasn't your fault, and there was nothing you could do to make Julian stay even if you had wanted him to. You just keep being the great, loving mother you are, and your girls will be just fine."

"I really hope so, Mom."

"They will be."

"And hey," Lynette said, "where's Daddy?"

"He ran to the store to get the girls some popcorn for their movie watching. That's the one thing we forgot to pick up this past weekend, and you know your father doesn't think anyone should plan a movie night without popcorn."

"Don't I know it."

"But enough about the girls. What are you planning to do this weekend? Something fun I hope, and have you met anyone yet?"

"Wow, so I guess we went from popcorn straight to Final Jeopardy."

CeCe laughed. "I guess we did, but honey, it's time."

"Yeah, maybe. But you know my girls are still my priority."

"As they should be. But that doesn't mean you can't go out with someone to have a good time."

Lynette wanted to tell her mom about Emmett, but she wasn't sure she should say anything until she and Emmett had gotten a chance to know each other a little better. "I know, and I am."

"Good, because it's not like you have to bring anyone around your girls. Especially with how crazy some folks can be nowadays. But if you meet a nice man that you believe you can trust, I don't see anything wrong with dating him. Oh, and as long as it's not some twenty- or thirty-year-old, either. Because lately, I've been hearing a lot of stories about all these young men who are going after beautiful women who are ten to twenty years older than they are. Especially women like you who have money."

Lynette chatted with her mother for a few more minutes, but all she could think was how she'd had no idea her mother was even paying attention to these kinds of stories. More than that, though, Lynette was glad she hadn't made the mistake of mentioning Emmett during their conversation, because her mother definitely would have wanted to find out everything she could about him—most of which Lynette still didn't know about him herself. Although, just before calling to talk to Chloe and Tabitha, Lynette had signed on to Facebook so she could search for Emmett's profile. She had searched for Pierce's, too—the guy she'd met in passing at the airport. But when she'd seen a few photos of Pierce with other women, she'd decided that it might be best to wait a while before possibly calling him. It was true that the women in those photos easily could have been friends, coworkers, or family members, because it wasn't as though Pierce had been hugged up with any of them. Still, Lynette couldn't be sure, and she also now wondered if dating more than one man at a time was actually a mistake.

But then who was she kidding? Because truth was, the real reason she had decided against contacting Pierce was because she liked everything about Emmett. Which meant she didn't feel the need to be with anyone else. Although, she had to admit, too, that her mother's comments did bother her. Yes, Emmett had made it pretty clear that he preferred older women, but at forty, Lynette still couldn't help wondering how long this sort of relationship could last. She wondered if maybe the day would come when she might start to feel insecure about dating a man who was ten years younger than she was. Not one, three, or five, but ten. Because wouldn't any forty-year-old woman soon begin feeling this way, if she found herself dating a gorgeous thirty-year-old man? But then, Lynette also thought about how it wasn't as though she was looking to fall in love with Emmett or get married to him—or to anyone else, for that matter. Especially not until her girls had graduated high school and left for college. So whatever this was that she was starting with Emmett was much more about fun and companionship than it was about anything else. Lynette simply wanted to have a good time with a good man who enjoyed her company as much as she enjoyed his. Which was the reason she told herself once again, there was nothing wrong with that. And for her sake, she hoped she was right.

CHAPTER 28

Kenya

Since Robert's attorney had agreed that he should try to reason with Terri one final time, Robert and Kenya had spent much of last night strategizing. Because with Terri being as irrational as she was, Kenya knew Robert needed to be careful about what he said to her during their conversation. Although, if Terri still refused to cooperate, Robert was fully prepared to use subtle threats, and he would certainly be speaking the kind of truths Terri wouldn't want to hear. Then, just to be safe, William had still hired the private investigator he had spoken about yesterday during their meeting. That way, if things didn't go well with Terri and filing a custody motion ended up being back on the table, the private investigator would already be ahead of the game.

Robert and Kenya sat down next to each other in Robert's home office and reviewed his carefully planned-out words.

"Are you ready?" Kenya asked him.

"As much as I'll ever be, I guess. But mostly I just want to get this over with."

"Yeah, me too," she said.

"Well, here goes," Robert said, pressing the speaker button on his phone and dialing Terri's number. It rang multiple times, but finally she answered.

"Why are you calling me?" she asked in her usual curt, irritated tone.

But Robert remained cordial. "If it's okay with you, there's something I'd like to talk to you about."

"Like what? You've come to your senses and canceled that visitation motion?"

"Well, I'm hoping that after you and I talk, I can."

"Oh, really? And what changed your mind about that?"

"I'm just wondering if we can come to some sort of an agreement. Not just for you and me as parents, but for Bobby's sake. So, would you at least be willing to hear me out?"

Kenya held her breath, waiting and hoping for a positive response, and she could tell Robert was doing the same.

"Fine," Terri said. "Go ahead. But if I don't like what you have to say, I'm hanging up."

"This won't take long, but please just give me a chance to explain."

"I said, 'Go ahead,'" she shouted just a little louder than before, and Robert and Kenya looked at each other.

"I first want to apologize to you for any- and everything I have ever said or done to hurt you. I know things didn't end well for you and me, but now all I want to do, Terri, is be a father to my son. And I don't want anything more than what you and I originally agreed upon, which is to see Bobby every other weekend, some holidays, and for part of his summer break. But for now, I just want to start having regular video calls with Bobby every day. Even if only for a few minutes. And then after a month of spending time with him that way, I would like to begin picking him up every other Saturday...and no, I'm not asking for him to spend the night right away because I know he and I need to rebuild our relationship."

"What relationship?" Terri spat, and Kenya shook her head.

But Robert ignored her sarcasm. "The relationship we had when he was much younger."

"No, what you mean is the relationship you had with him when his *parents* were still married and also right up until you married your *new* little wifey."

Now Robert shook his head, too, but Kenya had known it wouldn't be long before Terri spoke about her in a derogatory way. Because no matter when Terri communicated with Robert, she always did. Still, though, through all of Robert's obvious frustration, he continued speaking to Terri in the same pleasant tone and per Kenya's advice last night, he now pleaded with Terri to let him see Bobby.

"I'm just asking you to please consider what I'm saying. Please give me a chance to be a father to my son while he's still a child. Because as it is, he's already twelve. Which means he'll be graduating from high school just six years from now."

"Yeah, well, you should have thought about that," she told him. "You should have realized that when men divorce their wives, they also divorce their children. Period. And then when they have the audacity to get married to someone else, that's when they send a message, loudly and clearly, that they don't ever want to see their children again. So, to me, you made your choice back then. You decided that your new little wifey was much more important than your son. And I'm certainly never going to allow him to refer to that woman as his mother, either—oh and by the way, trick, I know you're sitting right there listening to this whole conversation, anyway. But honey, that's a good thing because now I can tell both of you at the same time...as far as I'm concerned, Bobby doesn't have a father. And he also doesn't have any siblings because those two little brats of yours belong to the two of *you*. They don't belong to me, which means Bobby will always be an only child."

Kenya frowned and thought, *What does that even mean? And what's wrong with this woman?*

"Look, Terr—" Robert said.

But Terri cut him off. "No, you look! You will never be a father to Bobby, so the best thing you can do is enjoy those other two kids of yours and forget about the son you walked away from."

Robert leaned closer to his desk with an enough-is-enough expression on his face, and Kenya knew he was preparing for plan B. Because being nice and cordial to Terri wasn't working.

"You know, Terri, I tried my best to do this the right way. I tried to talk to you as one parent to another, but since you still won't hear what I'm saying, let me tell you what's going to happen from here."

"No, you're not going to tell me—" she tried to say, but Robert never stopped talking.

"I'm filing for full custody. As in Bobby will be moving in with us full-time, and you will only see him on whatever days the judge orders us to let you see him. Which also means that those three-thousand-dollar monthly child support payments you receive from me will come to a screeching halt. You won't be receiving another red cent from me, and if you ever get a job the way you should have done a very long time ago, our attorney will be immediately filing a child support petition against you. He'll be asking for twenty percent of your net, which is the same percentage I've been paying you for years," Robert said, and he was so angry he was nearly out of breath.

But Terri was angrier. She was so livid that she cursed Robert out at the top of her lungs for what seemed like thirty seconds, and all Kenya could hope was that Bobby was outside playing with friends. But then suddenly, Terri pretended that none of what Robert had said to her was any big deal. "You know? I'm not worried in the least. So you do whatever you want."

"Oh, that's exactly what I'm going to do. Even if it means spending every single dime I have on legal fees. Even if it means taking out a loan for thousands of dollars, I'm prepared to do it because, Terri, I'm done playing with you. What I want is to be a father to my son, and I'm getting ready to do whatever it takes to make that happen. And I'm not waiting, either. Instead, I'm calling my attorney as soon as we hang up, so he can get the ball rolling as quickly as possible."

Kenya waited to hear more screaming, but Terri ended the call.

"Can you believe her?" Robert said.

"Of course I can."

"Well, I meant what I said. I know it's after six, but I'm calling William this evening at home so he can begin working on the custody motion right away."

"I'm sorry that talking to her didn't work, and I have to say, I really thought the idea of her losing her monthly child support payments would open her eyes. I'm glad you used it as a last resort the way we discussed, but I was so sure that this would change her mind about everything."

"Yeah, when you suggested that yesterday, I thought it would work, too. But Terri is straight crazy. She's evil, and nobody can change that," he said, but then he scrunched his eyebrows when he saw Terri's name and number appear on his phone screen.

"Oh my," Kenya exclaimed. "I can't believe she's calling you back."

"Neither can I, and I'm almost afraid to answer her," he said before pressing the Answer icon anyway.

But to Robert and Kenya's great surprise, it wasn't Terri calling at all. It was Bobby.

"Hi, Dad," he said.

Tears filled Robert's eyes. "Hi, son . . . how are you?"

"I'm good."

Kenya was stunned, but she was also over-the-moon excited for Robert and Bobby because this conversation had been such a long time coming. She did wonder, though, why Bobby didn't sound as angry, annoyed, and uninterested as he had on the past few occasions that Robert had spoken to him. He even sounded somewhat relieved, and this puzzled Kenya, too. But nonetheless, she was just happy that Robert was finally talking to his son because the tears now easing down her husband's face were priceless.

CHAPTER 29

Michelle

Michelle pulled into Aunt Jill's driveway. It was a beautiful Friday evening, and while Michelle would have loved nothing more than to be spending it with Chris, enjoying dinner at one of their favorite restaurants or at the new, upscale jazz club that had opened in Mitchell only a few months ago, she just couldn't face him. Not after having such a heart-to-heart conversation with Steven yesterday and now feeling more guilty and confused about every aspect of her life. Then, there was all the lying she kept doing to Chris. She told one lie after another, and even today she'd lied and told him that the reason she needed to go visit Aunt Jill was because her aunt needed her to review some business documents for her. But what else was Michelle going to say? Because it wasn't as though she could tell him the truth: that the real reason she'd planned an impromptu visit over to see her aunt was because she desperately needed to talk about her unfortunate predicament. She needed to confide in the woman whom she loved like a second mother, because she knew her own mother would never as much as entertain the idea of her leaving Chris and getting back together with Steven.

Michelle reached toward the button to turn off her

ignition, but as she did, her phone rang and she saw her future mother-in-law's number displaying on her console screen. She, of course, loved Audrey, but she didn't want to talk to her right now. Not when it would mean having to pretend with yet one more person. But Michelle also knew that if she declined the call, she would just end up having to get back to her, either later tonight or by tomorrow morning. So Michelle went ahead and answered it.

"Hey, Mom," Michelle said in as friendly of a tone as she could muster.

"Hey, my beautiful daughter. I didn't catch you at a bad time, did I?"

"No, not at all. I just pulled up to my aunt's, but I can talk."

"Oh, good. Please tell Jill I said hello, and actually this won't take long at all. I'm calling because four of our friends who RSVP'd for the wedding will now be out of town that weekend. So I was just wondering if it would be okay for me to add on two other couples that didn't make the cut for the original guest list. They're very dear friends of ours, and if possible, they would love to come. Oh, and I already checked with your mom to make sure she and Larry didn't have four people they needed to add on instead."

Michelle smiled because of how thoughtful and considerate Audrey was, and she loved that she was so unlike the many pushy, overbearing mothers-in-law Michelle had sometimes heard about from friends, patients, and acquaintances. So much so that just thinking about how kind Audrey was made Michelle feel that much worse about the conversation she was preparing to have with Aunt Jill—and about the fact that Michelle still didn't know if there would even be a wedding for these four new guests to attend.

"Yes, please go ahead and add them. I'm totally fine with it."

"Thank you so much. I really appreciate it, and I'll send the wedding coordinator their names and dinner selections. And hey, don't forget that Sunday is the day we're all going out to dinner together again. Us, you and Chris, your parents, and your aunt Jill," she said, referring to the monthly Sunday-after-church dinners they'd been getting together for since the beginning of the year. Something Audrey and Michelle's mom had thought would be a good way to help bond the two families, and actually, it had.

"Nope, I haven't forgotten, and I'm really looking forward to it."

"So am I. Okay, well, I won't hold you, but again, please tell Jill I said hello and that I'll see her in a couple of days."

"I will," Michelle said.

"I love you, my dear."

"I love you, too."

Michelle grabbed her large red leather tote, stepped out of her vehicle, and strolled up to the front door. But as soon as Aunt Jill opened it, Michelle walked in, dropped her bag onto the floor, fell into her aunt's arms, and wept.

Aunt Jill pushed her door closed and held on to her niece tightly. "Honey, what's wrong? Why are you so upset?"

"I'm in so much trouble, Aunt Jill," she said with her body heaving up and down. "And I just don't know what to do about it."

"Let's go into the living room," Aunt Jill said, leading Michelle in that direction.

But when they sat down on the soft brown sofa, Michelle cried much more intensely and covered her face with both hands.

"Sweetheart, you have got to calm yourself down and

tell me what's wrong," Aunt Jill said, leaving the room and coming back with several pieces of tissue in her hand.

Michelle took them from her and sniffled a few times. "Everything is so messed up."

"Why?"

"Last month, I ran into Steven at the grocery store."

"The young man you dated in high school and while you were in college?"

"Yes. I saw him right before Memorial Day. And then he contacted me on social media...and I called him last night."

"Oh my."

"I know. I never should have done that, but now that I have..."

"But you haven't seen him again, have you?"

"No...but I want to. I really do, Aunt Jill. But I also don't want to hurt Chris. Then, at the same time, I don't want to take vows with Chris when I know I'm in love with someone else."

"Oh, dear Lord. So, you still love him? After all these years?"

"I do. And I can't help it."

"Well, I guess I shouldn't be surprised. Not with how in love the two of you were with each other. Still, that's neither here nor there, because right now, you're engaged to some-one else."

"I know, but I also can't stop thinking about Steven. I can't stop wondering what life will be like without him."

"That may be, honey, but listen to your auntie. No matter what your feelings are about that young man, please, please, please don't start seeing him again. At least, not until you make up your mind about what you're going to do about

Chris. Don't betray Chris that way, because he hasn't done a thing to deserve that."

"I know. You're right."

"But you are still going to have to fix this. Which means, not only are you going to have to make a decision, you're going to have to make one you can live with."

"But that's just it. I have no idea what that decision is."

"Really?" Aunt Jill said, seemingly not believing her. "Well, let me ask you this: If Chris reconnected with an ex-girlfriend of his and then realized he was still in love with her, would you want him to keep that from you? Would you want him to marry you, even though he really wanted to spend the rest of his life with someone else?"

Michelle took a deep breath. "No. I would want to know the truth."

"And *why* would you want to know the truth?"

"Because I wouldn't want someone marrying me out of obligation or pity."

"Okay, then, why don't you think Chris would want the same thing? Even if it's not what he would want to hear?"

"I don't know. But what I do know is that he's going to be hurt, and Mom and Dad are never going to forgive me. Because as it is, you know they've already spent a lot of money on this wedding. Most of which they won't get back because we've already passed many of the refund deadlines."

"Yeah, but sweetheart, let's be honest. Money isn't what you're really worried about. What you're worried about is how your parents are going to feel once they find out Steven is back in the picture. Right?"

"I don't know...I guess."

"Of course you are. But let me tell you something. You can't live your life trying to satisfy other people. Years ago, your mom and dad stopped you from being with a man you loved, and you know I was never okay with that. I was never happy about them looking down on someone just because of what he did for a living. But now you have another chance to be with him. You have a chance to be happy. And please don't get me wrong. I love Chris, and I love his family, but is it really fair for you to marry him under false pretenses?"

Michelle heard and agreed with everything her aunt was saying, but she wasn't sure she could ever find the courage to tell Chris the truth. She also couldn't help thinking about the huge amount of shame she was already feeling. Not to mention what her best friends, coworkers, and church members were going to think about all of this. Sure, Aunt Jill had just reminded her that she couldn't live her life trying to satisfy other people, but living by that kind of philosophy was much easier said than done. At least it was for Michelle, anyway. Which meant that even after receiving all the great advice that her aunt had just given her, she was still terrified about her future. She was troubled, heartbroken, and baffled by her circumstances, and all she could hope was that God would give her the courage she needed to do the right thing. She prayed He would help her through all of what she was experiencing and give her heart and soul the kind of peace she was seeking.

CHAPTER 30

Lynette

Lynette was not happy. Because here she'd planned out a nice, quiet evening with herself, what with Emmett attending a business dinner. Yet, two hours ago, Julian had called to see if he could come by the house to talk to her. Of course, her first thought had been to wonder what he could possibly need to discuss with her, and then she'd wondered why they couldn't simply talk about whatever it was by phone. But then, when she'd asked him the latter, he'd practically begged her to let him come speak to her in person. He'd also sounded distraught, which was more the reason Lynette had relented and told him he could drop by to see her.

Still, she wondered what was so important that it couldn't wait until tomorrow or next week even. Although, given the way Julian had acted toward her the last couple of times she'd seen him—far too nice and attentive—a part of her did want to know what was going on. And yes, she still wanted to know if he and Crystal were already having marital problems. It would surely serve him right if they were.

But in the meantime, she called Kenya just to chat, and to her surprise, what she learned was that crazy Terri had finally given Bobby and Robert permission to talk on the phone to each other. Then she'd called Michelle, whose phone had rung a few times and gone to voice mail, and finally, Lynette had contacted Serena, who had big news to share, the same as Kenya had. Serena had met someone whom she truly seemed to like, and she was waiting for him to pick her up for dinner. Lynette, of course, hadn't been able to believe what she was hearing, but she was beyond happy for Serena and glad to know she was no longer dating that awful Tim guy.

Lynette flipped through her TV channels, trying to find something good to watch. But when the doorbell rang, she went to answer it, Julian came inside, followed her into the kitchen, and they took seats across from each other at the island.

"So what's up?" she asked, hoping she could get him out of there as quickly as possible.

But then the worst of the worst happened. Julian broke into tears and cried like a baby. He sobbed so uncontrollably, Lynette thought she was going to have to leave her seat to go console him. But eventually he settled down on his own.

Still, Lynette was speechless. She wondered if maybe his devastation had nothing to do with Crystal and if maybe something else had happened. She also hoped he wasn't ill.

So she finally said, "What's wrong, Julian? Why are you so upset?"

"I'm really sorry about this. I'm sorry to be dumping all my problems on you, but I just needed to talk to someone. And you're the only person I know I can trust."

"I find that really hard to believe because what about your wife?"

Julian swallowed hard and sniffled a couple of times. "Yeah, well, my *wife* is the cause of everything I'm dealing with right now."

"What do you mean?"

"She completely deceived me. She told me we were having twins."

Lynette wondered if maybe he was losing his mind because he and Crystal did in fact have two babies. "I don't understand what you mean."

"She told me we were having twins, but somehow she forgot to mention the part about her sleeping with someone else. She never told me that there was a chance those babies might not belong to me."

Lynette gasped with disbelief.

"Yeah, that whore has been lying to me all along."

"How did you even find out? Did she tell you?"

"Eventually. But it wasn't until I got suspicious and had a DNA test done behind her back."

"Why were you suspicious?"

"Because when the twins were born, I realized they didn't look anything like me. I mean, I know babies can sometimes not look like anyone when they first get here, but after a few months, nothing changed."

Lynette wouldn't tell Julian this now, but even though Chloe and Tabitha had only seen the babies twice, Chloe had mentioned from the very beginning that they didn't look anything like their dad or like her or her sister. But Lynette hadn't cared one way or the other, and she hadn't thought any more about it.

"Wow, so then who do the twins belong to?"

"She won't tell me, but you can best believe I'm going to find out. Although, it's not like knowing who their father is will change anything."

"That's really deep," she said.

"Yeah, it is. And even more so because I gave up the best

woman in the world for some tramp, and I don't know how I'll ever be able to forgive myself for that."

Lynette wondered what he wanted her to say, because it wasn't as though she could fix any of this for him.

"I am so sorry, Lyn. I know I keep saying that to you, but I am."

"And I forgive you. I told you that a while ago, but I can't help you with this."

"I know, but I'm just hoping you might...you know."

"No, I don't know. You're hoping I might what?"

"Think about taking me back."

Lynette wasn't sure if it was her mind or her ears that were playing tricks on her—or maybe it was both—because there was no way her lying, cheating, selfish ex-husband was even considering the idea of asking her to give him another chance. To let bygones be bygones. To take him back and pretend that nothing had ever happened. He couldn't have been serious, and it was the reason that Lynette didn't even bother responding.

"I know you're probably a little shocked about all of this, but I'm begging you. Please, let me make things up to you and the girls. Let me make things right with you. Let me prove to you how much I still love you, and that I will never— not for as long as I live—hurt you again."

"I just can't believe you," she finally said. "I will say, though, I knew four days ago...right before the girls left for Mississippi, that something wasn't right. I knew something was wrong with you and Crystal. But not in my wildest imagination did I ever think she'd gotten pregnant by someone else. And on top of that, she made you think those babies were yours?"

Julian's eyes watered up again, but he didn't allow any

new tears to roll down his face. He looked so wounded and devastated, though, and Lynette knew why. His mistress had beaten him at his own game, and there was nothing he could do about it. Sure, he could divorce her anytime he wanted, but biological father or not, he'd signed both of those birth certificates, and that meant, by law, he was the legal father of Crystal's children—and that if he tried to divorce her, he would be paying child support to two different households. He would also be paying Crystal a huge monthly sum in alimony. So now Lynette wondered if the real reason he was there, begging and pleading for her to take him back, had more to do with his financial situation than it did anything else.

"So what is this really about, Julian?" she asked. "Because if it's money you're worried about, I'm not giving you back anything I won in our divorce settlement, and I'm also not giving up a single dime of my monthly child support payments. And actually, when I chose not to request alimony payments, I did you a favor."

"Well, that's not really true, Lyn. I mean, yeah, you passed on getting alimony, but it's only because you took half of everything else."

"And you don't think I deserved it?"

"Look," he said, holding up his hands and calling a truce. "That's not what I'm saying at all. I'm just upset, okay? I'm hurt, and I'm trying to figure out what to do. And no, I'm not here because of money. I'm here because I still love you with all my heart, and I want you to take me back. I want to leave Crystal and work things out with *you*."

Lynette stared at him, and while she knew getting back together with Julian was never going to happen—and most important, that she no longer loved him the way a wife should love her husband—she also didn't want him to hurt any more than he already was.

"Look, I'm sorry about what you're going through, Julian. I really am. But I need to be honest with you. I'm not in love with you anymore. And I would never take you back under any circumstances. What we had is over for good, and I really mean that. So from this point on, all I can do is pray for you."

Julian leaned back in his chair, looking defeated and teary-eyed again, and soon after, he got up and left the kitchen. Then he left the house altogether. He never said goodbye, thank you for listening, or anything else. But that was so okay with Lynette because it was the same as she had just told him only minutes ago: All she could do was pray for him. She also couldn't wait to call Kenya back to tell her everything.

CHAPTER 31

Serena

Serena gave the kind, elderly delivery guy a generous tip, closed the door, and smiled at the two dozen beautiful long-stemmed red roses that someone had sent her. They were actually the most beautiful flowers Serena had ever seen. Although, she wasn't surprised by this at all. Not with them coming from one of the best floral shops in town and also because as she set the glass vase onto her kitchen island and pulled a card from the tiny envelope that was attached to it, she saw that these gorgeous roses were from Jake.

> This is just a quick note to wish you all the very best at your speaking engagement today. Love and blessings.

Serena reread his short message more than once because while he hadn't said *Love you* at the very end, the words *Love and blessings* still meant a lot to her. Especially since they'd only known each other for three days. Actually, if she hadn't experienced so many bad relationships, she might even start to believe that Jake was the one. That he was the man she'd been hoping and praying for all her life. But whether he was that man or not, what she couldn't deny was the fact that she was already falling in love with him. Yes, it had happened very quickly, but it also felt natural and real. Then, last night when Jake had taken her out for pizza, they'd had the time of their lives, laughing and talking about everything imaginable, and then there had been those sudden moments when they'd gazed into each other's eyes without saying anything. Yet Serena had felt so warm and happy on the inside, she'd barely been able to hide the way she was feeling.

She simply just enjoyed being with him. Jake certainly wasn't the kind of man she was used to dating, but something was very different about him. He also treated her as though they'd known each other for months and as though they were in an exclusive relationship. In four words: He treated her well. And he'd seemed just as excited as she was about their first date.

Serena checked her phone to see how much time she still had left to do her hair, apply her makeup, and get dressed, and then she called Jake.

"Hey, you," he said.

"Hey," she told him, feeling warm and happy again. The same as last evening.

"So are you about to start getting ready?"

"I am, but Jake, thank you. Thank you for sending me such beautiful flowers."

"I was hoping they arrived in time, and you are quite welcome."

"I was so surprised, and you didn't have to do that."

"I know, but I really wanted to. I wanted you to know that I'm thinking about you today and that I really enjoyed myself last night."

"I did, too. I had a great time. Better than I've had in years."

"Same here. And now I'm glad I mustered up enough

courage to come back into the coffee shop," he said, and they both laughed.

"I'm glad you did, too, because . . . I was in a very low place."

"Really? Well, if you were, it didn't seem like it. If anything, you seemed like the most confident woman in the world."

"Yeah, well, I've always been good at putting on a happy face. Even when I'm feeling completely torn apart on the inside," she admitted, and sort of shocked herself by sharing this kind of information with Jake. But the one thing she wouldn't tell him—at least not yet, anyway—was about the anxiety attacks she sometimes struggled with.

"Had something just happened?" he asked. "I mean, why were you feeling down?"

"I'd just gone through a bad breakup. As in, it just happened two weeks ago."

"I'm really sorry to hear that."

"Thank you, but the good news is that I'm in a much better place now. And I also don't want you to think that dating you is some sort of rebound thing for me, because it's not."

"Are you sure?" he said, chuckling, but Serena could tell he was serious.

"I'm very sure. I mean, don't get me wrong, it was a very painful situation for me. But that was mostly because of the way I was treated and because of how the breakup happened."

"Well, for whatever it's worth, I'm not here to hurt you or to try to deceive you in any way. I really like you, Serena . . . and while I know we just met . . . I more than like you."

Serena smiled and was thrilled to learn that she wasn't the only one feeling the way she was about their new relationship. Jake felt their special connection, too, and unlike a lot of men, he wasn't afraid to tell her about it.

"I feel the same way," she said.

"I'm glad to hear it."

"Well, I hate to run, but I really do need to get ready. And thank you again for the beautiful flowers. They really made my day...*you* made my day."

"It was no problem, and I'm glad you liked them. I was also hoping I could see you again tonight. But only if you're not busy."

"That would be great."

"Are you comfortable with coming over to my place? Or I could come to your house instead. That way maybe we could order carryout and watch a movie."

"Whichever you prefer," she said. "I'm flexible."

"Sounds good. I'll call you later to see what you want for dinner, then I'll pick it up and head on over."

"Okay, talk to you then," Serena said, now wishing that she had suggested they go to a restaurant and then to a movie theater instead. That way, she wouldn't have to worry about cozying up next to Jake on her sofa, only to have one thing lead to another. Because whenever two people shared the kind of intense chemistry that she and Jake did, temptation was hard to ignore. And Serena didn't want to take a chance on losing him—something that might happen almost instantly, once he learned she was celibate. Jake's interest in her might come to a screeching halt, the same as it had with Tim, and Serena didn't want that.

But then, as much as she hated to admit it, she also thought about Michelle and the disaster she had recently experienced with Chris. Michelle had broken her celibacy vow, but then discovered that the man she was getting ready to marry couldn't satisfy her. This, of course, made Serena wonder just how many other celibate men and women who

had saved themselves for marriage ended up hugely disappointed on the night of their wedding. Serena was sure it
happened all the time, even though by then, there was nothing either spouse could do about it. Still, Serena wanted to
do the right thing, which meant she would continue being
celibate, no matter what. Because after all, being celibate was
the reason she hadn't had sex with the likes of Tim, an awful
man who had slept around on Serena whenever he felt like
it. And while she wasn't sure why Michelle continued to be
so heavily on her mind, she hoped her friend had become
celibate again, too. Especially since Michelle no longer knew
whether she wanted to marry Chris or not. Meaning, if she
wasn't going to become his wife, there was no reason to have
sex with him at all. There was no reason for her to have sex
with anyone, not even Steven, until she finally decided who
she was going to take vows with.

ONE MONTH LATER

CHAPTER 32

Michelle

I can't believe I overslept," Chris told Michelle. "But if you want, we can still go get brunch from somewhere."

"No, remember, I have my nurse practitioner seminar this morning," Michelle reminded him.

"Oh yeah. I worked so many hours yesterday, I totally forgot you had that again. This is your third week going, right?"

"Yes, but I only have one more Saturday to go. So next week will be it."

"Good, because you know Saturdays belong to us. Starting with breakfast."

"I know, and I'm really sorry that my seminar was scheduled on the weekend."

"It's fine. I'm good, and just call me when you're on your way home."

"I will."

"I love you, baby," he said.

"I love you, too," Michelle told him, and ended the call.

Then she looked over at Steven, who shook his head at her in a perplexed and disappointed sort of fashion. But instead of commenting one way or the other, he leaned farther back onto the couple of pillows he was propped up on in his bed, pretending to watch the baseball game—the one he had quickly muted right after Michelle's phone had begun ringing.

Michelle—against every bit of advice her dear aunt had given her—was sitting right next to him and feeling guiltier than she had ever thought possible. She was so ashamed of what she was doing because here she'd gone from growing in her faith and becoming celibate...to having sex with Chris...to lying about attending some nurse practitioner seminar...to having sex with Steven three Saturday mornings in a row at his condo. She was such a hypocrite, and since she was consciously and willfully committing what she knew was a total sin, she wondered what was wrong with her. She wondered how she'd ended up in such unfortunate turmoil and how she now found herself lying to Chris at every turn. All so she could spend much of her free time sneaking around with Steven.

Sadly, over these past four weeks, she'd even met Steven a few times for lunch at a park—a park that not many people tended to frequent during the weekdays—and she spoke to him by phone at least twice every single day. She now spoke to Steven as much as and sometimes more than she did to her own fiancé.

But Michelle was in love Steven. She loved him with her whole heart, and there was nothing she could do to change that. She'd tried to end things with him, both in her mind and by phone, but Steven hadn't listened to a word she'd said, and the next thing she'd known, they'd begun seeing each other. Then, they'd expressed their undying love for one another, and soon, they had taken their relationship to a more serious and passionate level.

"So how long are you going to keep this up?" he finally asked, but he didn't turn to look at her.

"What?"

"Telling that man you love him. And leading him on when you've already decided to give him his ring back."

"Next weekend. I promise."

"You said that last weekend, yet here today is Saturday and you still haven't told him."

"I know, but I mean it this time."

"Well, baby, I hope you do because I don't like this. I don't like deceiving him this way. Which is what you and I are both doing. And I don't think you're feeling good about any of this, either."

"I'm not, but it's like I've been telling you all along, so many people are going to be hurt."

"I get that, but the sooner you tell him, the better off he and all of us will be."

"This is so hard," Michelle said. "And now I wish I had told Chris right away. I wish I had just been honest with him from the start."

"I wish you had, too, because now you're lying to him every time you talk to him. And you're also lying to your parents and your friends."

"I know, I know, I know, and I hate doing any of that. I hate that any of this is happening the way it is."

"Then why not go ahead and tell him the truth this afternoon?"

"After being here with you? After making love to you, you want me to go see Chris and end things with him just like that?"

"I do. Because it's like I said, the sooner you tell him, the better off everyone will be."

"I'm sorry, but I can't."

"Then what about tomorrow?"

"No. Next weekend will be the best time to do it."

"Why?"

"Because...well...for one thing, I don't want to do this after church."

"Okay, then what about Monday?"

"I also don't want to interrupt Chris's work week. You know the kind of work he does, and I can't be responsible for him making any surgical errors."

Now Steven turned and looked at her. "So now you're lying to me, too, right?"

Michelle stared at him for a few seconds and then glanced over at the television.

"You're just trying to buy time," he continued. "You're still trying to put off the inevitable, and it's a mistake."

Michelle turned her body toward him. "How is it a mistake? And what difference will it make? I mean, whether I tell him today, tomorrow, or seven days from now, how will that change anything?"

"It won't. But if you tell him this afternoon, that's seven more days we won't have to sneak around, and seven more days you won't have to keep lying, just so you can cover up the last lie you told him."

"I just can't do that. Not today. But I will next weekend."

"I still don't get it, but whatever you say. And I hope next weekend doesn't mean next Sunday night. I hope you're planning to tell him as early as possible on Saturday."

"I am."

"And then what about your parents?"

"Well, of course, I'm telling them, too."

"When?"

"Soon."

Steven shook his head again. "Wow."

"What?"

"Look, I know this isn't easy for you, and that it's going to take everyone close to you a long time to accept your decision. But you really need to take care of this."

"And I will. But, baby, you need to let me do this in my own timing. And anyway, why are you pressuring me so much about this?"

"You really wanna know?"

"I do."

"Because you didn't do it this weekend the way you said you would, and that worries me a little."

"Why?"

"Because it makes me wonder if you're still not sure about calling off the wedding. It also makes me wonder if you're more concerned about what your parents and everyone else will say—if you give up marrying a prominent surgeon for someone who won't be able to give you the kind of luxuries he can give you. Especially since this was the very reason you and I broke up the last time. You chose your parents and the inheritance they were leaving you in their will."

"But I was much younger back then, baby. I was young, and while the money never, ever meant more to me than you did, I was afraid to lose my parents. I loved you with all my heart, but I also couldn't imagine living the rest of my life without my parents being in it. I just couldn't. But that was back then, and this is now."

"I really hope you mean that, and I also hope you're really going to tell everyone the truth next weekend, because you're running out of time."

"Meaning?"

"Your wedding date is only two months away, and I'm guessing that everything is still steadily being finalized.

219

Which means you're going to disappoint more and more people as time goes on."

Michelle leaned her head back against the shiny mahogany headboard and closed her eyes. Because sadly, Steven was right about everything he was saying. Especially when it came to Serena, Kenya, and Lynette, who had just confirmed her final bridal shower agenda a few days ago. They'd spent a great deal of money and dedicated quite a bit of their time toward hosting an epic event for her, yet they had no idea that it would all end up being for nothing. Because while Serena did know that the wedding might be canceled, she had no idea that it was *definitely* being canceled or that Michelle was now spending so much of her time with Steven. And then as far as Lynette and Kenya were concerned, they knew absolutely nothing about Steven because Michelle still hadn't found the courage to tell them about him. When they learned the truth about everything, though, they were certainly going to be upset with her, and Michelle wasn't looking forward to having to explain any of this to either of them. Michelle also didn't want to entertain any questions or snide comments they were surely going to have, all because they would want to know, matter-of-factly, why Michelle was betraying one of the best men they knew.

Just thinking about having to face them was exhausting, let alone having to actually talk to them or see them in person. But Michelle couldn't worry about her best friends or anyone else. Instead, she had to come clean to Chris. She had to tell him the ugly truth about why she was ending their engagement and walking away from their relationship. It would likely be the most difficult thing she would ever have to do in her life, but she also had to believe that this, too, would pass—and that Chris would eventually overcome his pain, meet his soul mate, fall in love with her, and go on living the kind of wonderful life he deserved. Michelle told herself, too, that someday, Chris would finally forgive her. And most important, so would God.

CHAPTER 33

Kenya

I t still didn't make much sense to Kenya, but Terri had made a miraculous turnaround, and Kenya was happy about it. Terri still didn't have anything nice to say to Robert, but at least now, she mostly said nothing to him at all. Which meant that the threat of losing every dime of her child support payments, which were also her only source of income, had made her rethink all her cruel, conniving ways. Because while no one could believe it, things had become so much better for Robert and Bobby that not only did they converse by phone every day, they also video-chatted on at least two or three of those days. They'd done this every single week for the last month, but best of all, today was a day Robert, Kenya, Livvie, and Eli would never forget. And neither would Bobby, because this would be the first day in many years that Terri had allowed Robert to pick Bobby up and bring him to their home. Not to mention, with the exception of that morning Terri had shown up at Kenya's medical practice with Bobby in the car, none of them had even seen Bobby in a very long time.

But now here he was, walking through the door with Robert, smiling. Robert Alan Griffin Jr. was literally smiling, and Kenya wanted to burst into tears of joy.

"Hi, Bobby," Kenya said.

"Hi, Ms. Kenya," he said, calling her by the name that his mom had insisted he use ever since the day Robert and Kenya had gotten married.

"It's so good to see you," she said, reaching toward him but not knowing if he would allow her to hug him or not. But he did. Then Kenya noticed how neat he looked in his white short-sleeved polo shirt and jeans. And he had a perfect hair-cut, too, which meant that the one positive thing she could say about Terri was that she clearly cared about the way her son looked.

"Hi, Bobby," Livvie said. "I'm your little sister, remember?"

"I do. Hi, Livvie."

"Hey, Bobby," Eli said.

"Hey."

"So you wanna play video games?" Eli wanted to know right away.

"Eli!" Kenya said, laughing, and so did Robert.

"Maybe Bobby doesn't want to play video games with you," Livvie added. "Maybe he wants to watch the Disney Channel with me."

"I doubt it," Eli said, playfully elbowing his baby sister. "I mean, Disney is fine, but who would want to watch some TV show over playing video games? And you know I've got all the latest everything."

Kenya was glad Bobby was facing Eli and Livvie the same as she and Robert were, so that Bobby couldn't see her squinting at Eli. She did this because she didn't want Eli saying anything that might make Bobby feel uncomfortable. She especially didn't want Bobby feeling as though he was missing out on any of what Eli and Livvie experienced as Robert's children, even though he absolutely was because of his mother. Still, Kenya didn't want him thinking about any of that now because the new goal was for them to give him everything they could from this point on. Their time, their love, and yes, even some of the material things that any child might look forward to having.

"Are you hungry?" Kenya asked him.

"No, ma'am," he said, and this was yet one more reason Kenya had to give credit where credit was due to Terri. Because Bobby definitely had good manners.

"Okay, well, if you want anything at all, the kitchen is yours. And there's no need to ask."

"Thank you," he said.

"So, which is it gonna be, man?" Eli asked. "Do you want to play video games in my room or watch TV in Livvie's?"

"Can I do both?" Bobby asked, and although he was very serious, Robert and Kenya chuckled a little.

"Of course you can," Robert said. "It's only a little after ten now, and you'll be here until six. So, you'll have time to play video games, watch TV, and do anything else you wanna do."

"Cool," Bobby said, and then looked at Eli. "We can play video games first, and then we can watch something on television. Is that okay with you, Livvie?"

"Nope. But it's fine, though, because Mommy and Daddy said that for a while, we have to do whatever you want. And they also said that we're not supposed to do or say anything that might upset you."

Kenya and Robert looked at each other, and while Kenya couldn't speak for her husband, she wanted to break and run to another room. Because as much as she and Robert had said pretty much what Livvie had just announced to Bobby—word for word—they certainly hadn't wanted Livvie or Eli to repeat out loud what they'd told them. But that was kids for you, and thankfully it didn't seem to bother Bobby at all.

"Then, let's go," Eli said.

But before the children could leave the kitchen, they all heard a knock at the door leading into the garage and then they heard Robert's parents walking in.

"Heeeey," Mary sang. "Good morning."

"Good morning," Robert and Kenya said.

"Granny!" Livvie yelled. She ran into her grandmother's arms and then she hugged her grandfather. "Paw-Paw!"

"How's my sweet baby doing?" Charles asked her.

"I'm fine, Paw-Paw, and look who's here. It's Bobby. Our big brother."

"I see," Charles said. "How are you, young man?"

"I'm fine, sir. How are you?"

"I'm doing well."

"Hi, grandson," Mary said to Bobby. "It's so good see you."

"It's good to see you, too, ma'am."

"Hey, Granny and Paw-Paw," Eli said, hugging both of them. "I know you guys probably came to see Bobby, but we're about to go upstairs to play video games. We'll be back down to see you guys later, though."

All the adults laughed, and then Eli and Bobby left the kitchen with Livvie following behind—trying to convince Bobby that watching television in her room was still a better option for him.

"Oh my," Mary said, with tears rolling down her face. "It was all I could do to not grab that beautiful boy in my arms and squeeze him for hours. It was so good to finally see him."

Charles nodded. "It really is a blessing, and it just goes to show what the power of prayer will do, because Mary and I have been praying for this day for a very long time."

"We all have," Kenya said.

"Indeed," Robert said, as the four of them headed toward the patio doors and out to their screened gazebo. Normally in July, it would already be heating up a bit too much for them to sit out there, but today the high was only going to be seventy-five, and right now the temperature was only in the sixties. Although, this was the very reason that Kenya and Robert had talked about remodeling their gazebo and turning it into a four-season room with heating and air-conditioning.

"This still doesn't seem real," Mary said, pulling a handkerchief from her purse and patting her face with it.

"No, it doesn't," Kenya said, "but I'm so glad Terri finally came around."

"And Livvie and Eli seem so excited about having their brother here."

"I was thinking the same thing," Robert said. "And when they found out he was coming today, they couldn't seem to talk about anything else. Livvie even wanted to know when he was moving in with us."

"That's my Livvie for you," Mary said. "Always speaking her mind."

"Isn't that the truth?" Kenya said, and they all chuckled.

"So when is Terri going to let Bobby spend the night?" Charles asked. "Because then you'll be able to bring him over to our house for a visit, too."

"I don't know," Robert said. "But just the fact that she's letting me talk to him whenever I want, and she finally let me bring him over here, is more than enough for me right now. It's way more than I ever expected her to do, so I don't want to push my luck."

"I agree," Mary said. "I'm sure she'll eventually let him spend the night, though. And some weekends, too. Or at least I hope she does, because a part of me still wonders when the other shoe is going to drop."

Kenya leaned her elbow against the wicker sofa. "Yeah, you and me both. I mean, I'm definitely trying my best to give her the benefit of the doubt, but she changed so drastically. And she did it so quickly."

"Yeah, but it's like we've been saying all along, the reason she changed for the better is because she didn't want to lose those child support payments." Robert said.

"Oh for sure," Kenya said. "There's no doubt about that. But I still wonder what else is going on. What she's hiding, or like Mom just said, I'm wondering when something more is going to happen. Something we won't see coming."

"Well, for now," Robert said, "I think we just have to enjoy the time we have with Bobby and be grateful that we've even gotten Terri to the point we have."

"I agree," Kenya said, hoping she and Mary were very wrong about Terri and that they had no reason to feel uneasy. She hoped their new suspicions about Robert's ex-wife had no validity whatsoever.

CHAPTER 34

Serena

An entire month and a few days. That's how long
Serena had been officially dating Jake, and she
was still having the time of her life. He was everything any woman could want, and she couldn't thank God
enough for answering her prayers. Because not only had Jake
told her how much he loved her—more than once—he also
made sure she always knew where he was. He called her during most of his work breaks, and whenever he came to visit
her, he checked to see if there was anything he could pick up
for her on the way. And he loved God unapologetically. He
wasn't the kind of man who went to church every single
Sunday, mostly because he sometimes worked on weekends
and chose to watch service virtually, but he wasn't afraid to
mention God in everyday conversations, and he certainly
wasn't afraid to hold her hand and say grace at a restaurant,
which was what he'd just finished doing not more than a
minute ago.

Jake drank some water. "So how was your mom doing
today? You went by there this morning, right?"

"I did, and she's doing fine. And she's, of course, dying to
meet you in person."

"The feeling is mutual. But the next time she asks you about it, please tell her that the only reason she and I haven't met is because her daughter doesn't want us to."

Serena laughed and bumped shoulders with him, something she could easily do whenever they went out since Jake always requested booths over tables so they could sit next to each other. "That is so not true. I do want you guys to meet, and you're going to."

"Yeah, okay, 'going to.' Because from where I'm sitting, it doesn't seem like it's ever going to happen."

"It will. And I just want you to be sure about us."

"Sure?"

"Yes. Because if you have any hesitation whatsoever about being with me for the long haul, I don't want to introduce you to my mom or my sister."

"Well, you didn't seem to have a problem with introducing me to your best friends."

"No, but that's because they kept asking, and because introducing your man to your friends is a whole lot easier than introducing him to your family."

"Yeah, okay," he said, sort of smirking.

"What's funny?"

"Nothing. Although, you and I both know that the real reason you wanted me to meet your friends was so they could check me out and report back to you."

Serena laughed out loud. "I guess you know me well, don't you? Already."

Jake laughed with her. "I do, but I'm only joking with you, though, because it was fine. And you can introduce me to your mom and sister in your own time. Only when you're truly ready."

"Well, for the record, my girlfriends loved you, and so did

Robert, Chris, and Lynette's friend Emmett. But I still hear you regarding my mom and sister, so how about meeting them tomorrow after you get off work?"

"That's actually the surprise I wanted to tell you about. I'm off tomorrow, and I was already planning to attend church with you."

"Oh, good. Then you can meet my mom and sister before service. Or after, depending on what time we get there."

"I look forward to it, and when you get some time, I'd love for you to check your calendar to see when you have a free weekend."

"Why? Are you taking me on some sort of exotic vacation?"

"No, I'm taking you to Florida to meet my parents."

Serena smiled but tried to mask her excitement because while she was good and grown—forty years' worth of good and grown—she knew how special and important it was whenever any man wanted a woman to meet his parents. Especially after only one month of dating, and even more so when it came to meeting his mother.

"I'll take a look later tonight or tomorrow," she said, although what she wanted to do was pull her smartphone out and browse her calendar as soon as possible.

"Good, because once you let me know, I can request a day of vacation for that Friday. That way we can leave that morning and stay through Sunday afternoon."

"That would be wonderful."

"My parents are going to love you."

"I hope so."

"They are. My mom has been wanting me to meet the right woman for years, and now that I finally have, she's going to nearly lose her mind. In a good way, though."

"And you don't think it's too soon?"

"Not at all. Because it's not like we're the only two people that basically fell in love at first sight."

"No, but it's not the most common thing, either."

"But it happens. And when you know...you just know."

"I agree, and while this has never happened to me before...you know, dating someone and feeling as though I finally met my soul mate...I always knew it was possible. I knew being in a relationship could be so much better than what I had experienced, and baby, you really are proof of that," Serena said.

"All I know is that when I'm with you, and even when I'm not, you make me happy. Happier than any woman has ever made me, and that means everything."

Serena and Jake chatted for a while longer, and then their waiter brought out their Cajun seafood-in-a-bag orders, which included lobster, shrimp, sausage, corn on the cob, and red potatoes. Serena and Jake loved this place, as well as everything they had eaten. Now, though, they felt full, and they were relaxing in their booth and enjoying each other's company.

Jake looked at her. "I really do love you. I loved you from that first night we went out, but I was too afraid to tell you that."

"Why?"

"Because I didn't think you felt the same way."

"Well, I did. I knew that day when you sent me roses. I knew I was falling fast and hard, but I was afraid to tell you, too."

"You've been through a lot, and I haven't had the best luck with relationships, either, so we were just being cautious. But baby, I do love you, and please don't ever forget that," he said, kissing her.

But as Serena smiled and rubbed Jake's chin, she looked across the restaurant...and saw Tim and some woman being seated a few tables away from them. She immediately made eye contact with Tim and a nervous feeling whirled in her chest. Then she became anxious and felt as though she needed oxygen.

"Baby, what's wrong?" Jake asked. "Are you okay?"

Serena squeezed his hand with force and took several deep breaths. She inhaled and exhaled a number of times until she felt calm again...but now she was so embarrassed.

"What happened? Do you have anxiety attacks?"

"I do, and I'm so sorry."

"For what? Because you don't ever need to be sorry for something like that."

"I know, but this isn't the way I wanted you to find out. I wanted to tell you before it ever happened again, but..."

"But what?"

"Come on, Jake. You know as well as I do that not everyone believes anxiety attacks are real. And some people believe you can just pray them away. Some people believe you can do that with any form of mental illness. Versus seeing a therapist and getting the help you need."

"Well, I'm not one of those people. One of my cousins struggles with anxiety, and there used to be times when her anxiety attacks would become panic attacks, and she'd end up in the ER. And actually, it wasn't until she began seeing a therapist that things got so much better for her."

"Really?"

"Yes. So I'll say this again: Please don't ever apologize about your anxiety. Not to me or anyone else."

"For a while, I saw a therapist, too, and I'm so glad you understand. And thank you for telling me about your cousin," she said, but then she couldn't help looking toward Tim's table again. Being in the same room with him felt more awkward than Serena had thought it would. And then seeing him with the same beautiful woman who had shown up at his house the last time Serena had gone over there, well, that had quickly brought Serena's pain to the forefront of her thinking all over again. Pain she had been sure she had gotten past but clearly hadn't, because as much as she wished she could say she no longer had feelings for Tim, she couldn't. Even with how awful he had been to her. Still, she couldn't deny the way she felt, and to her, this was the saddest part of all.

Jake locked his fingers between Serena's. "Are you okay now?"

"I am. I'm fine."

"Good, but there is something else I want to know."

"What's that?"

"Who are that man and woman who just walked in? And why did seeing them upset you so badly?"

Serena swallowed hard and debated lying to Jake. But because she didn't want to ruin the best thing that had ever happened to her, she knew she had to be honest with him. She had to tell him the truth, even though what she wanted to do was vanish into thin air. She wanted to race out of there and never look back on any of this.

CHAPTER 35

Lynette

Emmett and Lynette had just arrived back at Lynette's home from Soriano's, the same restaurant she and her friends went to for their monthly Girls Day Out, and they'd had an amazing time together. Dinner had been delicious, and of course, just being with Emmett was always a great experience because not only did he know how to wine and dine a woman, he was also fun to be with, and he was a perfect gentleman. Lynette and Emmett even had a lot in common. That is, save for the fact that he loved rap music, and she loved only gospel and R & B—and unlike her, Emmett shopped all the time, for both himself and his home, and he never cared about how much anything cost. He had even purchased an expensive diamond bracelet for her, which she had told him she couldn't accept. Although, what Emmett did with his money wasn't Lynette's business, and she was just happy she was enough for him—something she believed because whenever they were out and about and beautiful young women walked by Emmett, he barely even looked their way.

But tonight, Lynette was taking things to another level. Because while she and Emmett had spent time together at his house on more than one occasion, this was the first time

Lynette had invited him into hers. In truth, she hadn't been sure if she ever would, but after a full month of dating him, she now felt a lot more comfortable about having him over. Although...she did hope she wasn't sending him any mixed signals, because no matter how much she liked him and wanted to keep seeing him, she still wasn't ready to have sex with him. And she wasn't sure when or if she ever would be. But the good news was that while Emmett had already tried talking her into doing so, he'd also been fine with her saying no. Something she had told him every single time he'd asked her.

After she turned off her home security system via the mobile security app on her phone, they entered the house, went down the hallway, and into the family room.

"Can I get you anything?" she asked.

"Some sparkling water would be great."

Lynette went into the kitchen, poured two glasses of Perrier, and brought them back into the family room. Then she sat next to Emmett on the sofa, leaving at least a foot between them, and picked up the TV remote.

"Is there anything special you want to watch?" she asked him.

But instead of responding to her question, Emmett slid closer to her. "Well, to be honest, I don't want to watch anything. I just want us to be together."

Lynette didn't move, speak, or breathe because it was this very thing that she had been afraid of all along. Just the thought of him trying to take their relationship to a more intimate level was too much for her, so she moved slightly away from him.

"So it's like that, huh?" he said. "Or maybe I should say, it's *still* like that?"

"I'm sorry, but I'm just not ready. And if I remember

correctly, you've told me more than once that you're okay with that."

"Yeah, I did, but we've been dating for what? A month now? And that's a pretty long time."

"Not to me, it isn't."

"Well, to me it is, and after a while you can only do so much kissing and cuddling, right?"

Lynette didn't respond.

"Or maybe the bigger question is, do you think you'll *ever* be ready?"

"At some point, I'm sure I will be. Just not right now."

"And why is that?"

"I'm just not ready."

"What are you afraid of?"

"Nothing."

"Is it our age difference? Because I thought you were a lot more at ease about that now."

"That's not it, either. That's not the problem."

"Then what is it?"

"I told you. I'm just not ready."

"I know you keep saying that, but there has to be a reason."

"I just want to be careful."

"Are you afraid I might give you something? Because if you are, we can get tested for HIV. We can get tested for anything you want. And, of course, I'll definitely use protection."

"When the time comes, I do want us both to get tested. I absolutely do. But that's not my only reason for wanting to wait."

"Then, what else is it?"

"I just want to make sure this isn't some fly-by-night relationship that we're in, and that you're planning to be around for a while."

"So you think I'm just hanging around long enough to sleep with you, and then you'll never hear from me again?"

"I didn't say that."

"No, but it sounds like that's what you meant."

"Well, I didn't. But what you have to remember is that while a month may seem like a very long time to you, it's not a very long time to me at all because I haven't dated for a good number of years. And even before I met my husband, I never thought it was okay to sleep with a guy only a month after meeting him."

"Really? Even if you knew he wasn't seeing anyone else? Because if that's what you're worried about, then I give you my word that I'm not."

"That's definitely reassuring, and I appreciate you telling me that. But I still want to wait. Just a little longer."

"But how much longer?"

"I don't know."

"Okay, baby, look. By now, I think you know that I really care about you a lot, and that I enjoy every second I spend with you. But I'm also a man who has needs. As in, if I could, I would make love to you seven days a week."

Lynette didn't know whether to run, scream, or do both. Because surely he didn't think she would ever want to have sex with him that often. So finally, she said, "You're not serious?"

"I'm very serious."

"Then, I guess I don't know what to say because I can't imagine having sex every single day. I just can't."

"Well, at the moment, we're not doing it at all. Not even one day a week," he said, laughing.

Lynette couldn't help laughing with him. "I won't even try to argue with that."

"I love hearing you laugh, though," he told her. "And I love being with you."

"I love being with you, too, and you know that."

"I do know. Which is why the very least you can do is meet me halfway, right?" he said, moving closer to her and wrapping one of his arms around her. "Because all I want to do is make you happy. Be everything you need me to be for you."

Lynette moved away from him again. Although this time, she'd slid so far right that there was no room left between her and the sofa arm.

"Wow, so you're really serious," he said. "You really don't want to make love to me."

Lynette sighed and then turned her body toward him. "That's not true. I never said that. I just want us to take our time, so we can get to know each other a little better. That's all."

"But you can't say how long that will be, though, right?"

"No, I really can't, but I'm hoping you'll be patient."

Now Emmett sighed. He was clearly frustrated with her, but instead of trying to pressure her any further, he picked up the TV remote and turned on the television. "So what movie are we watching?"

"You're upset, aren't you?"

"I won't lie, I'm definitely disappointed. But I'm not upset."

"I'm glad. And thank you."

"For what?"

"For understanding." she said, but then wondered what she'd gotten herself into because there was no way she would ever be okay with having sex with any man on a daily basis. As it was, she hadn't been intimate with anyone since separating from Julian. Actually, because of all of Julian's affairs,

Lynette had stopped him from touching her at all, many months *before* they'd separated. So even though Lynette was attracted to Emmett, and she had even thought about taking things further with him, she also didn't want to jump into bed with him too quickly. She wanted to be cautious, making sure Emmett was exactly who he said he was and that he wasn't a serial cheater like Julian. But most important, she wanted to make sure Emmett wasn't too good to be true.

CHAPTER 36

Michelle

Michelle was a nervous wreck. After chatting with Chris yesterday morning by phone, all while lying in bed next to Steven, she hadn't been able to think straight. Then, once she'd gotten home in the afternoon, Chris had insisted on coming over, which meant she had to do even more pretending, lying, and smiling, even though she had been dying inside. She'd seen no choice but to laugh and talk with Chris, cuddle with him, and act as though she still couldn't wait to marry him, and the entire performance had been exhausting. In fact, the whole evening had worn her out, and it was the reason she'd been glad Chris had gotten called in for another emergency surgery. This, of course, wasn't the most common thing to happen to him on a Saturday night, but nonetheless, Michelle had been relieved. Because while she'd lied and told him she wanted to become celibate again, she was to the point now where she didn't even want to sleep in the same bed with him. And sadly, she didn't want him touching her in any way. Not when all she could think about was Steven. Not when she knew how desperately in love she was with him. Not when she knew beyond a shadow of a doubt that it was *he* whom she couldn't wait to spend the rest of her life with.

Steven Matthew Price.

The man she'd loved for as long as she could remember.

The man she had never stopped loving.

The man she would defend to anyone who had a problem with him, including her parents.

This was also the reason that Michelle truly was going to end things with Chris next weekend as planned. She had thought long and hard about it, and she'd also prayed for God to give her the strength she would need before, during, and after she delivered the news to him. Then she had prayed for Chris's peace, understanding, and emotional well-being. All of which she hoped God would provide for him very quickly.

But now, it was time to tell her girlfriends the truth about everything that had evolved, which she would do just as soon as Serena finished her phone call. Actually, Serena had just walked into Michelle's kitchen, and Kenya and Lynette were already sitting next to each other at the island, talking among themselves.

"Baby, you are so crazy," Serena said, laughing out loud in a way Michelle hadn't heard her laugh with any man before. Plus, her laugher was so contagious, Serena, Kenya, and Lynette cracked up laughing, too. "Oh no, please stop," Serena said, laughing even harder.

"My goodness," Lynette said. "Now I want to know what in the world Jake is on that phone saying to her."

"Exactly," Kenya said. "What in the world *indeed*."

Serena waved them off with her hand. "Hey, baby, I just walked inside, so I'll call you when I'm leaving, okay?...I will...I love you, too," she said, and dropped her phone inside her handbag. "Jake said to tell all of you hi."

"Hi, Jake!" Kenya and Lynette said and laughed out loud again.

"You guys are a mess," Serena said, laughing with them.

Lynette scooched farther back into her chair. "Well, I'm just glad you gave that man a chance because, honey, you are glowing big time."

Kenya nodded. "Isn't she, though? And not only that, but I don't think we've *ever* seen you this happy before."

"That's because I've never been this happy before. Not about anything."

"Well, it shows," Kenya said. "And I'm with Lynette. I'm so happy you finally decided to give a really good man like Jake a chance. Even though he didn't fit your normal standards."

"I am, too, because ladies, I'm really in love with Jake."

"That's so wonderful to hear, Serena," Lynette said. "Good for you."

"What a blessing," Kenya added.

"We're all so happy for you, girl," Michelle told her.

"Thank you. It's a great feeling. Especially since I never thought something like this would happen. Not ever. And then when Jake told me that he'd only finished high school and that he worked in a factory, I won't lie, I wasn't thrilled about dating him at all. I mean, I was really attracted to him, and I really liked him as a person, just from talking to him. But you know I have always wanted to meet and marry a successful businessman. Someone who went to the right schools for both grad and undergrad, and someone who could give me the kind of lifestyle I've always dreamed of. But I will say that when Jake told me he earned six figures, that really helped a lot, and it made me at least want to give him a chance and see how things would go."

"Well, good for you," Kenya said, "because as you can see, things worked out for you and Jake just fine. And shoot, the next thing you know, he'll be popping the big question."

"I sure hope so because I would marry him in a minute."

"I don't blame you," Kenya said, and then looked over at Michelle. "Are you okay?"

Michelle and Serena finally sat down across from Kenya and Lynette, and Michelle covered her mouth with both hands, feeling guilty and ashamed of herself.

"What is it?" Kenya asked.

"Well, you know it has to be important if I called you guys over here on a Sunday afternoon," Michelle began.

"Yeah, I figured it was, but I never thought it was something bad." Kenya said. "I just thought you wanted to make some changes with the bridal shower maybe."

"I do want to make some changes. Because there won't be a bridal shower."

"What?" Lynette said. "Why, what happened?"

"Nearly two months ago, I ran into Steven again."

"The guy you used to date?" Lynette asked.

"Yes...and I'm still in love with him. Which is the reason I can't marry Chris, and I have to break our engagement."

"This can't be real," Kenya said. "You're not serious."

"I'm very serious. I've never been more serious about anything in my life."

Lynette locked her hands together. "And you decided this just based on seeing him again? Because it's not like you've had an opportunity to be with him. So how do you know this isn't some sort of living-in-the-past sort of thing?"

"Because I know it's not. I've been talking to him every single day for an entire month, and it's as though we never lost any time with each other. We picked up right where we left off, and if anything, the feelings we have for each other now are stronger than they were all those years ago."

Kenya stared at Michelle. "I don't understand. Because

are you saying that you're making this kind of a decision just based on a few phone conversations? With a man you haven't seen since right after college?"

Michelle wanted so badly to tell them that she had done a lot more than just *talk* to Steven on the phone—a whole lot more—but she just couldn't. She couldn't even tell Serena, for that matter, and she certainly didn't feel comfortable telling any of them that she sometimes met Steven for lunch at a state park. But Michelle did feel as though she needed to confess to Lynette and Kenya about her rendezvous with Chris, because surely her best friends wouldn't expect her to marry a man who couldn't satisfy her.

"There's much more to the story," Michelle told them. "A few weeks ago, I slept with Chris...and it was terrible."

"Oh my," Kenya said.

"'Oh my' is right," Lynette added.

But when Serena didn't respond at all, Kenya said, "Did you know about this? Because you don't look surprised about anything Michelle is saying."

Serena pursed her lips but still didn't say anything.

"Maybe that just wasn't a good night for him," Kenya tried to explain.

Michelle frowned. "No, I think you're either compatible with someone or you're not. That's just the way it is."

"But it might get better," Lynette said. "You know. Once you guys get used to each other. And once you've made love a few more times."

"I don't think so," Michelle said. "And I don't think you guys believe that, either. You just don't want to see me break things off with Chris."

"We don't," Kenya said. "Chris is a good man, and he loves you with all his heart. Or at least that's how it has always seemed to me. *But* I also don't want you to marry someone you don't think you can be happy with."

Michelle nodded in agreement. "Thank you, because I'm telling you, what I experienced with Chris won't get better. It just won't," she said, waiting for someone else to comment.

But instead, there was total silence. Likely because no one knew what to say next. Either that or secretly, Michelle's three best friends were judging her. And if so, this was even more the reason why she couldn't tell them she was sleeping with Steven. Michelle couldn't have them judging her even more than they already were. Not when she was already judging herself in such a cruel and self-loathing way and feeling horrible about everything she had done lately.

They sat for a few more seconds in awkward silence, but then Lynette finally spoke up. "So have you told your parents you're canceling the wedding?"

"No. I need to sit down with Chris first, and then I'll tell them."

"Do you think they'll be more accepting of Steven this time?" Kenya asked.

"I doubt it. Not when Steven still works for a fast-food chain. He'll never be good enough for them, and I'm okay with that. I mean, I don't want to become estranged from my parents, but I also don't want to live the rest of my life wishing I had married someone else."

Kenya leaned back in her chair and folded her arms. "Maybe things will be different with your parents this time around because, nowadays, most of us realize just how short life truly is. How precious it is, and how none of us should spend a single moment doing something we don't like or being with people we don't want to be with."

"Well, I know that's exactly how I feel," Michelle said.

"Which is why I can't marry Chris, and why I know I have to be with Steven. But I still don't see my parents changing their position on any of this."

"But you're their only child," Lynette said. "So even though the last time you and Steven were together your dad made a lot of crazy threats, I just don't see him cutting you off for good. I also don't see your mom doing that, either."

"Then, girl, after all these years, you still don't know my parents very well. Because, unfortunately, status, prominence, and appearances mean almost everything to them."

"But Steven was always such a nice guy," Michelle was glad to hear Kenya say.

"I know, and they would love him just fine, even with him working as a fast-food manager, as long as he married someone else and not me."

Lynette shook her head. "What a shame. What a terrible, terrible shame."

"Well, maybe there's still some hope for them after all," Serena said. "Because if I can change the way I think about people, learn to accept Jake for who he is and fall in love with him, then maybe your parents can change, too."

"Yeah, maybe," Michelle said, but in her heart of hearts, she knew better. In reality, she knew who her parents were, and there was no way they would accept Steven over Chris. Ever.

CHAPTER 37

Michelle

Michelle waited for the stoplight to turn green, but when it did, her phone rang. It was Chris, and while Michelle didn't want to talk to him any more than she had to, she was glad he was calling now rather than sometime later. Because this way, she could talk to him and then get him off the phone well before she arrived at the park to meet Steven.

"Hey," she said.

"Hey, how's it going?"

"I'm good. You?"

"It has already been a long day, so I'm a little tired," Chris said. "But other than that, I'm great. You headed across the street for lunch?"

"No, actually, I'm on my way to this new deli one of our staff members told me about," Michelle said, telling the truth about there being a new deli in town, but lying about being on her way to eat there.

"Where is it?"

"It's about fifteen minutes away. Over near the outside shopping mall. So I'm going to grab a sandwich from there and then sit at one of their outdoor patio tables to read."

"You've been leaving the area a lot lately. Because normally, you just walk over to one of the restaurants across the street from your clinic."

"I know, but I'm a little tired of eating the same food all the time. And sometimes it just feels good to get in the car and drive a little distance. It really makes you feel like you're breaking up your day."

"That's true."

"What are you doing for lunch?" she asked, hoping they'd be able to end this call very soon because she was now turning into the park entrance.

"My usual. Getting something from the hospital cafeteria. So I guess I'd better get going. That way I can eat and still have a few minutes of down time before my next surgery. But I'll see you tonight, right?"

"Uh, yeah," she forced herself to say. "What time will you be over?"

"Probably around six."

"Okay, I'll see you then."

"And baby?" he said.

"Yes?"

"Is everything okay with you?"

"I'm fine," she lied. "Why do you ask?"

"I don't know, you sound like you're in a hurry. And lately you've seemed sort of distant and not like yourself."

"Everything is fine," she said.

"Okay. If you say so. But I just wanted to check."

"And I appreciate that. I really do, but I'm fine. Really, I am."

"Well, like I said, I'll see you tonight around six."

"I'll see you then. Oh, and if you want, I can cook something for you," she said, trying to ease his suspicions.

"That will be great, but only if you feel like it."

"It's not a problem."

"Sounds good, baby," he said. "Love you."

"I love you, too," Michelle told him, but she felt awful about lying to Chris. She also felt relieved, though, because as she drove through the park and made her way around to the perfect, secluded area, she saw Steven's SUV parked not far from the picnic table he was sitting at. Then after parking her vehicle, she walked over to him.

"Hey, babe," she said, hugging and kissing him.

"I'm glad you made it."

"Me too, and thank you for picking up lunch for us," she said, sitting next to him and reaching for the grilled turkey sandwich that she'd asked him to get for her. Steven had also gotten her a bag of kettle potato chips and a soda.

Steven took a bite of his ham, turkey, and salami sandwich. "Mine is still pretty warm, and I hope yours is, too."

"It is," she said.

"So have you been busy today?" he asked.

"I have. Between eight a.m. and twelve noon, I saw seven patients."

"Yeah, you really have been busy, then."

"What about you?"

"You know how the fast-food business is. It's always busy. But I have great assistant managers who can run the place just as well as I can. So that helps."

"I'm sure it does," Michelle said, as they continued eating.

But then Steven changed the course of their conversation. "So this really is the last week that we'll have to sneak around like this, right?"

Michelle had been hoping they could just enjoy their lunch and some quality time together, but she also knew

Steven wasn't going to stop talking about any of this until her relationship with Chris was over.

"Yes," she finally said.

"You're telling him Saturday, right?"

"I am."

"And you're telling your parents, too, right?"

"I am, and just so you know, I told Serena, Kenya, and Lynette last night."

"Really?" he said, sounding shocked. "What brought that on?"

"I knew I couldn't keep hiding something like this from them. And, to be honest, I didn't want to. Not anymore."

"And what did they say?"

"They were surprised, of course, but they also want me to be happy. So no matter what happens, they'll be there for me. Just like they've always been."

"That's great to hear, and I'm glad you told them," he said.

Over the next twenty minutes, Michelle and Steven chatted and finished eating, and soon after, Steven hopped up and sat on the tabletop, and Michelle got up, moved in front of him, and hugged him.

But as Steven hugged her back, and said, "I really do love you, and I can't wait to make you my wife," they heard a car winding around the road that led to the area they were sitting in—an area that until this very moment, they'd never seen anyone else driving into.

Michelle turned her head to see who it was, and when she did, she pushed away from Steven. "Oh dear God, no. Please, Lord...no."

"Whose car is that?" Steven asked, as they both watched the black Mercedes S-Class rolling closer and closer to them.

"It's Chris."

"Chris? How?"

"I don't know, but what are we going to do?"

"There's nothing we can do. Except tell him the truth."

"Oh my God," she exclaimed, and her heart pounded so violently, she worried that it might beat straight through her chest. Then when Chris jumped out of his car and stormed toward them, she thought she would pass out completely.

"Michelle, who is this? And why are you out here with him?"

"Chris, I'm so sorry, but please, let's not do this here. Let me talk to you about this somewhere else. Let's go home."

"Home? Which home? Mine? Yours? Or his?" he said, pointing at Steven.

Michelle just stared at him.

"And have you lost your mind?" Chris asked. "I mean, are you really out here all hugged up with another man, when we're supposed to be getting married only two months from now? So no. We won't talk about it at home. We're going to talk about this now," he yelled, stepping closer to them.

"Chris, please, I'm begging you," Michelle said. "I know you're upset, but I can explain."

"Just shut up," he yelled, and then frowned at Steven. "Did you know you were messing around with someone else's woman? Another man's fiancé?"

Steven raised both his hands. "Man, for whatever it's worth, I'm really sorry. I'm sorry about all of this. And I'm sorry you had to find out this way."

Chris grabbed the sides of his head with both hands and turned away from them. "Ughhhh! I can't believe this!" he said, and then he turned back around to face them. "I knew you were lying about those Saturday seminars. Something just didn't feel right about any of it. So I had one of my staff members look up local seminars for nurse practitioners. I had her check to see if any were scheduled here for this month, and she couldn't find a single one. Not one. So when I could tell you were lying again this afternoon, I decided to keep following you. In fact, when I called you, I was already in my car driving, and the only reason I waited to drive all the way back to this area was because I wanted to see exactly what you were up to.

"But you know what? I'm done with you. I treated you like a queen, Michelle. But as it turns out, all you are is an ungrateful little whore. You're pathetic, and since we didn't use protection that night we made love, you'd better hope with everything in you that you're not pregnant. Because I'll never let you have custody of my child. You hear me? Never. I'd rather see you dead first!" Chris shouted.

Then he strutted back to his car and drove away like a madman.

But when he was out of sight, Steven locked eyes with Michelle and clearly wasn't happy. "I thought you told me that you and your fiancé were celibate? That you both wanted to wait until you were married?"

Michelle stared at him with no words to speak. She said nothing at all, and instead, she stood there, crying and feeling like a total fool—and wishing she had called off the wedding well before now. But even more, she prayed that her cycle would begin as soon as possible. Because as it was, she was already two days late, and then last month, right after she and Chris had made love, her period had been very light. Actually, what she thought more about now was that it had mostly only been spotting—spotting that had only lasted for three days. And the thought of that made her nervous because although she and Steven had used protection every time they had been together, she and Chris hadn't used anything. They hadn't even talked about it, likely because they knew they were getting married, but now Michelle knew that not talking about it had been a big mistake.

But there was no way she was pregnant. Not after being with Chris only one time.

Not at forty years old.

She just couldn't be.

CHAPTER 38

Serena

S erena paced back and forth in her bedroom, wondering why Jake still hadn't returned her phone
calls. At this point, she must have called him at least
twenty times to no avail, and she couldn't imagine what was
going on. She had first tried calling him yesterday evening
from her car, right after she'd left from chatting with her girlfriends over at Michelle's, but Jake hadn't answered. Then
when she had driven by his house and hadn't seen any lights
on, she'd dialed his number again. And when she'd gotten
home, she had called him once more and left a voice message. Still, there had been no response, and because of the
way Jake was seemingly ghosting her, she hadn't eaten in
more than twenty-four hours. She also hadn't slept. Instead,
she had tossed and turned and tossed and turned some more,
and while she had half expected that Jake would at least call
her during his first break this morning the way he always did,
he hadn't. He also hadn't called her this afternoon when he'd
gotten off work, or this evening.

Now, though, as Serena's thoughts raced back and forth
in her mind, she reflected on Tim and all the other men who
had disappointed her over the years, and then she thought

about the conversation she'd had with Jake on Saturday evening when they'd left the restaurant.

"The man you saw is a guy named Tim that I used to date," Serena had told him. "And the woman is someone he started seeing right after he and I broke up."

"Are you sorry that things didn't work out for the two of you? Is that why you got so upset when you saw them together?"

"I guess so. Things ended really badly between us, and I also discovered that he had been messing around on me all along."

"I'm sorry to hear that," Jake had said. "Because I know finding out something like that couldn't have been easy."

"It wasn't, and then to make bad matters worse, he wasn't sorry about anything he did. I mean, he apologized, but I could tell it wasn't genuine. And then the last time I saw him, he said a lot of hurtful things to me."

Jake had paused for a few seconds before speaking and then said, "Were you in love with him?"

"Unfortunately, I was."

"Are you still in love with him?"

"No. I'm not."

"But you still have feelings for him, though, right?"

Serena had debated how she needed to respond to Jake, but eventually she had decided that telling him the truth was best. "I guess I do. But again, I'm not in love with him," she had quickly reiterated to him. "I'm in love with you and only you."

But instead of acknowledging what Serena had just told him, Jake had driven the rest of the way to her house in silence. So now she wondered if being completely honest with him had been the right thing for her to do. Because maybe it would have been better to tell him everything except for the part about her still having feelings for Tim. Maybe if she hadn't bared her soul, she wouldn't now be regretting telling him anything at all. Although, as planned, he had still gone to church with her yesterday morning, and when he'd met her mother and sister, he had seemed fine. He had also seemed okay when Serena had been on the phone with him last night. Both during her drive over to Michelle's and when she had walked inside Michelle's home. So again, Jake not answering her calls didn't make sense. Or maybe his sudden loss of interest in her had more to do with his witnessing her unfortunate anxiety attack. He'd said he understood, but maybe he had begun rethinking his commitment to her and their relationship. Maybe he had started to wonder if there was possibly something else wrong with her, too, and that having anxiety attacks wasn't the only mental health issue she was dealing with.

Serena paced a few more times and then called Michelle. But Michelle didn't answer. Although, since Michelle had her own problems to deal with, her not answering had probably been a good thing because she certainly didn't need Serena adding even more drama to her plate. But nonetheless, Serena desperately needed to talk to *someone*, so she dialed Lynette's number, and Lynette answered right after the first ring.

"Hey, girl. What's going on?"

"Girl, I'm not even sure where to begin," Serena said. "But let's just say, something isn't right with Jake."

"What do you mean? Just yesterday evening, the two of you were laughing and joking around on the phone like two teenage lovebirds."

"I know. But then, when I left you guys, I called him, and

he didn't answer. I've called him multiple times, but he still hasn't gotten back to me yet."

"That's really strange."

"Yeah, tell me about it. This isn't like him at all, so I don't know whether to be worried, not worried, or outraged."

"Did anything happen before the girls and I saw you yesterday?"

Serena told Lynette about seeing Tim and his new woman and also about the confession she'd made to Jake. "Do you think I made a mistake? Was I wrong to tell him I still had feelings for another man?"

"Hmmm. That's a hard one. Because on the one hand, it showed Jake that you trusted him enough to be honest with him. But on the other, it might have him wondering if you really love him the way you've been telling him you do."

"But I really do love him. We even talked about that at the restaurant. Just before Tim and that woman walked in. We talked about how in love we are with each other and even about him taking me to Florida to meet his parents."

"That's really wonderful."

"I know, and I was so excited. But then Tim showed up. And then the other thing I had to admit to myself was that if I didn't still have feelings for Tim, I wouldn't have been so bothered by seeing him."

"Yeah, but it hasn't even been two whole months since you guys broke up."

"Still, I never thought I would feel so strongly about seeing him again. Not when I now have Jake. And I'm so in love with him."

"I think your feelings for Tim are more about you not getting any closure."

Serena knew Lynette was right, because even though she

hadn't told her girlfriends about her going over to his house to confront him that one last time, she certainly hadn't gotten the kind of closure or apology she needed and deserved. Which was the reason she wished more people realized just how important apologizing to others truly was. It usually made all the difference between someone being able to forgive and move on very quickly versus staying stuck in a moment that had passed a long time ago.

"I just don't know what to do," Serena said.

"Maybe you should just give Jake some space for the rest of the evening and then try to call him again tomorrow."

"Maybe so. But, how are you? And how are things going with that fine-looking man of yours, Emmett? Actually, I wanted to ask you about him last night, but I didn't want to take the focus away from Michelle and what she's dealing with right now."

"I know. She's really going through a lot, and I'm still shocked about all of it."

"I am, too, but I know she'll be fine."

"Well, as far as Emmett and me, for the most part, every-thing is going great, and I really like him. But girl, he keeps pressuring me about having sex with him."

"And you're not ready, I take it?"

"I'm not. I mean, it's not like I'm trying to be celibate the way you and Michelle are. Or I guess I should say like the way you are, and the way Michelle used to be. But I do want us to wait a little longer. Maybe even just another month or so."

"I totally understand that, and there's nothing wrong with feeling that way. But I will say this: I hope Emmett eventually becomes okay with waiting. Because Tim never did. Even though he pretended he was perfectly fine with my decision."

"Yeah, I know, and then with Emmett, you have to add in the part about him being only thirty years old."

"Exactly. So unless he's a lot different than most men his age, I'm just going to tell you straight out—either he'll start sneaking around with some other woman, or you'll just stop hearing from him altogether."

"You think so?"

"I know so. And actually, now that I'm thinking more about it, maybe that's the reason Jake has so mysteriously disappeared. He claimed right away that he respected my celibacy decision, but he was probably just lying to me like all the rest. And if that's true, then disappearing was the right thing for him to do, because I'm not going against my beliefs. Still, though, he could have at least had the decency to tell me."

"But you don't know that for sure, so I still say you should just try to call him again tomorrow."

"Yeah, maybe. But who knows, and I guess we'll see soon enough."

CHAPTER 39

Michelle

Michelle had cried so much, her eyes were nearly swollen shut. And she knew why. Her entire world had fallen apart in a matter of minutes. She'd lost everything. Or so it had seemed, because now, neither Chris nor Steven was speaking to her. Chris wasn't because he'd caught her with another man, and Steven wasn't because she'd lied to him about having sex with Chris. Then, there was this whole pregnancy scare that Michelle was dealing with, something she hadn't given a second thought about—not until Chris had threatened to take away any child of his she might be carrying. Interestingly enough, this possible pregnancy had been one of the first things he'd seemed to think about—which had actually seemed a bit bizarre—but the last thing Michelle wanted was to have a baby with him.

And she could kick herself for being so lax about protection. In the past, when she'd been sexually active, she'd always taken birth control pills, but when she'd become celibate, she hadn't felt the need to do that any longer. But as a forty-year-old woman who was also a medical professional, she certainly knew better. She knew that all it took was one time for any woman to get pregnant, and now all she could do was hope and pray she wasn't.

Michelle was a total mess, and now she wished she'd been brave enough to answer Serena's phone call from a half hour ago. But she just hadn't known how she could manage talking to Serena without telling her everything. She hadn't been sure how she could seek out her friend's advice without specifically telling her that she had slept with both Chris and Steven. Michelle simply couldn't do that. Not when she could still see the judgmental looks that had been plastered across Serena's, Kenya's, and Lynette's faces yesterday, right after she'd told them she was ending things with Chris and planning to be with Steven.

What am I going to do? And why didn't I handle things right away, before it was too late?

Michelle pondered her terrible decisions and tried to figure out what she needed to do next. Then she called Steven.

But he didn't answer.

She called him again. And again. And again.

But finally, when his phone went to voice mail a fourth time, she left a message.

"Steven, please call me back. I am so sorry about all of this, but if you'll just give me a chance, I'll try to explain everything to you. I really am sorry, and I still want to be with you. I still love you, so, so much," she said with tears filling her eyes.

Then once she settled down a bit, she dialed Chris's number. But he didn't answer, either.

"Chris, I am so very sorry. I am so sorry I hurt you the way I did, and I really hope you can forgive me. So if you would, please call me. Please call me as soon as you get this message."

Michelle set her phone on her nightstand and sat down on the side of her bed. But then she wondered if Chris had already told his parents the news. Or worse, she wondered if he had told *her* parents. Because the last thing she wanted was for them to learn about this nightmare of hers from someone other than her. Which was the reason that she got herself up from her bed, went into the bathroom, wet a towel with cold water, and washed her face. Then she wet the towel again and held it across her eyes, trying her best to alleviate some of the puffiness. After that, she brushed her hair, pulled on a Chicago Cubs baseball cap, and went back out to her bedroom to grab her purse and slip on a pair of ballerinas. Her T-shirt and athletic capris were a little wrinkled from her lying down in them, but that was the least of her worries. She couldn't have cared less about any of that because what she had to focus on now was her parents. What she had to do was drive over to their house so she could tell them the truth. The unadulterated truth. The kind of truth they wouldn't want to hear in a million years.

Michelle didn't usually ring the doorbell when she visited her parents because, one, she still had a key, and two, she generally called to let them know she was on her way. But not tonight. Not when she still hadn't figured out what she was going to say once she saw them in person. So instead of alerting them, she'd shown up unannounced and was now knocking on their front door. And to her surprise and total dread, she heard quick and heavy footsteps, which meant her father was completely outraged.

"Michelle, what in the world is going on?" her father shouted as soon as he opened the door.

But instead of responding, Michelle looked at him, walked inside the house, and continued down to the family room, where her mother was waiting.

"Michelle, Chris just called us in an uproar," Lucinda exclaimed. "He was so upset, and then he said the wedding was off. But when your father asked him why, he told him to ask you. So what did you do to cause this?"

"Mom, please," she said, looking at her parents and then sitting in one of the chairs. "You and Daddy both need to sit down. Please just sit down, so I can explain everything."

Lucinda did as her daughter told her, but not Larry.

"I don't need to sit down for anything," he said, folding his arms. "I just need you to tell me what this is all about. Your mother and I both need you to tell us what happened."

"About two months ago, I saw Steven at a grocery store, and he told me that he and his wife had gotten divorced. But then last month, he and I reconnected and began speaking by phone...and then I started seeing him."

"You what?" Larry shouted. "Why? Seeing him for what? When you're getting married to one of the best men you've ever met?"

"Daddy, I don't love Chris that way. I love him as a person, and I care about him, but I'm not in love with him. I never have been. Which is the reason I was going to call off the wedding myself anyway. I was going to tell Chris this weekend."

Lucinda scrunched her eyebrows. "Well, if you weren't going to tell him until then, why did you do it today instead? Why couldn't you wait a little while longer and think this thing through?"

"Chris caught Steven and me together at a park today."

"Lord have mercy, Lucinda," Larry said to his wife. "This girl has lost her natural mind."

"No, Daddy, I haven't. And I'm not a girl. I'm forty years old, and I know exactly what I'm doing and how I feel about it. And I don't want to marry Chris. I won't marry him."

"You *will* marry him," Larry said matter-of-factly. "You're going to forget this Steven lowlife, never see him again, and fix things with Chris. You're going to tell Chris you made a mistake. That you don't know what you were thinking. That with the wedding date being so close, you got a little scared. But now that you've had time to think about it, you realize how wrong you were. And then you're going to beg Chris to forgive you. You're going to beg him in a way like you've never begged anyone before."

"Daddy, I just told you that I'm not in love with Chris. I'm not. And I'm not marrying someone just to be marrying them. I won't live in a loveless marriage for the rest of my life," Michelle said, thinking back to what her patient Ms. Hattie had told her.

Lucinda was distraught. "Honey, why are you doing this? Why are you ruining your relationship with a man like Chris, just so you can end up with the likes of this Steven character?"

"Because I love Steven. I've always loved him, and Mom, he loves me. He never stopped, not even when he was married to someone else."

Larry waved Michelle off. "I don't care if he loves you with every ounce of his pathetic little life, you're not marrying that man. You're marrying Chris. A man who loves you and who can't wait to give you everything. So what more could you possibly want?"

"I don't care about any of that. The money, the status, none of that. And the only reason Steven and I aren't married today is because you wouldn't allow it, Daddy. And Mom, you went along with it. But now I'm making my own decisions. The way I should have done all those years ago."

Larry shook his head in disgust. "Lucinda, will you talk

some sense into this girl? Because she's not hearing a word I'm saying."

"I hear you just fine, Daddy. But I'm not marrying Chris."

"Well, you do what you want, but when it comes to this Steven guy, nothing has changed. Your mother and I still don't approve of him, and we never will. We'll never accept him as our son-in-law. He'll never truly be a part of this family. Is that understood?"

Michelle stared at her father, letting him know she wasn't backing down. "It is."

"Honey, what kind of life will you have with this man? How will he take care of you? Because isn't he some food worker?"

"I make more than enough money to take care of myself, and Steven makes enough to take care of him. So together, we'll be just fine," Michelle said, hoping Steven would get over his disappointment and would still want to marry her.

"I suggest you do what I said," Larry instructed. "Beg Chris to forgive you, and then beg him to take you back. Do it tonight. Before too much time passes. You get in your car and go see that poor man, right now, Michelle. You hear me?"

Michelle heard her father, but she was also tired of listening to his demands. Still, she didn't want to keep arguing with him. Or her mother. She also didn't want to disrespect the two people she loved more than life itself, even though they were the only two people who didn't want her to be happy. So instead of trying to make her case, which she knew wasn't possible, she said nothing else. She kept quiet because no matter what her mother and father said, she wasn't marrying Chris. Baby or not, she just couldn't.

CHAPTER 40

Kenya

I t was shortly after six p.m., and as Kenya mixed home-made tomato sauce and crumbled ground turkey in with the spaghetti she had just cooked, she glanced over at Robert, who was standing maybe four feet away and leaning against the cabinet. Kenya was preparing dinner for the four of them—her, Robert, Eli, and Livvie—and Robert was keeping her company.

"I still can't get over how great this weekend was," Robert said. "Especially Saturday."

"I know," she said. "Neither can I, because it really was wonderful."

"I mean, I actually got to bring Bobby over here. After all those years of pleading with Terri to let me see my son. But you know what else I can't get over?"

"What?"

"How happy he seemed."

"I agree, because that was never the case in the past."

"It was also very obvious that he never really disliked us. And that the only reason he never said much on the few occasions he did come around us was because of his mother."

Kenya nodded. "Well, you know I always thought his attitude had everything to do with his mom and all the horrible stuff she was telling him. Because when children know their mothers don't like someone, they either act standoffish around that person or they make it clear that they don't like the person, either. They do that because they don't want their mom to be upset with them or so they won't have to feel like they're siding with the enemy. Their mother's enemy."

"Exactly," Robert said. "Because the Bobby I've been talking to for this whole last month is not some angry, disrespectful kid. He's nothing like his mother, and again, you could tell he was really glad to be over here. He had a great time with Eli and Livvie, and I told you when I dropped him off at home, he wanted to know when I would be picking him up again."

"Yeah, you did, and that truly warmed my heart. I'm also really happy for you as his dad because I know this has been a rough few years."

"It really has been," he said, moving closer to her and pecking her on the lips. "And, baby, thank you."

"For what?"

"For supporting me through all of this. For realizing how important this was to me and that I just wasn't going to rest until we got it handled."

"I'm your wife, and I love you. Which means you don't have anything to thank me for. I mean, I do wish you'd chosen a different first wife, but I digress," she said, laughing.

Robert laughed with her. "Yeah, I wish I had, too. Believe me, I do."

"Although, if you'd chosen someone different, you might

still be married to her. And, of course, that means you and I never would have met, let alone started dating."

"That's very true, and actually it was my terrible experience with Terri that taught me how to truly appreciate a woman like you. Someone who honestly loves me and who has never felt the need to sleep around on me the way Terri did."

"I do love you, and there's not a man alive who could ever change that."

Robert gently held the side of Kenya's face and kissed her again.

Then Kenya stirred her spaghetti some more. "This is just about ready, and the garlic bread should be ready as well," she said, opening the oven and pulling a baking sheet out of it.

"You know," Robert said, "I was thinking about something else today, too. Like how great it would be for us to take Bobby on our little mini-vacation next month."

Kenya and Robert lived only about ninety miles from downtown Chicago, and while they sometimes drove there to shop or have a date night, they'd never purchased a family tourism package before. So, this time, they were doing just that, and the package they'd purchased included day passes for the Shedd Aquarium, the Museum of Science and Industry, and Skydeck Chicago. They were also planning to take the kids to Brookfield Zoo.

"I wish Bobby could come with us, too," Kenya said. "But I think that might be a little too much for Terri."

"Well, it's not like we won't take good care of him."

"Yeah, but taking him on a trip will make her feel even more like the five of us are trying to be one big family. And you know that's the one thing she definitely doesn't want. That's the part she hates more than anything because she doesn't want him thinking—not even for a second—that I'm some sort of mother figure to him. And you also know she's not happy about him having a brother and sister, either."

"You're right, and what a shame. But I still think I'll ask her. Because all she can do is say no."

When Kenya and Robert placed all their food on the round glass table near their patio doors, Robert called Eli and Livvie down for dinner, and they hurried to take their seats.

"Did you guys wash your hands?"

"Yep," Eli said.

"I did, too," Livvie added. "And I washed them really good, Mommy."

"That's great, honey," Kenya said as she and Robert sat down as well.

"Do you want to say grace, Eli?"

"Yes, please," he said, and they all bowed their heads. "Dear Lord, thank You for blessing my mom, my dad, Livvie, Granny, Paw-Paw, Auntie Lynette, Auntie Michelle, Auntie Serena, and all their family members. And thank You for letting us be with our big brother, Bobby, and for letting Livvie and I have so much fun with him. And thank You for letting Dad get to spend some time with his son. Oh and thank You, Lord, for the food we're getting ready to eat. In Jesus's name. Amen."

"Amen," Kenya, Robert, and Livvie said, but then Kenya smiled to herself. Because no matter how well she believed they were raising their two children, what she was most proud of was the fact that she and Robert were raising them up to know, love, and honor God. Kenya was also happy to know that while Eli was only eight years old, he always got so excited whenever he was given an opportunity to say grace. He did tend to mention so much more than just the food he was praying over, but Kenya was still happy about his willingness and enthusiasm about it. Actually, Livvie loved saying grace, too, but for some reason, Eli seemed to love being asked to do it more than any other child Kenya knew.

As Robert placed spaghetti on everyone's plate, one by one, Livvie said, "I can't wait for school to start again."

Eli looked at his sister as though something was wrong with her. "Not me. August is too early, and I wish we didn't have to go back until September."

Kenya and Robert laughed at Eli.

"Is that right?" Robert said. "Because what else does an eight-year-old have to do besides eat, go to school, and do his homework?"

"That's what I want to know, too," Kenya said. "Especially since right now, you're living the best years of your life. You have no bills to pay, no major decisions to make, no real responsibilities at all. So take it from us, you need to enjoy your childhood years as much as you can."

"And for as *long* as you can," Robert said.

"Yeah, but it'll be better when I get older," Eli said. "Especially when I turn sixteen, because then I'll be able to drive, and I'll have my own car, too."

"Not in this household," Kenya said. "Because in this household, children don't get their first cars until they're finishing up their last year in high school. Meaning, not until the last semester of your senior year."

"Then why does Bobby get to get a car as soon as he turns sixteen?"

Robert and Kenya looked at each other.

"No, it's like your mom said," Robert told him. "The children in this household won't be getting cars until they become seniors. And even though Bobby lives with his mom, the same rule applies to him as well."

"Well, that's not what Bobby said. Because on Saturday, he said his mom told him that you were buying him a car as soon as he gets his license. He said she promised him you would."

"Really? Then I guess I need to make sure Bobby and his mom understand the rules, too."

"Bobby said a lot of stuff," Livvie announced nonchalantly while twirling her pasta with her fork.

"Like what?" Robert said.

Eli sucked his tongue loudly. "Don't be such a tattletale, Livvie."

"You just told something, too, Eli. So why can't I tell Mommy and Daddy whatever I want?"

"Just be quiet, Livvie," Eli said, still trying to hush his sister up.

"No, let her talk," Robert said. "What else did Bobby tell you and Eli when he was here?"

Livvie cast her eyes at Eli and then back at her mother and father. "He didn't say it to us. But when I came out of my bedroom to walk back down to Eli's room, I heard Bobby in the bathroom talking to his mother."

"And what did you hear him saying?"

Livvie cast her eyes at her brother again. "Eli knows what he said. Because when you took Bobby home, Daddy, I told Eli all about it."

"Why won't you just be quiet, Livvie?" Eli yelled much louder. "Dad finally gets to see his son, Livvie, so why won't you just let him be happy? And let us finally have a big brother?"

Kenya and Robert looked at each other again, and now

Kenya knew it was time for her to intervene. And time to find out why Eli was so upset about whatever Livvie was trying to tell them. Because even though his baby sister sometimes got on his nerves the way most baby sisters do, Eli never became as irritated with her as he was right now.

"It's okay, sweetie," Kenya told Livvie. "You can tell us whatever you need to tell us because, in this house, we don't have any secrets. Remember?"

Livvie nodded yes.

"Okay, then go ahead and tell us what you heard."

Livvie cast her eyes at Eli yet again, and then put her head down. "Bobby told his mom that he was having a really good time, and that he wanted to know if he could spend the night with us. Then he told her that we didn't hate him the way she said we did. He said we all really liked him a whole lot. Even Ms. Kenya."

"And what did his mom say?" Kenya asked.

"I dunno. He didn't have his phone on speaker."

"Well, was that all? Or did he say something else?"

Livvie cast her eyes at Eli a fourth time and then dropped her head back down again. "He asked his mom why she couldn't just be happy for him. And then he asked her to please stop making things up. He wanted her to stop saying..."

"Go on, sweetie," Kenya said. "He wanted his mom to stop saying what?"

"That Daddy wasn't his real daddy and that his real daddy was dead."

Kenya was beside herself. She also mentally replayed what her daughter had just told them. Three different times. But she couldn't wrap her mind around any of it. Because surely not even Terri would lie about something this serious?

About her own son's paternity? Would she? Or was she simply making things up the way Bobby believed she was? It had to be the latter, though, because the former was way too unthinkable. Far too inconceivable and far-fetched. But worst of all, the latter would shatter Robert's heart into a million pieces.

CHAPTER 41

Michelle

M ichelle slowly opened her eyes and did what most people do every single morning: She confirmed in her mind what day it was, and then she thought back to the night before, trying to remember whether her day had ended on a good note or a bad one. But then she realized that hers had ended in disaster. She had gone to sleep devastated, and the more she thought about Chris, Steven, and all that awfulness that had transpired at the park, the more she wondered if she would ever be able to overcome any of it. She also wondered if Chris would ever speak to her again and whether he had finally told his parents about their broken engagement. Just the thought of how disappointed they were going to be made Michelle feel even worse because Chris's parents were such good people. And so was Chris, for that matter. Not to mention, her once-future-in-laws truly loved her, and they had always gone out of their way to let her know it.

Michelle lay in her bed, debating whether she was going to drag herself in to work or call in sick. But it wasn't long before she realized that maybe going in to work wasn't a good idea. Because truth was, she was both mentally and physically exhausted, and she knew her patients deserved better.

So, after forcing herself to sit up and swinging her legs over the side of the bed, she picked up her phone and dialed her assistant.

"Hey, Michelle," Trina said. "Good morning."

"Good morning. Also, let me say now how sorry I am to be calling you so early."

"It's no problem at all, and actually I'm just getting ready to head out to the clinic."

"Well, that's part of the reason I'm contacting you. I wanted to let you know that I won't be in today."

"Are you okay?" Trina asked.

"No, I'm really not, but I'll explain more when I'm back in the office."

"I'm so sorry, and is there anything I can do? Besides getting your patients rescheduled?"

"No, I think that will be all."

"Do you need to me to reschedule tomorrow's patients, too?"

Michelle wanted so badly to tell Trina yes, but she said, "No. I plan to be in tomorrow, but thank you."

"Okay, sounds good. But, please, if anything changes, don't hesitate to call me. You can call me for anything you need."

"I really appreciate that, and thank you again."

"You're welcome, and please take care."

"You too."

Michelle pressed the End button on her phone and called the physician she worked for to let him know as well that she wouldn't be in today. Then she dialed Steven, hoping he might answer her this time, but when the call went to voice mail, her doorbell rang. Of course, as she grabbed her silk robe, slipped it on, and stepped into matching slippers, she wondered if it was Chris. She actually hoped it was him. But she also knew it wasn't likely because by now, Chris was already at the hospital making early-morning rounds.

Still, she went downstairs to see who it was, and as she walked closer to her front entrance, she saw through the window section of her door that it was indeed Chris. But when she opened the door, he stood there looking at her in silence. His eyes were sad, and he was clearly broken. Michelle could tell he was as devasted as she was, if not more so, and she had no idea how she was going to make him feel better about any of this.

So instead of trying to figure out what to say to him now, she waited for him to walk inside, and then she followed him into her family room. Chris sat down on the edge of the sofa, and Michelle sat across from him in a chair.

But nonetheless, the silence between them continued, and Michelle wasn't sure what she should say first or how she should say it.

Finally, though, Chris said, "Why?"

"It's a long story, but first let me just say again how sorry I am. Because, Chris, I never, ever meant to hurt you."

"Well, you did. You hurt me in ways I didn't even know I *could* be hurt, and I didn't sleep all night long. I'm a wreck, and for the first time in my medical career, I had to reschedule my elective surgeries and reassign those that were urgent."

"I'm so, so sorry about all of this, Chris. I really am."

"Please don't say that anymore," he said. "Please don't keep saying you're sorry, because it's not helping. It's not making me feel any better about this, because what I really want is for you to tell me why this happened. I also want you to tell me who this guy is that you're messing around with."

"His name is Steven, and we dated during my college years."

"And?"

"We were high school sweethearts, but even once I left for college we continued dating."

"Yeah, okay, and...?"

Michelle could tell Chris wasn't going to make this easy for her. "We were in love, but my parents didn't approve of him. They even threatened to cut me off if I married him, so Steven and I finally broke up."

"Why didn't they approve of him?"

"Because he wasn't college educated, and they didn't think he would ever amount to anything. Or at least amount to anything that lived up to their standards."

"Well, has something changed?"

"What do you mean?"

"Did he finally get a degree? Or did he find success in some other way?"

"No, he still works as a restaurant manager."

Chris sighed. "Okay, look, baby. I don't care at all what this Steven guy does for a living. Because none of that even matters. My concern is you and why you betrayed me. Why you went behind my back with another man."

"I know, and I was so wrong for doing that. And I really am sor—" she almost said again, but then remembered how Chris had just told her he didn't want to hear that.

"So, what is this really about?" Chris asked. "Are you still in love with this man?"

Michelle took a deep breath. "I am."

"And when did you realize you weren't in love with me? Because you can't be in love with two people. I know some folks think you can, but to me that's just not possible."

"It's not that I never loved you, because I did. And I will always care about you. But to answer your question, yes, I'm in love with Steven. I've always loved him."

"I just can't believe any of this. I can't believe you would string me along like this, when you knew full well you wanted someone else."

"But that's just it. I hadn't seen or heard from Steven in years. At one point, he was even married."

"And then you just somehow miraculously reconnected? Only months before you were getting ready to marry me?"

"Yes. I saw him at the grocery store. But even after that, I tried to forget about him. I tried to make you and our wedding my priority."

"Well, clearly you didn't try hard enough. Because if you had, we wouldn't be in the mess we're in right now."

"I know, but I can't change how I feel. I can't pretend that Steven doesn't exist."

Chris dropped his head back and sighed again.

Michelle paused for a few seconds and then said, "So have you told your parents yet?"

"No," he said, now looking at her with sad eyes again. "I haven't told them anything because I'm hoping you and I can fix this."

Michelle tried not to show any emotion, but deep down, she wanted to tell him the truth: that fixing things between them wasn't an option. She wanted to explain to him how even if Steven decided not to be with her, she still couldn't marry Chris. She still couldn't be with a man that she wasn't in love with.

"So you don't have anything to say?" he asked.

"I just don't think that's possible."

"Baby, what is it about this guy? I mean, I know you're not sleeping with him, so what is it? Or maybe you have."

Michelle hated this, but she also didn't want to lie to Chris. If she could help it, she didn't want to lie about anything to anyone ever again.

"So, have you?" he asked. "Have you been sleeping with this man?"

"I have."

"Wow," he said, shaking his head. "Wow."

"I know this isn't what you want to hear, but I also want to be as honest with you as I can, Chris."

"I don't believe you. Not when you've made such a big deal about being celibate. Because even after we made love that one time, you all of a sudden decided you wanted to begin practicing celibacy again until after our wedding. Yet, now, you're telling me you've been sleeping with this Steven guy?"

Michelle didn't bother responding because there wasn't a whole lot she could say.

"Did you use anything? Any protection?"

"We did."

"So, if you're pregnant, there's no chance the baby could be his, then?"

"No, but I'm hoping we won't have to worry about that."

"But what if you are? What if you're carrying my baby, Michelle? Then what?"

"Then we'll just have to deal with it."

"Yeah, okay, whatever you say. But when is your cycle supposed to begin?"

Michelle paused for a few seconds. "Three days ago. And last month, all I had was a little spotting."

Chris reached his hand out to her. "Baby, come here. Come sit next to me."

Michelle didn't like where she believed this conversation was headed. But she did what Chris asked her to do.

When she sat next to him, he kneeled in front of her on one knee. "Baby, I'm begging you. Please don't ruin things for us. Put an end to this Steven thing, once and for all. I want you to end things with him so we can get married as planned. Because I forgive you. I forgive you for everything, and for as long as I live, I will never bring this up to you again. I mean, I know when I called your parents, I jumped the gun. But it was only because I was so upset with you. I was hurt. And angry. And disappointed. But then when I went home, I thought things over. I thought about how we all make mistakes, and that what matters is that you and I love each other. I also haven't told my parents anything, and last night, I called your dad back, too. I told him how you and I would make this right. That we would fix this, and everything would be fine."

Michelle listened to every word Chris was saying, but she knew there would be no fixing of any of this. Still, she didn't have the heart to tell him that.

Chris held both of Michelle's hands. "Baby, you know how much I love you, right? And what if you really are pregnant? What if we're about to have a beautiful little baby together? Do you think this Steven guy is going to be okay with that?"

Tears filled Michelle's eyes, but she still didn't say anything. She just didn't have any words to speak, but like Chris, she did wonder if she was pregnant. And if she was, she wondered what that would mean for her and Steven—the man who was the love of her life. The only man she had ever truly been in love with.

The man who had professed his eternal love for her, yet now wasn't even speaking to her.

CHAPTER 42

Michelle

Since early this morning, Michelle had been trying to get in touch with Steven, and although it was now six thirty in the evening, he still wasn't answering. Chris, on the other hand, had tried calling Michelle three different times, but because Michelle hadn't felt there was anything left for them to discuss, she hadn't responded. She also didn't know what else Chris expected her to say, what with her answering all of his questions this morning to the best of her ability and then telling him she was in love with someone else. Although, with the way Chris had pleaded with her to forget about Steven—and with the way he had insisted they should still become husband and wife—she knew it would likely be a while before Chris finally accepted their fate.

Now, though, as she drove closer to Steven's house, mentally preparing what she would say to him when she arrived, her phone rang, and she saw her mother's name appear on her console screen. Of course, with everything that had evolved, Michelle's first thought was to let the call go to voice mail. Because the last thing she wanted was to have words with her mother, and she certainly didn't want to get herself all worked up before seeing Steven.

But then she decided that maybe if she spoke to her mother now, Lucinda wouldn't have a reason to call her again for the rest of the evening.

So, Michelle clicked the Accept button on her car screen. "Hello?"

"Hi, honey. How are you?"

"I'm good. How are you?"

"Well, given the circumstances, I guess I'm doing as well as can be expected."

Michelle rolled her eyes and kept driving.

And Lucinda got straight to the point. "I understand Chris came by to see you this morning."

"He did."

"But it doesn't sound like things went too well with the two of you."

"They didn't."

"I'm really sorry to hear that because, sweetheart, Chris is a good man. A man who loves you in a way I doubt any other man will ever love you."

"Really? And how would you know that, Mom?"

"Because I just do. Chris has always loved you, and until this Steven person came back into the picture, you loved him, too."

"You're right. I did love him, but not in the same way I love Steven. Because with Steven, there's so much more. Steven is my soul mate, Mom. And if I didn't already know that before, I definitely know it now."

"*Soul mate?* What does that even mean, Michelle?"

"That we're connected in a very special way. That when we're not together, we feel as though something is missing. That as long as we have each other, the world seems like a much better place to live in. And we also think alike on so many different levels. But more than that, I've never felt more comfortable with anyone than I do with Steven, because not only does he fill my heart with so much joy, even my soul feels at peace."

Lucinda chuckled a little bit. "Oh my, well, honey, please don't take this the wrong way, but it sounds to me like you're trying to live out some sort of romantic fairy tale."

"No, I'm talking about real life. I'm talking about the kind of love that Steven and I share with each other."

"Okay, I hear what you're saying, but like I said, this sounds more like some sort of fairy tale. Or maybe some kind of unhealthy fantasy you're caught up in."

"That's because you and Daddy don't have that kind of relationship," Michelle exclaimed, and then regretted her words as soon as they left her lips.

"Excuse me?" Lucinda said.

"Mom, I didn't mean that. You and Daddy have a wonderful marriage. I've witnessed that for years. I've always been proud to know that my parents get along so well and that they truly love each other. But you also care a lot about money, status, and appearances. Sometimes more than you care about anything else. Including people."

"That's not true. Your daddy is one of the most loving men I know."

"I'm not saying he isn't," Michelle said. "I'm just saying that not everyone can graduate with a master's degree, a law degree, or a doctorate. And some people don't even want to go to college in the first place. Some people just want to be happy. They do want to earn enough money to take care of themselves, but they also want to have the kind of joy in their lives that money can't buy."

"Sweetie, what in heaven's name has happened to you?"

Lucinda asked, as though she hadn't heard a word Michelle had said.

"Nothing, except that I finally realized I have to live my own life. I have to do what's right for me and not what's right for you and Daddy. Or anyone else."

"Even if it means you'll never be able to bring your own husband inside your parents' house?"

"Yes, Mom. Even if it means that."

"I'm really sorry to hear that, because I was so sure you wanted better for yourself. Your father and I both thought you wanted better."

Michelle turned down Steven's street and saw his SUV parked in his driveway. "I'm sorry we don't see eye to eye on this, but Mom, this isn't about you and Daddy. This is about me being happy."

"Maybe you just need more time to weigh your options. Because while I was hoping I wouldn't have to bring this up, Chris told us you might be pregnant. Is that true?"

"I don't know," Michelle said. "But even if I am, I'm still not marrying Chris."

"That Steven guy has really gotten inside your head, hasn't he?"

"Mom, I'm going to hang up now, okay?"

"Fine. I'll talk to you later," Lucinda said.

Michelle pulled into Steven's driveway and turned off her ignition. Then she closed her eyes and promised herself she wouldn't cry. She promised herself that even though it would kill her to not see her parents anymore, she wouldn't let them control her destiny. Because parents or not, no one had the right to do that to anyone.

Michelle finally left her vehicle, strolled up the walkway, and rang the doorbell. To her surprise, Steven opened the door almost immediately—and he looked more devastated than Chris had been this morning.

"Can I come in?" she asked.

Steven stepped back slightly, making room for her to walk inside. Then he closed the door and motioned for her to proceed ahead of him with his hand.

"I know that saying I'm sorry isn't enough," she said, sitting down next to him on the love seat and turning toward him. "But I am. I'm sorry and ashamed. I'm also very disappointed in myself."

"I feel the same way. Because while I do wish you would have told your fiancé the truth weeks ago, I realize now that we never should have started sleeping together before that happened. So, we were both wrong, and now we're paying the consequences."

"You're right. I should have ended things with Chris first," she said, remembering how that was what her aunt Jill had told her to do from the start.

"Well, what's done is done now, and we all have to live with that. We all have to go on with our lives. Even if that means you and I will never be together."

"But why can't we be together?" Michelle asked. "Because I really am done with Chris for good. I told him that this morning, and I meant it."

"Yeah, but things are no longer that simple."

"Maybe not, but all I know is that you're the only man I want and need. You're everything to me, Steven, and I can't imagine living my life without you."

"I can't imagine living my life without you, either, but baby, you lied to me. You told me that you and your fiancé were celibate. But then yesterday, I find out that not only did you have sex with him, you also might be pregnant. And if you are, how do you expect us to continue on, business as usual? And how do you expect me to ever trust you again?"

"Because you can. I know I lied, and I apologize for that. But, baby, I was so confused about everything."

"I understand that, but you should have told me the truth. You should have just been honest with me because had I known there was any chance you might be pregnant by someone else, I never would have gotten so close to you again. I never would have allowed myself to fall even harder for you than I did years ago."

"But there's a chance I might not be pregnant."

"Yeah, but there's also a chance you are. You could be having another man's baby, and we can't just simply ignore that. And then there's still this whole thing about you lying. I mean, why do that about something so serious?"

"I don't know. I just didn't feel comfortable telling you that Chris and I had slept together."

"Why? Or more important, why didn't you guys use some kind of protection?"

"I don't know that, either. We just didn't. I mean, I was even planning to start taking birth control pills one month before the wedding, but when I realized I wasn't going to marry Chris, I sort of stopped thinking about birth control altogether. It was really stupid of me, though, and I should have been more careful."

Steven rubbed his face with both his hands and looked straight ahead.

"But no matter what," Michelle continued, "whether I'm pregnant or not, this doesn't have to change anything for us."

Steven finally looked in her direction again but this time with his eyes watering. "Baby, I really do love you with all my heart...I love you from the bottom of my soul...but I don't know if I can handle something like that."

Michelle touched his arm. "Something like what?"

"Becoming a father to a baby that I will always wish was mine."

"I know it won't be easy, but with prayer and total commitment to each other, we can do this. I know we can, and I also promise that I will never, ever lie to you about anything else."

Steven looked away from her again.

But Michelle pulled him closer, and they hugged each other tightly.

"This really hurts," he said. "But as much as I hate to admit it, if we don't stay together, I know my pain will be unbearable."

"It would be for me, too, so baby, please don't give up on me. Please don't give up on us."

"But what about your parents? Do they know about all of this?"

"That's actually a whole other story, but yes they do, and they're not happy about me breaking up with Chris. Or about me being with you."

"Of course they're not, but there is something that I haven't been fully honest with you about, either."

"Oh no...what is it?" Michelle hurried to say.

"It's not bad news."

"Oh, good," she said, feeling relieved.

"Still, it's not something you're going to be expecting to hear."

Michelle frowned a little with curiosity. "Okay."

"So, you know how I became a restaurant manager right after you got out of college?"

"Yeah."

"Well, I stopped being a manager a long time ago."

"Really? Why? And why didn't you think you could tell me the truth about that?"

"Because I wanted to make sure you really were still in love with me...for me...and not because of what my annual salary is. Or because I finally earn the kind of money that would make your parents happy. Although, knowing them, what I do now still wouldn't likely be good enough for them because I still don't have the kind of education they think I should have."

"What my parents think about you no longer matters to me. So just go ahead and tell me. Who do you work for now?"

"I don't. I own three franchise locations of my own. And before you start wondering why I live in such a small condo, well, this isn't my primary residence. This is one of my rental properties that I rent to Airbnb guests."

Michelle didn't want to believe what she was hearing, but she could tell that Steven's words were very real. "So, when you told me yesterday that your assistant manager was covering for you during my lunch hour, you made that up?"

"I did. I know it was wrong, but it's like I said. I needed to know that you loved me for me. And as soon as you broke off your engagement, I was going to tell you everything."

Michelle stared at him in shock. But in all honesty, she understood his reasoning. Especially because of how terribly things had ended between them before. She, of course, wasn't happy about him lying to her, but truth was, they'd lied to each other, and now they could make a fresh start. They could move past all their early issues and go on with their lives. Even if the blood test she would be taking at her clinic tomorrow morning turned out to be positive. This certainly wasn't the outcome she was hoping for, but she also knew that whenever anyone disobeyed God's Word—something she'd done a lot of as of late—there were always going to be consequences. But then there was also an opportunity to repent and to seek forgiveness, so regardless of the outcome, she knew she would be fine. She and Steven would be fine, and that's all that mattered to her.

CHAPTER 43

Lynette

Lynette was a bundle of nerves. But rightfully so, because although she'd told Emmett this past weekend that she still wasn't ready to make love with him, she was now preparing for what she hoped would be the best night of her life. Or at the very least, it would be an amazing night to remember. Still, though, she was nervous and hesitant for three reasons. For one, she hadn't been intimate with anyone for more than two years. Two, she worried that, by tomorrow morning, Emmett would regret having wasted so much of his time with a woman who was ten years his senior. And three, although her relationship with God wasn't nearly where it needed to be, the idea of willingly committing a sin—that she knew for sure was a sin—troubled Lynette to some degree. She wasn't sure why, exactly, because having sex outside of marriage certainly wasn't new to her. In fact, before Lynette had married Julian, they'd had sex all the time, both while they were dating and throughout their entire engagement.

But then Lynette knew, too, that part of the reason she was suddenly thinking so much more about her faith and the importance of doing the right thing was because of

Michelle and the unfortunate predicament she'd recently gotten herself into. Michelle had become celibate, but then she had slept with her fiancé anyway. Worse, Michelle had realized just how in love she still was with her childhood sweetheart and how she *wasn't* in love with Chris. Yet now, there was a chance she was carrying Chris's baby.

Early this morning, Michelle had gotten Kenya, Serena, and Lynette together via a virtual group call, so she could share many of the details she hadn't told them about before today, but Lynette was still having a hard time believing all that had transpired. Actually, there was one *specific* thing Lynette couldn't seem to get beyond, which was this whole idea of fornicating and then suffering the consequences the way Michelle had. Lynette also thought about the scripture that her mother had quoted to her pretty regularly when she was a child, Galatians 6:7, which said, "Be not deceived; God is not mocked: for whatsoever a man soweth, that shall he also reap."

She had always remembered that scripture word for word, but maybe Lynette was overthinking things, because it wasn't as though she was perfect. She also didn't want to lose Emmett, something Serena had told her that she believed would definitely happen, should Emmett ever grow tired of waiting on her. That particular conversation had taken place barely forty-eight hours ago, but ever since then, Lynette hadn't thought about much else. So much so that she had replayed Serena's words over and over in her mind. And over and over again. She'd thought about nothing else— for two whole days—and then if that hadn't already been enough, Lynette had made the mistake of inviting Emmett over for another visit last night. And things had gone so far that Lynette had found herself wanting to go all the way just as much as Emmett. Because truth was, Lynette had needs and desires, too, and she really enjoyed being with Emmett. She didn't love him, because after all the pain she'd had to endure with Julian, she knew it would be a while before she could love any man the way she had loved her ex-husband. But nonetheless she still liked Emmett a great deal, and right or wrong, she didn't want to lose him the way Serena had insisted she would.

Which was the reason that, a few hours ago, she had called him up to tell him she was ready. He, of course, hadn't believed she was being sincere and had thought she was simply joking around for the fun of it. But then when he had discovered how serious she was, he'd told her he would be there around seven. So now Lynette was sitting in front of her makeup vanity in her bedroom, applying the finishing touches of her makeup. She had also twisted her hair up in a classic chignon and put on a pair of understated pearl earrings. But as she sat debating whether she should slip on a necklace or a bracelet, she decided against both. To be honest, she wasn't sure what she should or shouldn't wear for her evening with Emmett. So she kept things pretty basic and slipped on a classic above-the-knee black satin nightgown with spaghetti straps, and then she covered it with a near floor-length matching robe.

Lynette looked good for forty, if she had to say so herself, and all she could hope was that Emmett felt the same way. She hoped he wasn't expecting the body of a twenty-year-old, though, because while she did take good care of herself physically, she was still a forty-year-old mother who had given birth to two daughters. And Tabitha had been born by C-section. So again, Lynette wasn't twenty years old. She was twice that age, and there was nothing she could do to change that.

After another half hour or so passed, Lynette went downstairs and a few minutes later, her doorbell rang. Emmett was right on schedule. Although, instead of simply being happy and excited about his being there, Lynette felt more like a schoolgirl—the same as she had felt that day when Emmett had asked her if she wanted to go out with him sometime. He'd also told her about his IT business and given her his business card. But now more than a month later, they had quickly moved beyond the idea of just getting to know each other better, and instead, they were expanding their relationship in a whole new way.

But when Lynette opened her front door, what she saw were two middle-aged men standing side by side.

"Good evening, ma'am," one of them said. "I'm Agent Hernandez, and this is Agent Pearson, and we're with the Federal Bureau of Investigation."

Agent Pearson acknowledged Lynette with a nod, and both men showed her their badges.

"We're so sorry to bother you this evening," Agent Hernandez continued, "but we really need to speak with you."

Lynette held the top of her robe together, making sure it didn't slip open, and then invited the two agents in.

"Please excuse my attire," Lynette said, because even though she was decent, a robe and gown weren't something she would normally wear in front of strangers.

"It's no problem at all, and we won't keep you very long," Agent Pearson told her.

"Please, both of you have a seat," she said, sitting down across from them in the living room.

Agent Pearson continued. "The reason we're here is to inform you that, as we speak, Emmett Johnson is being arrested, and his home is being searched by federal agents."

Lynette's heart jolted more than once. "What?"

"We've had Mr. Johnson under surveillance for the last six months, and because you recently began seeing him, unfortunately, you were under surveillance as well."

"Oh my dear Lord," Lynette exclaimed.

"We're sorry that we had to involve you in this process, but the good news is that we know you're completely innocent in this matter. Still, we do need to ask you a few questions, and then as we continue our investigation, we may need to contact you again. You will also be hearing from the U.S. Attorney's Office. Their Complex Frauds and Cybercrime Unit."

Lynette chuckled a little, even though not a single thing was funny to her. "Okay, wait a minute. So what exactly did Emmett do? I mean, why is he being arrested?"

"He's the mastermind of a credit card laundering scheme," Agent Hernandez said. "Sadly, Mr. Johnson has defrauded millions of dollars from several different credit card companies. And he's been doing it under the guise of an IT consulting firm he owns."

Lynette shook her head, and she felt numb. She'd had many moments when she'd wondered if maybe Emmett was too good to be true, but not because of the amount of money she believed he earned. It was because he had always been such a gentleman. From the moment she'd met him, he'd begun treating her with the utmost kindness and respect—and he was the kind of man you wholeheartedly wanted to trust. He also never gave Lynette a reason to not trust him, but now she knew that some of the nicest people in the world lived very secret lives—criminal lives, even. And in this case, Emmett had fooled her completely. He had wined and dined her and romanced her in some of the most thoughtful ways, yet the man she had been seeing was a professional criminal—and he was going to prison.

CHAPTER 44

Kenya

"Well, my friend, I'm sorry to say I don't have the best news," William said to Robert via video chat.

Robert and Kenya had both just arrived home from work not more than half an hour ago, and their attorney was calling to give Robert an update on Bobby's paternity mystery.

"I'm almost afraid to hear," Robert said, sitting down at the island and positioning his phone against a fruit bowl so he wouldn't have to keep holding it.

"Is Kenya nearby?" William asked. "Because I really want her to hear this, too."

"I am," she said, standing up and moving directly behind Robert so that William could see her.

"Well, as you know, the private investigator I hired had been sending me regular reports about Terri all along, yet not much had ever really shown up. But when you called me on Monday night to tell me what your daughter said about Bobby's father being dead, that made me wonder if maybe I had missed something. So, when I went back into the office first thing the next morning, I reviewed all the reports again."

"And did you find anything out of the ordinary?" Robert asked.

"No, but just to be safe, I thought it might be good to see if Terri has been making other large deposits. Meaning, in addition to the payments you give her every month. And while there is no need for you to know how I discovered what I'm about to tell you, I wanted to contact you about it as soon as possible."

"Okay," Robert said. "Go ahead."

"Terri deposits another two thousand dollars into her account every single month. And she's been doing so for years."

"Really?" Kenya said. "From whom?"

"Well, that's the strangest part of all. The checks Terri has been depositing are signed by a woman I know. She's the wife of a judge I had known for years."

Robert looked at Kenya confused. "Why would a judge's wife be paying Terri any money at all? Let alone two thousand dollars a month? And when you say someone you *had* known, are you saying the judge you know is now deceased?"

"That's exactly what I'm saying. His name was Neil Jamison, and just minutes ago, I spoke to his widow, Vivian."

"I still don't understand why she would be paying so much money to Terri," Robert said.

"Because, unfortunately, my friend...Bobby is Neil's son."

Robert sat down in one of the island chairs with tears in his eyes. "Man, please tell me this isn't true. Tell me this is some kind of mistake."

Kenya caressed her husband's back, and soon tears filled her eyes, too.

"I'm really sorry, Rob. I'm so sorry to have to tell you any of this."

"Did this Neil guy have a relationship with Bobby?" Robert wanted to know.

"No. And the only time he actually saw him up close was when Vivian demanded that a DNA test be taken."

"So, he was having an affair on his wife?" Kenya asked.

"Yes, and when Bobby was born, Neil and Vivian had already been married for ten years. But it wasn't until you and Terri got divorced that Terri called Neil threatening to go public about their affair and the fact that he'd had a baby out of wedlock. So once the DNA results confirmed that Bobby was in fact Neil's son, they gave Terri what she wanted. But they did it under the conditions that Terri would never contact them about anything ever again and that she would allow Bobby to continue believing that you were his biological father."

"This is crazy," Robert said. "So they knew I thought Bobby was my son?"

"Yes. They did. But they also didn't want to deal with a public scandal. Not with Neil being an elected judge who sat on the bench for more than twenty years before he passed away. And because Vivian doesn't want their children to know about Bobby, either, she agreed to continue paying Terri until Bobby graduates from college. But at the same time, Vivian also told me that Terri was more than fine with that, and I believe that's because she wanted to collect child support from both you and Neil. Which is likely the reason, too, that she never made good on her threat about having you pay her through the court system. Something I always thought was odd, anyway, because women like Terri will normally take their ex back to court for any reason they possibly can. And especially if they don't believe they're getting the amount of child support they're entitled to."

Kenya nodded in agreement. "That's what I believe, too, because this is definitely the kind of dirty thing Terri would do and then never feel a single shred of remorse behind it."

"So now what?" Robert asked William. "What do we do now? Because here's the thing: As far as I'm concerned, Bobby is still my son. I still love him just the same, and that's not going to change."

Kenya agreed with him. "Exactly. So yes, William, how do we proceed from here?"

"Well, the question is, how do you want to proceed? Is Terri still not answering your calls?"

"She's not," Robert said. "And I've been calling her ever since Livvie told us what she heard Bobby saying. Actually, I called her that night, three times on Tuesday, and then again yesterday. And now Bobby's phone is going straight to voice mail, and I can't get him on video chat either. Which means Terri was probably so upset about him saying he wanted to spend the night with us, she's now taken his phone away from him completely. And I rode by their house yesterday, too, and again about an hour ago, but her car wasn't in the driveway. It could have been in her garage, though."

"Well, you tell me what to do, and I'll do it," William said.

Robert looked at Kenya, and she knew exactly what her husband was planning to say. And she fully supported him.

"I want full custody of Bobby, and if Terri doesn't agree to give me that without a fight, I want her arrested for black-mail, extortion, or whatever it is she's guilty of. I know the judge's wife won't be happy about this information going public, but I need to do what's best for Bobby. I need to protect *him*, and I also won't lie to him about who his father is. He deserves to know the truth, and the truth is what I'm going to tell him."

"I understand," William said. "And I'll get things started right away tomorrow."

"Thank you for everything, man," Robert told him.

"Yes, thank you for everything, William. We really appreciate all your help with this," Kenya said, and then the doorbell rang. Eli and Livvie were still at day camp, so Kenya knew it couldn't have been any of their neighborhood friends stopping by this early. But as she walked through the kitchen, down the long hallway, and into the front entryway, she opened one of the stained-glass French doors and saw Bobby standing in front of her.

"Hi, honey," Kenya said.

"Hi, Ms. Kenya. Is my dad here?"

"He is. Come on in. Are you okay?" Kenya asked him when she saw tears rolling down his face, and then she wrapped her arm around his shoulders. Bobby also looked exhausted, like he had walked all the way from his house to theirs—about ten miles—and he'd done so in humid eighty-five-degree weather.

"No," he said with tears now flooding his face. "My mom is moving us away, and she said I'll never see my dad again. She said I'll never see any of you again. And Ms. Kenya, I don't want to go with her. I don't want to stop coming over here to be with all of you."

"Oh honey, I am so sorry, and you won't."

"Thank you, Ms. Kenya," he said, still weeping but now hugging Kenya as though his life depended on it. But as Kenya hugged Bobby back, she glanced up and saw Robert, looking on at them and crying, too—and smiling with absolute joy.

CHAPTER 45

Serena

When Serena saw Tim's number displayed across her phone screen, her stomach stirred a bit. She was preparing to walk inside her mother's house, but when she decided to answer Tim's call, she refrained from ringing the doorbell.

"Hello?"

"Serena?"

"Yes?"

"Hey, it's Tim, but I'm sure you already saw that on your caller ID screen. That is, if you haven't already deleted my name and number from your contact listing," he said, chuckling a little.

"No, actually, I haven't, but I'm going to," she told him.

"And I don't blame you."

"So why are you calling?"

"I wanted to properly apologize to you. Something I should have done that day you came by to talk to me."

"Really?" she asked, not knowing whether Tim was being genuine or not.

"Yes, really. I was wrong, and I knew I was wrong. But when you confronted me, instead of owning up to what I did behind your back, I got defensive, and I made it personal."

"Yeah, you did. And I didn't deserve that, Tim."

"No, you honestly didn't, and the things I did to hurt you were on me. None of it was your fault."

"Well, I'm really glad to hear you say that, but Tim, I still want to know why you said you were okay with me being celibate if you really weren't. And if you wanted to date other women, why couldn't you just tell me, so I could have gone on with my life?"

"Because I was mad at you."

"Why?"

"It's a man thing."

"Meaning?"

"When you wouldn't let me make love to you, I felt rejected. I felt like you were waiting for someone better."

"But I told you from the very beginning that my decision had nothing to do with you personally. And that it had everything to do with my faith in God and how I was trying my best to stop doing things that I knew God wasn't pleased about."

"I know that. I remember all the reasons you gave me, but I was raised in church, too, and I know a lot of the most common scriptures. So what I also found really interesting about you was how you were always so adamant about not having sex, yet you were also walking around not talking to your own sister. She would call you all the time, and you would totally ignore her. You never really told me why you were so angry with her, but I do remember you saying you hadn't forgiven her for something. Something that happened way back when you were kids."

Serena frowned. "Yeah, that's true, but that's not the same thing. It's not even close."

"Not honoring God's Word is not honoring God's Word.

So, it's not like you get to pick and choose which scriptures you want to abide by. I mean, I'm far from being a devoted Christian, but even I know that much."

Serena had never quite looked at things the way Tim was explaining them—even at forty years old—but she also couldn't argue with what he was saying. "I still don't think it's quite the same thing, but I also won't deny that you have a point. And for the record, my sister and I have finally talked, and we've also forgiven each other."

"That's really great to hear, Serena, and I'm happy for both of you."

"Thanks."

"Well, I won't hold you, but again, I just wanted to apologize. I wanted to do things the right way because when I saw you at the restaurant on Saturday, I could tell how uncomfortable you got. And if you want to know the truth, I felt uncomfortable, too. I felt bad because of all the terrible things I said to you, and I felt guilty."

"I appreciate you calling me. It really means a lot, and I accept your apology."

"Okay, well, you take care of yourself, all right?"

"I will, and you, too."

Serena dropped her phone in her leather tote and rang her mother's doorbell as planned.

Juanita opened it with a huge smile on her face. "Hey, sweetheart."

"Hey, Mom," Serena said, walking in and hugging her. Then they went into the kitchen and sat down at her mother's breakfast table.

"I know you said you were coming by, but I thought you would be here a little later. I haven't even cooked anything yet for dinner."

"It's fine, Mom. I just wanted to come see you. And talk to you."

"Well, I'm glad...and you know I am *especially* glad you and Diane are on so much better terms these days. She finally told me that the two of you had a really long talk about everything."

"We did, and I'm glad, too."

"She didn't tell me what 'everything' actually meant. But all I care about is that the two of you worked out whatever you needed to work out with each other."

"Well, that's part of the reason I wanted to come by here, Mom. Because you need to know the reason I never had much to do with Diane."

"Okay, why then?"

"It was partly because Diane's father came around all the time, but mine never came around at all. I never even got a chance to meet him."

"But that wasn't Diane's fault."

"No, it wasn't. But I'm just telling you how bad that always made me feel."

"I know it did, but I always told you that if you ever wanted to try to find your father, I would do all I could to help you with that. And you've always known his full name and where he was born because it's on your birth certificate."

"I know, but all these years I was just so angry at him for never trying to find *me*. I despised him for not caring whether I was dead or alive, because it just seemed so cruel. But now, I do want to at least see him and find out if I have other siblings or grandparents that might still be alive."

"I don't blame you. And sweetheart, I'm really sorry. I had no idea all of this was affecting you in such a terrible way."

"That's because I never talked about it to you, which was a

mistake. I'm also glad I talked to Diane because when I told her about all the bragging and boasting she used to do, she basically told me that she did it on purpose."

"Bragging and boasting about what?"

"Mom, you remember the way Diane would go shopping with her dad and then come home bragging about all the clothes and other things he would buy for her. And she would brag about the summer vacations he and his wife took her on, too."

"She was just a child, though, Serena."

"Yeah, that's what she said, too, but she also told me something else. Something that I'm not sure she will ever tell you."

"Like what?"

"That she grew up dealing with a lot of emotional struggles, too. Mostly because you always compared her to me, and you bragged to everyone about my grades and the university I went to."

"Really? She told you that?"

"She did, and I think what hurt her was that you made her feel as though she was never going to be good enough. And that she was never going to accomplish as many things as I have."

"I only said some of the things I said as a way to motivate her. I was just trying to inspire her and encourage her to become the best person she could be. I wanted both you girls to do far more than I ever imagined for myself. But I guess I went about it the wrong way, and for that I apologize. I'm really sorry, sweetheart, and when you leave, I'm going to call Diane over here. That way, I can talk to her and tell her that I never meant her any harm."

"I think that's a good idea, but Mom, please know that

we're not mad at you in any way. Because we know you did the best you could with what you had, and you did it on your own."

"I did, but I wasn't perfect. I still made mistakes. But one thing I hope you know is that I love both you girls more than anyone or anything in this world. I always have."

"We do know that, Mom, and we love you, too," Serena said, reaching for her mom's hand.

"So now that we have that out of the way, what's going on with Jake?" Juanita asked. "Because Diane and I really like him a lot. I know we already told you that, but we really do."

"I haven't heard from him, Mom," Serena said, being more vulnerable with her mother than she had ever been.

"Why not?"

"I don't know. Things were fine at church, and then I talked to him early that evening, but that was it."

"Have you been calling him?"

"Every day. More than once."

"And you didn't have any kind of disagreement? Nothing happened?"

"No. But we did have a conversation about my breakup with Tim. Something I know I haven't told you everything about. But long story short, Jake and I saw Tim and his date out at a restaurant on Saturday."

"And?"

"It was awkward, but when Jake asked me if I still had feelings for Tim, I told him yes. But I also told him I wasn't in love with Tim, and that he's the man I'm in love with."

"Well, you were just being honest. Although not every man is secure enough to handle that kind of truth."

"Yeah, I realize that now, and Lynette said something very similar."

"Well, maybe you should just go by there."

"I did. On Sunday night. But I didn't see any lights on."

"You should go back, though. Because sweetheart, Jake is the one."

"Why do you say that?"

"Because he really loves you, and I saw the way he looked at you. Like you were the love of his life."

"I don't know, Mom. Because why would he just stop talking to me for no reason? And if there is a reason, why hasn't he been man enough to tell me about it?"

"I don't know the answer to that, honey. But what I do know is that when you were talking to some of our other church members, he told me that he was glad to finally have a chance to meet me . . . and that he'll let me know when he's ready to make things more official. He said he wanted to take you to see his parents first, though."

"What? Why didn't you tell me about that, Mom?"

"Because Jake wanted it to be a surprise. But now that you're sounding like you're giving up on him, I wanted you to know."

"I just don't want to be that woman who runs after a man who doesn't want her. As it was, I was almost at the point of doing that with Tim."

"I understand that. Believe me I do, but I'm telling you, if Jake isn't returning your phone calls, there's a reason. Because it's like I said, he loves you. Honey, he really is the one."

CHAPTER 46

Serena

Serena walked up the two steps leading to Jake's front door and thought about her mother's words. *Because it's like I said, he loves you. Honey, he really is the one.* In all honesty, Serena didn't know whether to believe those words or not, but because Serena truly did love Jake, she wanted to give him the benefit of the doubt. She wanted to try contacting him one more time—this time in person—but if for some reason he wasn't home or refused to let her in, that would be it. Not because she didn't want to be with him for the rest of her life, if she could, but because she was slowly but surely starting to recognize her worth. She didn't think she was better than Jake, or anyone else for that matter—at least not anymore. But she also wouldn't place more emphasis on finding a man than she did on maintaining her dignity. Because in the past, she had done this kind of thing all the time, and it hadn't gotten her anywhere. Instead, what it had done was cause her a great deal of pain and anguish. But again, she wanted to give Jake the benefit of the doubt, so she took a deep breath and rang his doorbell.

Then, when he didn't answer right away, she rang it again—and then a third time. However, when he still didn't come to the door, Serena turned to walk away.

But just as she did, Jake finally opened it.

"You must be really busy," Serena said.

"I'm not busy at all."

"Well, I know you saw how many times I called you, and I know you got my messages."

"I did."

"Well, why didn't you answer? Or at least have the decency to call me back?"

"Because I'm not the man you want."

Serena looked away from him, but then she soon locked eyes with him again. "Look, Jake, I don't know what I did or what happened, but will you at least invite me in so we can talk about this?"

"I'm not sure what we have to talk about, but fine," he said.

Serena followed him into his living room, which wasn't far from his entryway, and took a seat on Jake's black leather sofa.

Jake sat at the far end of it. "So, what is it you want to talk about?"

"You and me."

"Okay, talk."

"Why are you being so cold and acting like you barely even know me?"

"Because you pretended to be so in love with me and then last weekend, I realized who you really were."

"Why? Because I admitted the truth about still having some feelings for an ex? Someone I just broke up with two months ago?"

"That's not what I'm talking about. I would never get upset with you for telling the truth."

"Well then, Jake, I'm at a total loss. I don't have a clue what's wrong with you."

Jake looked at her with no emotion, and if anything, he seemed hurt. "It's what you said to your friends."

"What friends and when?"

"Sunday night. You know, when you met your friends over at Michelle's."

Since Jake hadn't been there with her, she wondered how he could possibly know about anything she had talked about that evening. Because what she knew for sure was that Michelle, Kenya, and Lynette would never repeat anything she told them.

"Look, Jake, I'm really trying here, but if you're just saying all of this because you've met someone else, then why don't you just tell me that? And stop playing games."

"'*And then when Jake told me that he'd only finished high school and that he worked in a factory, I won't lie, I wasn't thrilled about dating him at all,*'" Jake said, mocking Serena's diction and tone of voice. "And what was it you said about colleges? Something about how you always wanted '*someone who went to the right schools and who could give me a certain kind of life-style*'? And then this was my favorite part of all: '*But I will say that when Jake told me he earned six figures, that really helped a lot, and it made me at least want to give him a chance and see how things would go.*'"

Serena was horrified. And while she wanted to deny every single word Jake had reiterated, she couldn't. Not when he had repeated her conversation to her friends nearly verbatim. But what bothered Serena even more was that she had no idea how he knew any of this.

"I don't know what to say," she said. "Except I'm sorry . . . but, Jake, who told you all that?"

"You did."

"How?"

"You never hung up your phone. I guess you just set it down next to you or dropped it in your purse."

"And you listened to everything we talked about?" Serena asked, trying to turn the blame on Jake, but deep down, she couldn't have been more ashamed of herself.

"No, but I listened long enough to hear how you feel about men like me. Men who don't fit your typical standards. You know, laborers like me who work their behinds off in a factory for sometimes twelve hours a day, seven days a week."

"Jake, you know that's not how I feel about you. I mean, there was a time when I did think that way, but you changed all that. You made me see that none of that mattered. And that I didn't need that kind of man in order to be happy."

"Well, you say that now, but down the road I won't be enough for you. Especially since I have no desire to go back to school to get a degree. I also have no desire to sit inside someone's corporate office. So if that's what you're looking for, then I wish you well."

"But baby, it's not what I want. Not anymore, and that's what I'm trying to tell you."

"Well, if you remember, I asked you in the very beginning if what I did for a living would be a problem for you. Remember when I said I wanted to know so that neither of us would end up wasting our time with each other?"

"I do remember, and I also remember that I told you that it didn't bother me."

"Okay, well even if that's true, what if I told you that I'm not a journeyman yet? That I'm still in the apprenticeship program, and right now I earn less than fifty thousand dollars a year?"

Serena smiled at him because for the first time in her life, that kind of news didn't matter to her. Then she slid her body across the sofa until there was no space left between them and laced her fingers together with his. "Jake, baby, please listen to me. And please believe me. I don't care if you earn twenty thousand dollars a year. As long as you have a steady job with good benefits, and you don't mind going to work every day, I'm good. But more than that, just answer me this: Do you really love me? I mean as much as you've been saying you do for the last month?"

Jake gazed into her eyes. "I love you so much that it hurts. Over these last few days, my heart was physically in pain because I didn't know what I was going to do without you. I mean, I knew I couldn't be with a woman who didn't think I was good enough, because I would never do that. Even though I really do love you. But I honestly didn't know how I would ever find another woman who I'm so compatible with. A woman who I know, beyond a shadow of a doubt, is my soul mate—especially when I never even used to believe in soul mates. So baby, when I tell you how much I love you, I mean that with every part of my being."

"And I love you, too, baby. You're my everything. So what I can promise you now is that the only one you will ever come second to in my life is God. But you'll never be second to anyone or anything else."

"I feel the same way. It's God, you, and everyone else," he said, kissing her with full passion. "Oh, and just so you know, I really am a journeyman. And I only said what I said to make a point and to make sure you were serious about what you were telling me."

"Well, I hope you believe me. Because I really don't care about any of that."

"I do believe you. Because the genuine look on your face said everything."

EPILOGUE

One Year Later

What an amazing difference an entire year could make, and Serena was having the time of her life. It had certainly taken her decades to arrive at such a happy place, but through God's grace, she was finally here, and she was beyond grateful. Of course, marrying the love of her life last month had been the highlight of all that she had experienced, but she was also happy about all the changes she had made along the way. Because there had certainly been a time when she had struggled so much internally that she had believed material possessions and sky-high salaries were the only keys to being successful. She had also believed that having those two things was the only way a person could truly be happy, but lots of heartbreak had forced her to begin thinking differently. Dating the wrong men for all the wrong reasons had been her downfall, and it hadn't been until she'd had the pleasure of meeting Jake that she had come to understand what true love was actually all about and what rightly defined the attributes of a good man. Because while Serena had thought for years that she knew what having a good man fully meant, what she had ultimately discovered was that she hadn't had a clue. That is, not until Jake had so perfectly come into her life at a time when she had been feeling at her lowest. And then, if that hadn't been enough, he had proven to be not just one of the best men she knew, but he was also the man and husband of a lifetime—intimately and emotionally—and she thanked God for him daily.

Serena was also thankful for the close relationship she now had with her sister, Diane, who had also gotten married, and the fact that the three of them—Serena, Diane, and their dear mother—had become closer than ever as a family. They spent most every Sunday afternoon together after church, and Jake and Darryl had become more like brothers than brothers-in-law. So, life for Serena and her entire family couldn't have been better. Although, there was one thing that hadn't worked out as well as Serena had hoped, which was meeting her father and getting to know him better. She had finally found him and met him for the very first time, but sadly, he had passed away four months later. Still, Serena was glad she had taken it upon herself to search for him when she had because little had she known, their first meeting would be the only time she would get to see him in person. Serena and her father had, of course, spoken by phone a few times as well, which she was thankful for because while her father hadn't offered her any good reasons for not being in her life, talking to him had given her a chance to forgive him. Serena had also learned so much from him about her family history, and she had even gotten a chance to meet her younger brother and sister.

So again, all was well, and life for Serena couldn't have been better, and she was grateful.

But then, the great news, too, was that life was also going wonderfully for her three best friends, because once Michelle had learned for sure that she was pregnant by Chris, Steven had still kept his word and stood by Michelle from beginning to end. Then, four months ago, right after Michelle had given birth to a healthy, beautiful baby girl, named Riley, Chris had found a way to forgive Michelle, too, and he had soon given up on the idea of trying to take Riley away from her. He had also admitted to her how busy he was with his medical practice and weekly surgery schedule, and then told her it was best for her to have primary custody altogether. They did agree that Chris could pick up his daughter as often as he wanted, though, and that his parents were welcome to see her anytime as well.

Then there was this whole idea of Steven being the best bonus dad any child could possibly ever want. Because oh, how he loved sweet little Riley. Steven fully respected Chris as Riley's biological father, but he still treated her as though she were his own, and that made Michelle happiest of all. Of course, in the beginning, Steven's parents hadn't been too happy about his marrying a woman who was pregnant with another man's child, but they had since come to terms with it and had genuinely welcomed Michelle and Riley into their family. They had even happily attended Michelle and Steven's private wedding ceremony two months ago, and Michelle, Steven, and Riley usually saw Steven's parents nearly every weekend. Sadly, though, Michelle's parents hadn't been as compassionate and forthcoming, because not only had they not attended the wedding, they still hadn't been on the best terms with Michelle for most of this past year. However, now that their beautiful granddaughter was here, Larry and Lucinda had finally reached out to Michelle, asking if they could come by to see her—something that Michelle had been fine with as long as they abided by one condition: Her parents needed to show her husband the kind of courtesy and respect he deserved. Larry and Lucinda had also been required to apologize to Steven for treating him the way they had and to acknowledge him and Michelle as the married couple they were. Because the one thing Michelle had talked about a lot was something she had read in one of her go-to inspirational books. She talked about the part where the author had stated plain and simple that if you didn't like her husband, you had already decided that you didn't like her. And that if you criticized or offended her husband in any way, then you were criticizing and offending her, too. But most important, the author had shared how this particular truth applied to everyone—friends, acquaintances, strangers, and even family members. Of course, Serena hadn't been sure Michelle's parents would even consider doing any of what Michelle had been asking them to do. But maybe they had truly wanted to see their granddaughter more than any-thing, because with absolutely no hesitation or objections, they had agreed to all conditions.

But no one had likely experienced a more trying and life-changing existence than Bobby had. Thankfully, he now lived with Robert, Kenya, Eli, and Livvie permanently, and he was thriving in more ways than one, but the initial part of his journey hadn't been easy. Because from the very start, he had missed his mother tremendously, no differently than any child would, and he hadn't understood why his mother had done so many terrible things. But then as the weeks and months had begun passing, things had gotten better for Bobby. His grades in school had risen, he had come to love being a big brother, and life as a whole had become much happier for him than it ever had been—and for the first time in his young life, he seemed at peace. There was still the whole Terri situation though, because as much as Terri had lied about Bobby's paternity to Robert and collected years' worth of child support payments from him—and blackmailed a judge and his wife—there was still a part of Kenya that felt sorry for Terri. Serena knew this because all these months later, Kenya sometimes spoke about the fact that she didn't wish jail time on anyone. And especially not on a mother.

But there was a blessing that had come from all that had taken place, because once Terri had been charged, arrested, and sentenced to prison for two years—only because she had stuck to her plan of moving Bobby out of state and never allowing Robert to see Bobby again—she had undergone a full mental evaluation and had been diagnosed with narcissistic personality disorder. To be honest, though, Serena knew that none of them should have been surprised to learn this because Terri had shown so many signs of that particular disorder for years—not limited to but certainly including how superior she thought she was to everyone else and how she believed she deserved special treatment. She also had no problem taking advantage of others, and her sense of self-importance and entitlement had been off the charts the entire time Kenya and Robert had been married. And Terri also had never been willing to recognize the needs and feelings of others, namely those of Robert, Kenya, Eli, Livvie, Robert's parents, and most important of all, her own son, Bobby. Either that or Terri simply hadn't had the ability to care about this kind of thing because of her illness. Still, Robert and Kenya were happy about Terri getting the help she needed, especially for Bobby's sake, and they also hoped that when Terri was released from prison, she would be a better mother to him. She still wouldn't have custody of Bobby, but at least she would be able to spend time with him and work on salvaging their mother-son relationship, something Kenya had told Serena she was praying for. Kenya also prayed for Terri's mind to be healed—and that there would come a time when the two of them would find themselves getting along the way every mom and bonus mom should be getting along for the sake of their children.

Then there was Lynette, who had experienced more in this last year than she had in a while, but thankfully, her entire life had become so much better. In fact, she had even begun dating an amazing guy named Pierce. At first, Lynette had talked about how she wasn't sure whether she wanted to contact him or not because after meeting him at the airport, she had gone onto his Facebook page and seen him posing in multiple photos with various women. But as it had turned out, those women in Pierce's photos had been family members—his sisters, aunts, and cousins—all of whom Lynette had gotten a chance to meet at Pierce's birthday party a few months ago.

Serena, Michelle, and Kenya had liked him right away, and given the disastrous situation that had occurred with Emmett, they were also glad to know that Lynette was now happily dating a man who was ten years older than her, rather than ten years younger. Although, to be fair, Serena knew Emmett's being a convicted criminal had absolutely nothing to do with age, and that it had everything to do with greed. Still, none of them could believe such a nice guy had turned out to be so slick and deceptive. The man had stolen millions of dollars, right from the comfort of his own home—well, actually from the comfort of his cushy home office—and he had also successfully hired several other highly intelligent IT professionals to help carry out his scheme. But, of course, when it came to trusting criminals, the problem was that no criminals could be trusted, and as a result, it had been

Emmett's so-called "most trusted" independent contractor who had blown the whistle on him and then had made a solid plea bargain that had kept him out of prison.

Still, although Lynette hadn't been in love with Emmett, she had liked him a lot. Which was the reason that when Emmett had been arrested, she had been hurt and disappointed. Then, when he had called her a few days later, she had purposely accepted the phone charges because she wanted to ask him why. And when she had, Emmett had told her something she couldn't believe. He had, in fact, created the scheme so he could live the wealthy lifestyle he was living, but after a while he had only kept it going because the idea of stealing large sums of money had become an addiction for him. He told her how there had been times when he had wanted to stop what he was doing—especially when he had begun dating her—but no matter how hard he had tried, he just couldn't. Emmett had also wanted to know if he could still stay in touch with Lynette, but of course she had told him no, and then wished him well. Still, when Lynette had learned that even with accepting the best deal possible from the U.S. Attorney's Office, that Emmett wouldn't be getting out of federal prison until twenty years from now, she had truly felt sorry for him.

And then there was Lynette's ex-husband, Julian, who had divorced his second wife but still hadn't given up on trying to get back together with Lynette—something that was never going to happen. But the good news was that Chloe had finally forgiven her father. It had taken her a while to do so, but now that she had, she and Tabitha sometimes spent entire weeks with Julian, even during the school year, and he now went out of his way to make his daughters a priority. Then, even though Lynette was no longer in love with him, she did wonder why men like Julian had to nearly lose everything before they learned their lesson. She wondered why getting married, having two beautiful children, and becoming a hugely successful businessman hadn't been enough for him. But then, Lynette had also told Serena that there was something else she had thought a lot about lately: She and Julian had never truly kept God first in their lives. They had gone to church pretty regularly, and Lynette was certainly a good person, but she had somewhat turned away from her Christian upbringing—meaning she had sort of become what her mother would call a lukewarm Christian.

Lynette had also talked about how, once she and Julian had gotten married, money, status, building beautiful homes, and taking exotic vacations had taken precedence over their lives. It was true that Julian had been the ringleader in all of this, but Lynette had admitted to Serena, Kenya, and Michelle that she needed to take some of the blame, too. Why? Because living a wealthy lifestyle was something Lynette had quickly gotten used to and enjoyed. She certainly knew nothing was wrong with being successful and wealthy, but when success and wealth became much more important than a person's relationship with God, that's when it became a problem. That's when a person could find themselves struggling in ways like never before.

But thankfully, today was a new day for Lynette, and she was finally in a place she could be proud of. Because not only had she made noticeable changes spiritually, she had also made them mentally and emotionally, and as a result, she was happier than she had been in years. Lynette was totally at peace, and Serena was happy for her.

And now, as Serena looked at all three of her best friends, she realized she was happy for *all* of them. She was also happy for herself and grateful to be sitting here at Soriano's for their monthly Girls Day Out. Serena loved Michelle, Kenya, and Lynette no differently than had they all been born to the same mother and father, and she thanked God for their friendship and sisterhood. Because after all, not only had they each grown in such an amazing way personally—and they had become much fiercer women of God—their bond had also become stronger than ever. It was rock solid. But then, Serena wasn't surprised by any of this because the four of them were true sister friends forever. Now and always.

ABOUT THE AUTHOR

KIMBERLA LAWSON ROBY is a *New York Times* bestselling author, speaker, and podcast host. She has published 28 books, including *The Woman God Created You to Be: Finding Success Through Faith—Spiritually, Personally, and Professionally*, as well as her novels, such as *Casting the First Stone*, *The Best-Kept Secret*, *The Reverend's Wife*, *Better Late Than Never*, and *A Christmas Prayer*. Kimberla is the recipient of the 2013 NAACP Image Award for Outstanding Literary Work—Fiction, and in August 2020, she was named by *USA Today* as one of the 100 Black novelists you should read. Kimberla resides in Illinois with her husband, Will.

ACKNOWLEDGMENTS

As with every aspect of my life, I thank God for absolutely everything. Your love, grace, and mercy continue to make all the difference in my life, and I will forever love, trust, honor, and depend on You with all I have in me.

To my dear, wonderful husband, Will—the love of my life for more than three decades—for all your unconditional love and support. I love you with my whole heart and soul, and I thank God for you every single day of my life.

To my dear brother and sister-in-love, Willie, Jr, and April Stapleton, and my dear brother and sister-friend, Michael Stapleton and Taja Wallace, for always supporting your big sis; to my dear bonus son and sweet daughter-in-law, Trenod and LaTasha Vines-Roby, and our grandchildren, Alex, Trenod, Jr., and Troy; to my mom's three living siblings: my dear uncle, Ben Tennin and my dear aunts, Fannie Haley and Ada Tennin (and Uncle Thomas); to her siblings-in-law: my dear uncle, Charlie Beasley and my dear aunts, Vernell Tennin and Ollie Tennin; to the rest of my dear family (Tennins, Ballards, Lawsons, Stapletons, Youngs, Beasleys, Haleys, Greens, Robys, Garys, Shannons, Normans, and everyone else I am related to); to my dear cousin and sister, Patricia Haley-Glass (and Jeffrey); my two best friends and sisters, Kelli Tunson Bullard (and Brian) and Lori Whitaker Thurman (and Ulysses); my dear cousin and sister, Janell Green; my dear friends and fellow sisters in publishing, Trisha R. Thomas (Thank you so much for all your book cover design inspiration!), Trice Hickman-Hayes, and Marissa Monteilh Pointer; and to the sweetest and most supportive spiritual mothers any woman could ever hope for in life: Dr. Betty R. Price and Ms. Gwendolyn G. Young—I appreciate and thank God for each and every one of you, and I love you with all my heart.

To my publishing attorney, Ken Norwick; my amazing publishing house, Hachette Book Group/Grand Central Publishing: Beth de Guzman, Kirsiah McNamara, the entire sales force, publicity team, marketing team, and everyone else at GCP; to all the bookstores and retailers who are kind enough to carry my work; every newspaper, magazine, radio station, TV station, website, and blog site that promotes it; to all my social media followers and to all the fabulous book clubs that continually choose my books, year after year, as your monthly selections—thank you a thousand times over for everything.

And finally to the best readers in the whole wide world—**thank you for being so wonderfully kind, loyal, and hugely supportive of me as an author**. I am forever grateful to you, and I love you all so very much.

Much love and God bless you always,

Kimberla Lawson Roby

E-Mail: kim@kimroby.com
Facebook: www.facebook.com/kimberlalawsonroby
Instagram: www.instagram.com/kimberlalawsonroby
Twitter: www.twitter.com/KimberlaLRoby